Match Made in Heaven

The Cricket Club
Book 5

MARGAUX THORNE

ARE YOU SIGNED UP FOR DRAGONBLADE'S BLOG?

You'll get the latest news and information on exclusive giveaways, exclusive excerpts, coming releases, sales, free books, cover reveals and more.

Check out our complete list of authors, too!

No spam, no junk. That's a promise!

Sign Up Here

www.dragonbladepublishing.com

Dearest Reader;

Thank you for your support of a small press. At Dragonblade Publishing, we strive to bring you the highest quality Historical Romance from some of the best authors in the business. Without your support, there is no 'us', so we sincerely hope you adore these stories and find some new favorite authors along the way.

Happy Reading!

CEO, Dragonblade Publishing

Chapter One

London, England August 1849

Looking back, Miss Ella Chesterfield probably should have listened to her mother.

And stayed home. In bed, like everyone else in her family.

But she didn't. And here she was, picking up her pace, ignoring her older sister's violent glare.

"You still haven't told me why we had to leave so early," Lady Cordelia grumbled, rubbing at the corner of her eye. "What kind of a lady goes for a walk at nine in the morning?"

Ella scoffed as she carefully guided the tired and grumpy Cordelia across the street to the park entrance. Though it was deemed too early by her sister, the road was already loud and bustling with hansom cabs, carriages, carts, and everyday laborers fighting for purchase as they made their way to their morning destinations. "I suppose this lady does," Ella replied evenly as her heartbeat quickened.

Hyde Park opened before them, large and wide, as did Ella's fragile hope. Most of fashionable London appeared to agree with Cordelia, and the lustrous park was empty save for the occasion gentleman who crossed their path, necktie unbound and askew, steps unbalanced and certainly not straight, smelling of a sickening mixture of alcohol and powdery perfume.

In those clumsy exchanges, everyone did their best to nod

and look away as quickly as possible, which was hardly difficult for Ella. Her sights were already spoken for.

The man in question just needed to make his entrance.

If only her sister would stop ruining the moment with her complaining. The previous night, Cordelia had acted excited at the prospect of a walk with her youngest sister. Since she'd married the marquise six months before, Cordelia had spent most of her time at her husband's estate in Ipswich, out of the familial loop. Ella had been flattered by Cordelia's open elation at the chance to spend the morning with her. However, she should have reminded her dear sister that her mornings started earlier than most women's—especially married ones.

"Stop muttering under your breath," Ella admonished her sister with a playful smile. "We're here now, so just enjoy it."

"I am enjoying it!" Cordelia snapped. "I just don't understand why Regent's Park wasn't good enough for you. Hyde Park is three miles away from home."

Ella tilted up her nose, feeling the soft burn of guilt climb up her neck. Since her family lived in one of the exclusive crescent rowhouses across from Regent's Park, Cordelia's assumption wasn't unwarranted. But what Ella was searching for couldn't be found in Regent's Park. *He* only came to Hyde Park at nine on Monday mornings, because *he* didn't wish to be disturbed. Ella had no plans to disturb him; she only wanted to watch him ... and hope that *he* might disturb *her*.

"Don't people walk in Ipswich?" Ella teased, turning the tables on her irritable sister. She wound her arm around Cordelia's, tugging her along. "Don't tell me that married life has changed you so much. I wouldn't be able to bear it."

Cordelia laughed, and that light, beautiful sound pinched Ella's heart, reminding her of how much she'd missed it these last months. Lovely and confident, Cordelia was only a year older than Ella, and the fourth daughter of Lord and Lady Weston to make a brilliant match. Ella had been elated for her sister, but this marriage had hit her the hardest. Alexandra, Constance, and

Suzanne's marriages had seemed predestined and inevitable. Older and more mature, they always appeared to have one foot out of the house. But Cordelia had been Ella's true friend, her partner in crime. Ella had childishly convinced herself that they would have more time together.

But then the marquis had come sniffing around last season, and Lady Weston made sure that Cordelia was everything he desired in a wife and could do no better. For once, Ella agreed with her intrepid mother. But the sting of loss still smarted. And to Ella's disappointment, it wasn't letting up anytime soon.

"Of course we walk," Cordelia returned cheekily. Her voice dropped to a furtive whisper that had Ella instinctively lowering her head to hear more. "But there's so many … *other* things to do as well, that are … *equally* stimulating."

"Ugh." Ella dropped her sister's arm with a huff. "Did you really come all the way out here just to tell me about your husband's … nighttime *prowess?*" Her feet stalled as a nervous expression floated over her sister's porcelain face. Now, it was all making more sense.

Ella's torso slumped despite the best efforts of her cage-like corset. "Wait. Did *Mother* order you to come with me today to tell me all about your husband's nighttime … *prowess?*"

"Oh, Ella, really!" Cordelia rolled her eyes devilishly. "It's not only during the night."

"How lovely for you," Ella answered drolly. "And don't *Ella* me! I know she did, so you might as well come clean."

Cordelia marched ahead, and Ella watched her sister's delicate shoulders inch toward her ears. Her elegant, gloved hands strangled her parasol as if it had threatened to steal her expensive reticule. And after a few weighted seconds, Cordelia released a stream of bluster. "Perhaps Mother didn't say it in so many words …"

"Ha! I knew it!" Ella cried. Cordelia's cracking under pressure was inevitable. As was her habit of doing anything their mother ordered. It wasn't that she was a pushover, rather someone who hated saying no to others. It just wasn't in her sweet nature.

Ella caught up to Cordelia's side, nudging her with her elbow, attempting to assuage her sister's guilt. "Let me guess how Mother said it." At once, Ella straightened her spine and clasped her hands demurely in front of her, stretching the crown of her head toward the sky. "Now, Cordelia," she began in an exceedingly clipped accent, more than a little nasally, "be sure to tell Ella all about your husband's beautiful form. Impress upon her the many joys and secrets of wedded bliss. Describe to her—in restrained detail—everything she is missing out on by being such a stubborn and obstinate girl."

Cordelia snorted, covering her mouth with her hand. "It's like Mother is right here!"

Ella pulled a face. "Hardly. Mother doesn't leave her room before noon. She says that's why her skin is so youthful and tight."

Cordelia cocked her head. "I thought it was the ammonia cream?"

"Not anymore. Father told her to stop using it because he couldn't stand the smell. He always thought something was burning."

"Ah." Cordelia clicked her tongue, fighting back a sly grin. "Well, yes, Mother did say something similar to all that. Not quite as salacious, though. She may not be as demure as the other mothers, but she still has limits."

Not as demure was a kind way of putting it. Lady Weston was nothing like the other mothers who preferred to speak about potential husbands in innuendo and bland hints involving adorable forest creatures. Lady Weston despised naïve women and made sure her daughters knew what was ahead of them regarding the opposite sex, and more importantly, what was expected.

"Mother? Limits?" Ella *hmphed*. "If she has them, I haven't spotted them yet."

Her older sister went on, ignoring her comment. "She *was*

very adamant about my mentioning Lord Lucas, though."

"Oh, was she?"

"Yes," Cordelia drawled, overlooking the acid in Ella's tone. "She wanted me to ask why you don't … encourage him a bit more. He's a good man. A viscount. He can't help that he … that he …"

Ella helped her sister finish her sentence. "That he can't control one eye?" She shuddered. "Cordelia, my love, he's nice enough, but do you understand how difficult it is to hold a conversation with a man who has one eye constantly veering off to the side?"

"He tries to keep it straight!"

"I know! That's what makes it worse!" Ella lamented. "The poor creature wrestles it back to center, and then slowly but surely it creeps over again as if my small talk makes it want to jump off a cliff. I never have any idea what he's saying because I'm utterly entranced by the eye's Sisyphean endeavor. It's too much for me to endure."

For a moment, Cordelia's expression sparked with thunder, and Ella thought that she'd gone too far making fun of the poor viscount, but then a smile twisted her lips and she broke out in giggles. "Oh, poor Lord Lucas!" she groaned, clutching her stomach through the hiccups. "He really isn't so bad. And Mother likes him. You know that means she's going to start meddling soon."

Ella sent her sister a swift side-eye. "Soon? Mother's already meddling. And let's not confuse things. Mother likes Lord Lucas's title more than she likes the man."

"That's not true," Cordelia replied unconvincingly. "She … she thinks he would make a good, proper companion for you. Someone to provide a nice, easy life."

The lackluster word fell between them like a lump of coal in a child's stocking. Ella scowled. "Companion. *Companion.* You get a husband with the kind of bedroom prowess—*that apparently isn't limited to the nighttime*—that even our mother boasts about, and I get a companion. And she wonders why I'm shuffling my feet to the altar."

Cordelia patted Ella's hand. "You know that's not what I meant." Her voice took on a soft, almost pitiful tenor, making Ella feel even worse. "I just don't want you to be bored or feel left behind with Mother and Father ... Alex and Constance and Suzanne have talked to me about it. The house must seem so quiet and lifeless."

"I wish you all wouldn't talk about me when I'm not around," Ella spat, unable to mask her hurt. It was bad enough being left behind—now her upcoming spinsterhood was the prime topic of conversation. "It's not fair. You're all a part of this married club, walking from room to room with smug, arrogant, *knowing* expressions. It's beyond annoying."

"We're hardly smug."

"All married women are smug," Ella contested. "You're just too nice to notice."

"I am not!"

Ella frowned at her oblivious sister. "You are, but don't worry. I still love you."

"Thank you so much," Cordelia grumbled. She swiveled her slender neck around, her eyebrows crowding into one. "Why have we stopped?"

Ella avoided her sister's discerning stare and pinched a few pieces of lint off her skirt. When she spoke, her voice was abnormally high. "No reason. I just thought you might need a rest."

Cordelia's frown deepened. They stood at the corner of South Carriage Drive and Serpentine Road, with the popular walking path, Rotten Row, waiting ahead of them. "I don't need to rest. Do you?"

Ella shrugged. "Not particularly."

Cordelia eyed her suspiciously. Using her parasol, she motioned forward. "Then should we continue?"

Ella shook her head, feeling the seconds pass by, pounding in tandem with her expectant heart.

He wasn't late; he couldn't be. He never was. Could she be early?

"I suppose I just like this spot, is all," Ella replied easily, gamboling over to a nearby oak tree. She plucked one of the low-hanging leaves and inspected it as if it were a fascinating new discovery. She twirled it lazily, desperately trying to seem as casual as possible.

Cordelia's shrewd gaze never strayed, branding Ella with her penetrating attention. "You practically pulled my arm out to get me here at this time and now you're acting like you have all the time in the world. You're acting weird."

The leaf quit twirling. "I am not."

"You are." Cordelia followed her over to the old, gnarled tree. Without asking, she flattened her hand up against Ella's forehead, almost knocking her straw bonnet from her head.

Ella jerked back, but her sister was insistent. "What are you doing?"

"I'm checking!" Cordelia replied, biting her lip. She held her hand against Ella a few more seconds before dropping it with a sigh. "You don't feel that warm."

Ella turned away in a dramatic huff. "Because I'm not. I'm perfectly fine."

Cordelia wasn't in the believing mood. "The doctors have told you that you mustn't overdo it. That's when your flares start."

Ella hugged herself. It wasn't that she felt violated by her sister's action, only she hated when others thought they knew her body better than she did. At twenty, Ella was far from the child who'd suffered from scarlet fever those many years ago. However, she was the only person who seemed to recognize that. "I know," she rasped, an indignant shiver zipping up her spine. "I am always careful."

Cordelia's sarcasm hit with the skill of a boxer. "You mean with all those ridiculous walks?"

Ella sulked. "I hardly walk this far every day."

"And what about your cricket club?" Cordelia harped. "I still can't believe Mother allowed you to join that team."

Ella's skirts bloomed as she spun around to face her sister. "You say you don't want me to feel lonely and then you ridicule the club I've joined. That club is the only thing that has helped my head stay above water ever since you … ever since … you left."

The second she heard her voice crack, Ella snapped her mouth shut. But it was too late. Cordelia's concern transformed into more pity, and Ella had to reach down deep to keep the tears at bay.

"Oh, Ella," she whispered. Cordelia reached for Ella's hand, providing a special safety blanket of comfort. "I'm sorry. I know it's been hard being alone." Her smile was pale and winsome, and cut straight to Ella's delicate heart. "If I could have taken you with me, I would have."

Ella sniffed, swiping at her nose. "I'm sure the marquis would have appreciated that."

Cordelia's lips widened in that smug, *married woman* way. "I'm not worried about the marquis. The man is completely infatuated with me. I can do no wrong in his eyes; sometimes I feel like an imposter, like I tricked him into thinking I could be his perfect marchioness."

"You're not an imposter," Ella grumbled. "You're perfect and you deserve every happiness. And I miss you."

Cordelia squeezed her hand one more time before letting it go. "I know. I miss you too. But that's why I need you to try now. I want you to find the same happiness I did. Then we can *both* be smug married women."

Ella finally raised her head and met her sister's unflinching, guileless countenance. Alexandra was considered the true beauty of the family with her raven locks, crystal-blue eyes, and alabaster complexion, but Cordelia was youth and vitality exemplified. Her features were more subdued, her hair more russet colored, her blue eyes paler, like the sea before a storm, but a sweet kindness emanated from her that was fruitless to ignore. Cordelia was the sun, her energy both brutal and life-giving.

Ella was more like their father, pale and blonde, with a petite frame that bordered on too skinny. Pretty enough, they'd say, especially for a wealthy viscount's daughter. She'd also heard *fair*, a time or two. Ella was fair. Not plain. Not extraordinary. Just *fair*.

"It's not like I'm against marriage," she began thoughtfully. "I don't *want* to be alone. You know that."

Cordelia nodded. "Well, that's a start. Do you … have someone in mind?"

Ella locked eyes with her sister. The name was on the tip of her tongue, but it refused to budge. There once was a time when she could have told Cordelia anything. Their childhood was filled with late nights under blankets, recounting dreams and fairytales that they wished would come true. But the past six months had pushed those nights and that childhood firmly in the past, to where Ella couldn't remember if those idyllic, enchanting moments had been real or just a figment of her imagination. Divulging secrets now—even to Cordelia—felt wanton and reckless. Childish.

And besides, everyone knew that once you said a wish out loud, it could never come true.

Ella was far from superstitious, but she'd never desired anything as badly as she wanted this man. This elusive, favored man—

Hoofbeats pounded into the dirt.

Ella's stomach immediately squeezed; her knees shuddered underneath her two stiff petticoats. Her tongue went dry.

Yes. Right on time. *His time.*

Ella's heart soared out of her chest, fluttering and pumping like the gallows of a great and mighty ship. Her eyes alighted down the lane, quickly and certainly, fixing on the man she waited every seven days to see, rain or shine.

Cordelia lined up next to her, shepherded by Ella's rampant fixation.

There he was.

Lord Oliver, Duke of Winchester, barreled down the park path atop his high-seated phaeton with his sleek and brutal cattle galloping at full, breakneck speed.

Ella was flooded in a fog of adoration, but even through that cloudy mist, she could hear the abject apprehension and pure, unadulterated fear in her sister's plaintive whisper.

"Oh, no, Ella … no," Cordelia murmured. The words sounded ragged and helpless. "Not him. Anyone but him."

The notion to be angry came upon Ella all at once. Swift and unrelenting, it clawed at her periphery, knocking, banging, trying to catch a thread of her sanity. But it was too elusive. Ella let the caustic feeling float by. All her attention, all her wanting, was for the man raging toward her, color high, hands strong and sure on the reins, the occasional grunt and whistle commanding the beasts before him as if he was Helios on his chariot, riding across the sky with his four-winged steeds demanding the day to commence.

And, as always, it was over too quickly.

A rush of wind slapped against the women as the duke rode past in a whirl of dirt, barely flicking them with anything remotely suggestive of an acknowledgement.

"Why is he driving like that? It can't possibly be safe," Cordelia exclaimed as they pivoted to watch him speed down the drive.

For some odd reason, that rankled Ella, even though her sister *was* right. The duke was driving one of the new, sleek phaetons and he sat up high, perched precariously on the box over the front axle. Light and airy, these two-horse vehicles were open to the elements on all sides and difficult to control for even the more experienced driver.

But if the rumors were true, Lord Oliver was an experienced man. In all things.

"He likes to race his cattle," Ella said. "He does it here, this early, so he can be alone and not put anyone in jeopardy." She wasn't precisely sure that was the reason, but it sounded right to her ears. She added, "It's very gentlemanly of him, actually."

"Gentlemanly, yes," her sister replied wryly. Ella could almost hear Cordelia's fine eyebrow arch in disdain. "That is exactly the word I would use to describe the Duke of Winchester."

Ella let that slight slide. What could she truly say, anyway? Did Cordelia actually think that Ella relished this obsession in her life? She'd heard the same stories that Cordelia had. All of London was aware of the duke's rakish behavior, his gaggle of mistresses, his sordid parties. The rogue was hardly discreet; he wore his debauchery on his sleeve!

Nevertheless, the moment Ella had witnessed his dark beauty and debonair suavity at her parents' ball the previous month, all self-preservation had flown out the window. She'd been hooked like the hapless fish that she was. Ella had been too terrified and overwhelmed to even be introduced to the duke at the ball by her friend, Lady Everly. Instead, she'd hidden, blending into the wallpaper, watching as the duke escorted their other friend, Lady Maggie, out to the dance floor. All eyes had been on him, so he couldn't possibly have known that hers had been the hungriest, had held the most yearning.

After that one pivotal scene, Ella had sought out every opportunity to know this man, to gather his personal information like a wartime spy. That was how she'd found out about these morning race sessions. That was when she'd set out to make him notice her.

Only he never did. This was her third Monday, and Lord Oliver had yet to tip his hat to her as he'd sped past her aloof façade. But Ella was patient. Scarlet fever had taught her that, when she'd been holed up in her room all those years ago, waiting for death to take her and offer a reprieve. Even after the worst had passed, a long convalescence had ensued. Books had been Ella's friends, and she'd gravitated to the great adventures. *Swiss Family Robinson, Ivanhoe, The Death of King Arthur*—heroes and kings fighting for love and family in far-off, exotic places that were beyond the realm of Ella's small, insulated existence.

The moment Ella had laid eyes on Lord Oliver, she'd known that he was those characters come to life. He was the real thing.

And one day, she vowed, he would speak to her. And in that blessed instance, she would no longer hide. And her days of traveling this world alone would be over.

"Ella?" Cordelia reminded her so much of their mother when she affected that wary tone. "He's a cad."

Ella pulled back her shoulders. "You don't know him."

"I know *of* him."

"Well, that's not the same, is it? Besides, he helped my friend this summer. He didn't need to, but he did. Lady Maggie said he was … surprising."

Cordelia huffed. "Surprising?"

"Please, just stop. I'm not in the mood for your comments."

Ella picked up her feet and trailed behind the phaeton's indentations in the dirt, keeping a watchful eye as the duke careened down the path. *He was going rather fast.* The wheels wavered side to side as if he was finding it difficult to keep them straight.

Cordelia trudged in her wake. "Mother will not be happy."

Ella scoffed. "Are you insane? She'd be ecstatic. Her entire mission in life is to see us married off well. It's no secret. The entire *ton* knows of her greed. She already has two marquises, one earl, and one viscount as sons-in-law. A duke would be her crowning glory. It would complete her card set."

Cordelia skipped up beside her, gasping as the phaeton hit a bump, all four wheels launching into the air before landing down safely. She blew out a nervous breath. "I had no idea you were so interested in helping mother complete her set." She gave the duke one last long look before sighing in resignation. "Can we go now? Have you taken your fill? I assume he was the reason we were here."

Ella's shoulders slumped. She was about to relent, but when she opened her mouth to respond, nothing came out. Or, at least, she couldn't hear herself. The crack of wood was too loud. The scream from the horses splintered through the park, bouncing off the trees in a cacophony of terror.

As Lord Oliver's phaeton took the turn for the Serpentine bridge, his reins snapped.

And all hell broke loose.

Chapter Two

"WHERE ARE YOU going?" Cordelia screamed.

Ella stopped. She blinked down at her feet, realizing that she'd taken off the moment she heard the wheel break off the phaeton. That had been the splintering noise. The duke had hugged the turn too closely. His wheel had skirted against the large rocks on the side of the path, causing it to skip into the air, smashing off as it hit the ground on impact.

Another scream—this time a man's—whipped Ella's attention back to the bridge. The horses were spooked and couldn't be contained. The vehicle swerved from side to side, smacking into the low brick wall on each end.

Panic fueled Ella as the phaeton tipped too far over the edge. She wanted to close her eyes to the monstrous event, but something inside her forced them open, needing to bear witness.

And then Lord Oliver fell. Or jumped. Ella couldn't be sure from so far away.

"Go!" she screamed, whipping back to Cordelia. "Get help! Quickly! Now!"

Cordelia's face was leached of color. "What? Where are you going?"

Again, Ella's feet were moving without her command. They gained momentum, and soon she was running at full speed toward the bridge. "Get help!" she cried over her shoulder.

Her eyes stayed on the water, and she pleaded with the Lord that soon she would see the duke's head pop through the surface, where he would take a massive breath.

But it didn't come.

Ella's lungs burned; her leather boots ate into the path eventually veering off to the grassy area bordering the lake. Scattered bits of the phaeton bobbed in the murky water, and Ella froze at the edge, unsure of what she could do.

When she saw a portion of his torso through the nebulous depths, she stopped thinking and threw herself into the cold water. Swimming had always come easy to Ella, but she'd never done it with this many layers of clothing on. She called up all her muscles to fight her dress and petticoats, which bloomed around her like she was a type of wayward jellyfish. The lake wasn't deep at first, and she was able to trudge along the muddy bottom, though the silty ground made it feel like tiny hands were grabbing her, forcing her under.

How long can a man stay underwater? Seconds? Maybe minutes? Ella had no idea how long it had been. Hours, in her frazzled mind.

The ground dropped out from underneath her, forcing Ella to swim the last bit. She stretched out her freezing hand and found his shoulder. Cupping underneath the duke's armpit, she tugged the rest of his body to the surface.

Instantly, Ella rearranged him so that his face was facing up. She forced herself not to panic. The duke's color was off; he looked the same, placid shade as the foul water he'd just been pulled from. They weren't far from the bank, but it took all of Ella's reserves to yank his body to the grass. She searched around for help, but no one was there. It was up to her. Only her.

When they were close enough to the grassy edge, Ella climbed out of the lake and attempted to pull him out. Again and again she yanked and tugged, but the man was simply too large. She could barely feel her hands now. Her feet were like icicles.

Disregarding the pinpricks of heat searing her toes into life, she ground her boots into the soft grass and pulled until she thought the tendons would snap from her neck. Ella screamed and cried, losing all hope that everything she'd just done might have amounted to something.

She managed to pull his torso over the edge of the lake, but his legs and feet still bobbed precariously in the water. Ella decided that would have to be good enough. She changed tactics.

Maneuvering herself on the slope, she placed his head in her wet lap, smoothing the duke's inky hair off his high forehead. She caressed his high cheekbones, pressed her shaking fingers over his pale, puffy lips.

She wondered if she'd lost her mind. Something insane inside her wanted to kiss those lips. Kiss life back into him, just like the fairytales promised.

His eyelid twitched, and Ella startled. She started at the thin, bluish pieces of skin, hoping that it would happen again. But nothing.

Breathless, shivering, she waited. And waited. But nothing more happened.

She'd read once that people blew into the mouths of drowning victims, inflating oxygen into their lungs. Could she do it? Ella bent over his torso, which seemed to turn more and more into a block of ice the longer he lay there.

Ella licked her lips, trying for warmth, trying to encourage life to flow from her into the duke. She'd never kissed a man before.

She leaned to him, feeling the heat of her breath ricochet off his pallid skin back to her. She closed her eyes, opening her mouth the tiniest bit.

And then it went dark.

Ella's head snapped up, but she was covered in … scratchy wool.

A blanket. Someone had thrown a blanket over her head.

Two hands took her shoulders from behind and launched her farther onto the grass. She tore the wool from her eyes and sat stunned as an older gentleman reached under the duke's arms and, with one great lunge, hauled his entire body from the water. The man wasted little time, beating against Lord Oliver's chest, slapping his face with a startling lack of care until the duke began to cough.

Water sprayed from his mouth and ran down the side of his cheeks. But still, his eyes remained closed.

"Are you all right, miss?"

Ella jumped at the voice behind her. She covered her face with her hands as heady, uncontrollable emotions bombarded her. He was alive. He was alive! Because of her.

"Miss?" A hand was on her shoulder now, and that small bit of kindness proved to be too much.

Ella broke as swiftly as the phaeton's wheel had done, and she began to sob. Large, ugly cries escaped her chilled chest as a crowd gathered around the scene. She could only sit there in her tears as two men shepherded in a cart from down the path. With steady hands, they picked up the duke and placed him in the back as if he were just an ordinary man.

Ella got to her feet. "Where are they taking him?" she shrieked, running to the wagon. Arms held her back as she fought to climb on. Leaving him seemed impossible. How could they just take him away from her? Why were they holding her back? "Please," she sobbed.

"It's all right, miss." It was the older gentleman who'd hauled the duke out of the lake. Through her tears and confusion, Ella could see his face was softened by age and kindness. He whispered to her as if she were a hysterical child. Perhaps she was. "He'll be all right. But he needs help. You've saved his life, but you can't do any more. You need to help yourself now."

Ella's face contorted in disbelief. "Me? I'm fine."

"Ella!" She turned to see Cordelia running toward her. She only had a second to brace herself before her sister threw her arms around her. "Are you all right?"

Ella couldn't take her eyes off the cart. It was already hurrying down the path. The duke was getting farther and farther away from her.

"Ella? Ella?"

Words. So many words pounded along the periphery of her mind. People kept trying to talk to her, touch her, guide her away, but Ella couldn't move. Her body felt stuck to this spot like a ghost who couldn't leave the place they'd been killed, doomed to haunt it forever.

The cart was getting away. Soon it would be out of the park. Soon the duke's life would be in somebody else's hands.

No longer hers.

"I was going to marry him," Ella said to herself. Her vision blurred. Everything started to spin. "I was going to be his wife."

And then she hit the ground.

Chapter Three

Two days later

THIS DAY SHOULD have gone differently.

Lord John Sutton clenched his fists in his lap, holding himself back from punching a hole in the carriage floor. He bobbed along like a cork in the waves as the driver remained vigilant in hitting every divot along the narrow London road.

They'd say he wanted this, wished for it, even prayed for it.

They'd say he wasted little time, moving into his brother's townhome, spending his precious money, drinking his even more precious wine.

But the *ton* didn't know Jack. And he doubted very much that they knew Oliver. Jack was the only one who did, and they hadn't had a true conversation in ... how long?

Jack waded through the grief and muck in his mind, grateful to focus on something other than the odds of his brother surviving the crash. The answer remained elusive. Surely, they talked each time Jack made port? It was true that Jack never stayed in London for longer than a few days before heading out to the open sea again, but he usually made time to visit his mother, kiss her on the cheek, and prove that he hadn't been shipwrecked or eaten by cannibals. He must have seen his older brother in passing.

Jack relaxed his fists long enough to fill his hands with his throbbing head. The brothers had been thick as thieves for the majority of their lives. With only the two of them, their parents had doted on them equally, despite one being a future duke. Oliver had never been singled out, paraded in front of others, or given a greater share of anything, whether it be toys or space. Jack could only assume his parents had known that those accoutrements would come later anyway.

And yet that knowing had never scarred their family like Jack had seen it scar others who were held by the yoke of primogeniture. Oliver was always going to be the duke. And Jack wasn't. And neither of them had cared a fig one way or the other.

So where had it all gone wrong? Could Jack pinpoint a time, a second when their casual, fruitful relationship had gone sour?

Finally, a conversation came to him. It wasn't their last, but Jack clung to it regardless. Could it possibly have been fifteen years ago?

Instead of filling him with anger and regret, the amorphous memory only infused Jack with contentment, and not a small amount of the kind of sadness that only homesickness could deliver.

It had started in this very carriage as it carried him to the docks that pivotal day. Jack recalled the sun hitting him in the eyes like a hammer as he'd opened the door and stepped out into the busy thoroughfare. Then he'd closed his eyes—yes, in an effort to block out the vibrant rays, but also so that he could inflate his lungs with the sea air. It smelled like freedom. It smelled like a different, more deserving home. An adventure in the way that most sixteen-year-old boys expected new beginnings to be.

If anyone had felt the cloying tug of jealousy that day, it was the eighteen-year-old boy Jack had left behind in the carriage.

"Tell Father and Mother that I'll miss them," Jack shouted to Oliver while he looked side to side, taking in all the bustling sights flowing past him.

His brother laughed, dragging Jack's attention back to the

carriage. Oliver lifted an imperious brow, stretching his neck out the window. "You already hugged them over a hundred times this morning. They already know you'll miss them."

Jack's rueful frown was good-natured. He ripped his new sailor's hat off his head, twirling it around in his trembling fingers. "Just tell them again, will you?"

Oliver nodded in that debonair, *noblesse oblige* way that he'd taken up ever since he'd started Oxford that fall. His eyes lifted from his younger brother and widened at the noise and commotion as a returning ship—a lean and sharp clipper—nearly collided with a shabby tugboat on its way to mooring.

"I'm not jealous of you, you know."

Jack's mouth split into a wide smile. It was something they said to each other. The statement almost served as an embrace. Something familiar. Like touching the person next to you in the dark just to make sure they were still there.

He hitched his hat back on his head, standing taller. "I'm not jealous of you either."

Confidence settled back into Oliver's broad shoulders. "Good. Because I'm going to be a duke someday." The haughtiness in his voice was belied by the crinkles forming at the corners of his eyes. "The last thing I would want to do is travel the world with a bunch of stinking men I don't know, exploring ancient worlds, eating spicy foods, savoring exotic women. No thank you. Not the life for me. Sounds awfully boring, actually."

Jack nodded, feigning seriousness. "You make a good point," he conceded. "But, then again, I would hate to be welcomed into the poshest clubs, be fawned over by scandalous and talented opera singers, all while hunting and fishing to my heart's desire. Nor would I want to be shackled to the most beautiful girl in London. Sounds absolutely horrid."

Oliver's aloof expression vanished. The sun glinted off every one of his white teeth. "She *is* beautiful, isn't she?"

There was a part of Jack that yearned to keep teasing his brother, but it proved impossible in this instance. "She is. I can't believe she actually likes you."

"Not just *likes* me. She *loves* me, brother."

An uncomfortable feeling stole over Jack, like someone had thrown a wet wool blanket over his shoulders. Love was all well and good in books and plays, but to his young self, it seemed to come with too many limitations. Now, lust, on the other hand … Jack approved of lust. He understood that. Lust made perfect sense.

Oliver continued to beam. "And Father loves her just as much as Mother does. How is that possible? Those two never agree on anything! She's absolutely perfect." His chin lowered along with his voice, but nothing could tarnish the glint in his eyes. "I'm going to look for a ring after I drop you off. One as big as your head!"

Jack snorted, all his biased notions about love being confirmed right before him. Love turned men into milquetoasts— even future dukes. "I hate to tell you this, Ollie, but dukes don't get married before they turn twenty. It's hardly the done thing."

"Well, I hate to tell *you* this, Jackie, but duke's sons don't run off to work on merchant vessels. Speaking of not-done things."

Ouch. That was a joust to the stomach. Jack caressed his solar plexus, right where he was sure the imaginary blow had hit. He'd deserved it. He'd only meant to tease his brother, but he must have forgotten that milquetoasts weren't usually known for their sense of humor.

However, it was nothing Jack hadn't heard before. His father and uncles had spent the last year begging him to go to university and become a member of the clergy, or—if his blood truly pumped for the sea—to join the Royal Navy. He'd considered it, only because they'd asked him to, but those options never fueled his ambitions like running his own company did. Jack craved money and success. Even though his family always prided itself on regurgitating the saying "Money is the root of all evil," it was only because they could afford to. Jack, as a second son, could not.

His hand dropped to his side. "You know why I'm leaving."

Oliver's fierce countenance matched his brother's. "And you know why I'm proposing. There's only one Jo. I could live to be one hundred and never meet another girl that is made for me like she is."

The wind kicked up, almost beckoning Jack away, and he had to hold on to his hat before it was blown off his head. "I know that," he said. Not even begrudgingly. Because it was true. Seeing his brother fall in love with Lady Josephine had made the past year exciting, and a little maddening. The sweet girl hadn't taken Oliver away from him so much as she'd opened Jack's eyes to the future. Sharing Oliver with the dukedom has always been easy—he'd grown up doing it. But sharing him with a wife would be infinitely harder. And realizing that had sharpened Jack's dreams of leaving home and learning the ropes on a merchant ship, hoping one day he'd be smart enough, savvy enough, courageous enough, to run his own.

So, he supposed the next time he saw Lady Jo, he should thank her. She'd lit the fire. And now he was standing at the docks saying goodbye to the person he loved most in the world, hoping that it wouldn't be their last moment together.

Jack glanced over his shoulder. Like ants, the shipman and cargo haulers, the passengers and warehouse directors, moved in a frightening way that seemed second nature to all but him.

"You'll get the hang of it in no time," Oliver stated, surprising Jack with his observant take. He patted the side of the carriage, like putting a period on a sentence. "Promise that you'll be back for the wedding?"

Jack nodded. He didn't dare talk. A tidal wave of tears and bumbling was building, and his resistance was fading quickly. He wasn't sure how to board a ship as a crew member for the first time, but teary-eyed wasn't it.

Oliver shrugged his great, wide shoulders, reminding Jack so much of their father. "So … I'll be seeing you, then?"

Jack nodded once more.

Oliver cocked his head and tried for a close-mouthed smile. "Try not to wind up dead."

Jack had to reach all the way down to his stomach to spit out the words. "I will," he replied gruffly.

With one last knowing look, the brothers took each other in, spending an extra few seconds trying to imprint each other's faces so that, if needed, they could live in that last moment for the rest of their lives. Then Oliver broke the spell, escaping back into the carriage as he hit the top of the ceiling, instructing the driver to move on.

His whole life had been ahead of him, as had Jack's.

But it wasn't supposed to land them here.

In this same goddamned carriage.

Jack wished that he would have offered his brother the same warning. *Try not to wind up dead.*

But would he have listened? Oliver made a habit of never listening to others. Jack always liked to think he was an exception—that Oliver would always heed him—but deep down knew that wasn't the case.

The carriage lurched to a halt.

Jack yanked the shade out of the way and peered out the window. A crescent of stately rowhouses trailed down the road, seemingly growing into the burnt-orange horizon that soaked through London's hazy sky. He shuddered through a haggard sigh and grabbed his hat next to him. Throwing it on his head, he hauled himself out the door. Time was precious. Lingering in the past was not.

Thankfully, he only had to give the door two raps before a severe, ancient-looking butler came to his rescue and directed him to the drawing room with shaking, craggy limbs. Although it was nothing like the sprawling home he'd grown up in, Jack could tell money and care went into the upkeep of the fine room. There were no loose threads on the damask curtains, no frayed corners on the thick Turkish carpet. Viscount Weston clearly wasn't hurting for funds, like some of the *ton's* finest families who failed to grow with the times.

Jack tried to sit on the velvet settee, but was on his feet in minutes, wearing out the rug, checking his watch so many times that he didn't even bother tucking it back into his waistcoat pocket. Everything about him felt raw, naked to the elements. Being here in this well-appointed home, waiting for some well-heeled chit, was the last thing he wanted to do, especially while Oliver was laid out in his bedroom, unconscious, fighting for his life. Fighting for all their lives, really.

For two days he'd shown no progress. Not even a slight improvement. No moving. No speaking. Not opening his eyes. Barely breathing. Jack should be there at his side! Providing … what? *Something*. Anything.

But his mother—who'd never shown any inclination for religion before this—suddenly was a full believer in the Lord's mysterious miracles, and she was desperately hoping the girl in this fashionable house would be a conduit for one of them. Maybe his mother was right, Jack conceded. If the rumors were true, and this woman had managed to entice a proposal out of the feckless, profligate Duke of Winchester, then maybe the impossible was still alive and well in Victoria's London.

Needless to say, desperate times made believers out of everyone. And Jack spent his days and nights with a bunch of superstitious sailors who would pray to an old shoe if they thought it could deliver them a fortuitous wind, so although he wasn't the first to drop to his knees and press his palms together, he wasn't above lifting an ear to a hopeful story.

Footsteps echoed along the shiny parquet floor outside the room. Jack turned to the door. The knob was twisted slightly before going still, as if the person on the other side had changed their mind. Exasperated, Jack charged forward, about to whip open the door himself when the latch finally clicked and a small, unassuming woman entered the space.

At first, Jack thought it was a child come to tell him that Miss Ella was delayed writing letters or arranging flowers, or whatever it was ladies did to fill their interminable days. But as she ventured toward him, he realized that children didn't hold themselves in such a stately and collected manner.

Nor did they reek of sherry.

Head bowed and demure like a geisha from the Far East, the girl misjudged the distance between them and halted a hairsbreadth away. For long, ungainly seconds, she stood there, and all Jack could do was wonder how much she'd had to drink while he stared at the dark blonde hair pulled tight across the crown of her head. The part in the middle was so aggressive that he spotted a couple of perfectly round freckles peeking out through the veil of hair. She was thin, giving Jack the impression that her skeleton was holding up her pale-yellow dress and not much else. She reminded him of a bird, one that had little hope of making it through winter without the help of a strong and determined mate.

Again, Jack meditated on his brother's intentions. This plain girl? How could she entice the duke when he needed neither the money nor the social advancement?

His eyes immediately went for her stomach, which was as flat and unremarkable as the rest of her. Jack was no expert on the subject, but a woman in difficult, delicate times surely showed more than that. If Oliver had put the girl in a bad position, wouldn't it have been more apparent?

Time gnawed away at him, eating at him like Prometheus's ever-present vulture. This wasn't the moment for these meandering questions. Nor was it for shyness or fear.

She hiccupped.

Or drunkenness.

"Are you …" Jack stopped when the girl's narrow shoulders bounced in surprise. He tried again, softening his tone. The silly woman might jump out of her translucent skin if he raised his voice above a whisper. "Are you Miss Ella?"

She hesitated a beat and then nodded.

Jack ran a frustrated hand over his face. *Christ,* he couldn't throw the woman in the carriage and speed off without her at least speaking first. Getting to the point was imperative. "The same Miss Ella who saved Lord Oliver's life two days ago—"

Another hiccup. Or was it a sob?

Jack rolled his eyes. He didn't know what he wanted her to be less, drunk or hysterical.

"Do not toy with me, Lord John. I do not think I can take it."

Jack hesitated. The tenor of her sentence was rather unexpected. As was hearing his given name. No one called him Lord John. Ever.

Her voice was deep and husky, completely foreign to the picture she presented. That low, toe-curling sound wasn't the voice of a shy girl who'd snuck into the sherry bottle, but of a woman. Jack widened his stance, rooting his feet in place in case any other surprises emerged to topple him over.

Face still downcast, Ella went on, "Please don't make me wait. Tell me now ... is he still alive?"

She lifted her head. Slowly, with undiluted authority, she met his gaze, holding it with the blazing heat of steady conviction. It was that courage, that tenacity, that stilled the words on Jack's tongue, though the dark brown eyes were equally arresting. Time—which had ridden him like an impatient jockey over the last two days—seemed to slow.

The girl—Ella—arched a brow in mild irritation. "Sir?" she said, seeming vexed. *With him!* "Please ... will he live?"

Jack continued to peruse her face, wondering what it was that had captured his brother's attention first. Was it the eyebrows that framed her eyes, bushy and a darker shade than her wheat-colored hair? The high cheekbones that were at present drained of color, but Jack suspected were infused with soft pinks at the best of times? Or maybe the lips that lacked the plumpness of a seductress's, though still yielded an enticing invitation as she gritted her teeth in irritation behind them. These were all small things, barely noticeable to men with big appetites, men with far-reaching tastes that could only be bothered with bigger and better and more, more, more.

Men like Oliver.

On the other hand, maybe he appreciated the fact that the girl enjoyed a tipple.

Now it was all starting to make sense. *Goddamn you, Oliver! Couldn't you have picked a respectable girl to bring home … for Mother's sake?*

This girl couldn't possibly provide the miracle his mother needed. And yet she wouldn't rest until Jack delivered this little drunkard. Again, he bristled at the waste of his time.

A tapping noise yanked Jack from his fury.

For some reason, he swept his hand to his heart, but that organ was not the source of the noise. His heart was pumping much faster, at the speed of a hummingbird's wing. He dropped his head and noticed Ella's dainty yellow slipper punching into the floor as she waited for him to connect his brain to his mouth.

Jack settled his hands on his hips. "I thought a girl like you would have figured out the secret by now."

Her brows pulled together in confusion. She shook her head for a couple seconds too long, causing her body to sway with it. "What secret?"

Jack leaned in, to the delicate lobe of her ear. He also did this for a few seconds longer than necessary, enjoying the way she held her breath, as if he were about to tell her the answer to life's greatest mystery. "You should always dab a little perfume after you've been at the bottle." He flicked a smooth swath of skin right behind her ear with the tip of his finger, causing her to jerk away in a rush. "It won't mask all the smell, but it helps."

Ella's mouth and eyes battled to see which one could widen the most in indignation. Her eyes won. "How dare you! I haven't been—*Hiccup* … It's medicine!" Glaring at him, she breathed into her hand and held it to her nose. She closed her eyes, her shoulders deflating.

Ha! Serves her right. "Medicine, sure, yes …"

"It is! I haven't been able to get warm. My brother-in-law

assured me that a capful of sherry would do the trick."

"Who's your brother-in-law, Blackbeard?"

"No," Ella replied uncertainly, taking his snide comment much too seriously. "Marquis Tykesbury. He's visiting with my sister, Cordelia. He left me the bottle … in case I needed it."

Jack twisted his lips wryly. "And let me guess, you've needed it all day long."

"Hardly all day—"

Jack shrugged, throwing up a hand. "I don't care. And to be honest, it isn't my business. But if it's possible, I need you to sober up. Quickly. I won't have you meeting my mother smelling and weaving like a doxy after a long night of work."

Ella's eyes and mouth were at it again. Had Jack thought her lips thin? They were actually quite full … when she was furious. Her upper body seemed to shake like she was a volcano ready to blow. Not a tendril of her hair fell out of place, though. She was a perfect English doll: fairly complected, petite. Her mouth set in a grim line. She probably read the Bible each night before bed— when she was sober enough to make out the words.

The fact that that aroused him should send him straight to hell. And yes, Jack *was* aroused. He'd always had a thing for priggish, disapproving women. His cock thickened, and the hairs on the back of his neck hadn't relaxed since she entered the room.

"How dare you—Wait." Her bluster evaporated as she lifted her nose, blinking into space. "Your mother? She wants to speak to me? Why?"

"Because my brother is dying," Jack stated bluntly, ignoring the stab to his heart. "My poor, grieving mother believes that you are the only one who can revive him, and I love her too much to tell her that she's mad." He cocked his head, studying her. "But I think I might just have to, because you are clearly not up for the task. Good day, miss."

He slammed on his hat and strode for the door. His hand was almost around the handle when a steel-like paw circled his forearm, yanking him back. This time there was no rehearsed look, no perfected smirk. His incredulity was purely of the moment.

Ella regarded the arm in her hand as if she didn't have the slightest idea how it got there. "I'm sorry. You can have this back," she said, swiftly dropping her hold. She paused to take a deep breath, fighting for composure. "I told you that I am not ordinarily like this. In fact"—she put up her hands in a defensive position—"I've never had a drink before in my life. And I only had one—all right, a few—today, which is probably why I'm acting so … so … forward."

Jack crossed his arms, masking his thoughts with a tight smile. "You're right. I don't believe you."

She rolled her eyes. "Why does your mother think I can help … help … Lord Oliver?" Her composure finally slipped. Her voice cracked in the back of her throat as she said his brother's name. Clenching her jaw, she continued, "Surely family should be with him in his time of need. I pulled him from the water—"

"You saved him." Jack swept a quick glance down her waif-like body, where he was certain he would need a magnifying glass to find any semblance of muscle. His next words sailed out of his mouth, more patronizing than he would have liked. "Although I don't see how."

Ella's chocolatey eyes narrowed at his rudeness. "You are rather quick to judge, my lord."

"I call it like I see it."

She pulled her shoulders back. "Well, you do not see me— *Hiccup*."

Jack raised his fingers to his temple, massaging the headache he could sense soaring his way. He was at a loss. Disappointing his mother was beyond his ken, but this woman … He watched as she meandered behind the settee. She reached out to hold on to the back frame but again misjudged the distance and almost toppled to the floor, catching herself right in time. This woman was an absolute mess.

Nevertheless, Jack was a captain. He'd dealt with messes

before. People were his specialty. If he could handle twenty-five no-account, filthy sea dogs for weeks at a time, he could manage this slip of a girl. For one night, anyway. And then he'd send her back to her home and her beloved sherry.

He stood in front of her once more, snapping his fingers to get her attention.

Ella swatted his hand out of her face. "You're intolerably rude, do you know that?"

Jack considered it a rhetorical question. "Stop talking and listen to me. My mother asks that you sit with Oliver tonight. She thinks you'll be able to help him. She's desperate and I'm desperate to give her whatever she needs. Can you handle this?" He lowered his head, repeating softly, "Can you handle that?"

The long lines of her throat undulated in a low wave before she eventually nodded.

"Good." He reached for her elbow. Ella jerked slightly as he held her. "Relax," he drawled. "I just don't want you falling before we get there. We don't need two people in comas tonight."

Ella whipped her elbow out of his hand. "I'm perfectly capable—"

In a flash, Jack was at her side, righting the ship when she stumbled.

"Care to finish that sentence?"

"Oh, be quiet," she murmured, allowing him to usher her out the door. But even as she became more malleable, Jack noticed a change in her as they headed down the hallway. Her limbs tightened as tension seemed to climb over her like a pernicious weed infecting a garden overnight. "B-but I don't understand," Ella stammered, losing the low, husky tones that had so captivated him. It was almost like she was speaking to herself. "I don't understand what your mother thinks I can do. I'm just the girl that pulled him out of the river."

When they reached the foyer, Jack began barking orders at the butler, demanding the lady's things, asking for a word with the viscount or viscountess. When he had the household rushing to do his bidding, he finally came back to her. Ella appeared lost to him, retreating into some inner turmoil. Jack wasn't even sure if she knew she was twisting her fingers raw. Gently, he reached for them, noticing how swollen and red they'd become. Painful even to look at.

He took his time unwinding the inflamed fingers. "Come now, you're more than that."

She blinked up at him, her pale eyelashes flickering as if he'd spoken in a foreign language.

"What do you mean ... more than—"

She broke off as a lady's maid lumbered down the stairs and placed a thin green cloak over Ella's shoulders. The viscountess was quick on her heels.

"What is going on?" Lady Weston demanded, lifting her chin. It was clear where Ella got her petite stature. But that seemed to be the only feature she'd inherited from her mother. Lady Weston was as dark as her daughter was fair, with lovely violet eyes and midnight hair piled lusciously on the top of her head. She halted on the fourth step from the bottom, remaining a head taller than everyone. Jack was in on her trick. He didn't think it was necessary. Her bellow was the type that generals practiced when they thought no one could hear them.

Jack bowed, quickly introducing himself and explaining why he needed Ella to leave with him at once. "I apologize for my behavior, my lady, but my mother says the doctors cannot do it all. She maintains that a man's body cannot be revived without his heart and spirit. She is under the impression that my brother will not wake unless his fiancée is there waiting for him."

Ella spun to face him. "Fiancée?"

Lady Weston's head jerked like a startled owl's. "Fiancée?" Then, as if her first word had never happened, she pivoted, brushing an errant black hair off her forehead. "Oh, yes, *fiancée*."

It wasn't a question this time. But it still didn't have the might of a statement. The older woman looked to her youngest daughter, eyeing her carefully. Something pricked at Jack's insides as Ella ducked, once more only showing the crown of her bowed head.

He shifted his weight to his other leg as he contemplated the scene. The viscountess would make a champion poker player. What tics and indications she'd revealed in her countenance had all been washed away in a matter of seconds.

Jack turned his focus to Ella, who released a slight tremble. "You *are* engaged?" he asked.

Did Ella chirp? He squared his shoulders, lifting her chin with the pad of his finger. Apparently, Ella was more like her mother than he'd thought, because she'd also managed to wipe her face clean. A blank slate, Ella withstood his scrutiny with placid, marble-like features.

Using his bulk as intimidation, Jack stepped closer to her, searching for guile, but all he noticed was that the heat running through his veins seemed to bleed into her, causing a flush to swim up her porcelain neck into the hollow of her cheeks. "The old man at the lake ..." he began quietly. "He heard you. He heard you say you were going to marry my brother. Did you say it? Is it true?"

"Of course it's true!" the viscountess cried, skipping down the last four steps, finally demurring to Jack's height. She nudged him out of the way with her hips and threw her arms around her daughter in a hug that was supposed to be comforting, but one Jack considered a little too congratulatory. Lady Weston pulled away, rubbing Ella's upper arms as if to wake the chill in her bones. Her words were to Jack, but her gaze never left her daughter. Her smile was wide and toothy as she said, "My daughter wouldn't declare anything so wonderful if it wasn't true. Obviously, she forgot herself in the drama of the day. Saving a life can be very taxing, can't it? I'm afraid you caught me off guard, my lord. You see ... the engagement is new, and I was surprised that you even knew about it. We haven't told anyone." Looking over her shoulder at him, she shrugged coquettishly. "Your brother had ideas about the announcement. You know how he can be."

Jack's eyes turned to slits. If the events of the last two days proved anything, it was that he wasn't sure if he *did* know his brother anymore.

The lady charged at him then, poking and prodding his shoulders before tugging Ella's cloak even tighter around her neck. "Go, go, you two. The duke needs you. Why are you still here? Don't keep him waiting. The sooner Ella can revive her love, the sooner the wedding can take place!"

Jack gave her one last discerning glance before taking the hint and turning toward the door, which the austere butler opened with relish.

But just as Jack had Ella at the threshold, she resisted, tugging out of his hold, throwing her mother a beseeching look. "What am I thinking? I can't do this. I can't do this. *I can't do this.* What does the duchess possibly think I can do?" She shook her head back and forth like she was in the middle of a fit.

She lunged for her mother, clinging to her arms for dear life. "I can't do this. Please, Mother. What about my condition? Didn't Father say I needed to rest?"

Lady Weston smiled sweetly at Jack as if apologizing for her daughter's outburst. However, the way she ground the words out through her teeth wasn't as saccharine. "Yes, and by the smell of your breath, it seems you've been doing exactly that." She clicked her tongue at Jack. "Poor thing, she's been beside herself with grief."

Ella ignored her. "But what about Cordelia? She's leaving tomorrow. I don't know when I'll see her again."

Lady Weston patted her hands. "You'll see her at the ball soon, and you write such personable letters!"

Ella lowered her chin, positively glowering. "Mother," she growled. "This is a family matter. Surely, *surely*, I shouldn't impose."

The viscountess tipped her head to her daughter's until their foreheads almost touched. Jack had the sick feeling of being a fly on the wall, that something was happening here that was completely lost to him. The mother spoke slowly and firmly. "But you *are* his family now, my love. And you're not imposing if they ask."

"Do you know what *you're* asking me to do?"

Lady Weston tilted her head back, that smile never vanishing. She cupped her daughter's cheek. "Yes, my dear. I'm asking you to do what you've always done. *Love him.*"

Chapter Four

MEETING ONE'S POTENTIAL in-laws was trying enough; meeting them after downing half a bottle of sherry, after telling a horrendous lie about their deathly-sick son, did not help matters.

Oh, Ella had really put her foot in it this time.

How in the world had this happened? She barely remembered pulling Lord Oliver out of the Serpentine. Her mind was as brackish and muddled as the disgusting water. She'd spent the better part of the past two days in bed, shivering under an avalanche of blankets, trying to recover and come to terms with the catastrophic event.

Her parents had been furious at her daring rescue, and Cordelia had had to fill her in on the pertinent parts. Even now she had a difficult time believing that she'd had the strength, nay, the courage to run toward the crash instead of running for help. What had gotten into her? Having been told her entire life that she wasn't strong enough, wasn't healthy enough, it was beyond Ella's reasoning that she'd thought she could do anything worthwhile for the duke.

And yet she'd dragged him from the lake. She had risked her life to save his.

And, unfortunately, in her heady, arrogant delirium, she'd

also told everyone within earshot that she was his fiancée.

It could happen to anyone, right?

Probably not.

Cordelia had had to tell her that part too. Ella certainly didn't recall that boldness. Perhaps in a pique of self-care, her brain had flung away the memory, hoping to never hear of it again. Saying it in her heart was one thing, but saying it out loud? *Brazen. Insane.*

And now Ella was paying the price, sitting across from this hulk of a man, being jostled about in a carriage by a driver who didn't care to avoid the holes as he hurried down the road. The last hole jounced Ella so bad, her head almost hit the carriage ceiling.

She should have known her mother wouldn't help her. Just as she should have known that Cordelia would have informed her mother about Ella's obsession with the duke.

Ella's stomach had almost hit the floor when Lord John said the unfortunate word: *fiancée.* Her mother's face, on the other hand, had never beamed brighter, because Ella knew a plan was being hatched. It had been inevitable. Lady Weston was known for many things: her beauty, her vivacity, her love for her husband, but most of all she was renowned for her ambition. A duke had somehow—sadly, unconsciously—fallen into her web. And nothing, not even a lie and a coma, would help the poor man out of it.

Ella would have to see this through. To what end, she had no idea.

She just had to get through the night. And let every step dictate her next. She would find a way off this hazardous ride. There was no other option.

But first things first. She needed to make sure she could walk in a straight line.

Ella searched about the carriage. The finest one she'd ever traveled in, it was resplendent with navy satin silk covering. The ceiling was pleated in blue damask, with a rosette in the middle with the same damask pattern acting as a border throughout. Her seat was plush and tufted with velvet, which certainly helped with the frantic driving.

She cleared her throat. "Is there any water?"

Lord John sat back in his seat across from her, thighs splayed wide. Shadows and light took turns slashing across his face from the shade bumping against the window. His hair was short, abnormally so, cut close to the skin and sun-bleached to the point where she thought he might be bald. Even the gentlemen who loved to ride and hunt weren't as tanned as he. If Lord John had pulled a golden earring out of his pocket and fastened it to his ear, she wouldn't have been surprised.

After appraising her long enough to make her squirm in her seat, the lord finally leaned forward with a put-upon sigh. He reached into the mahogany drawer against the wall and pulled out a small bottle and glass, then unscrewed the top and sniffed it. Scrunching his nose, he returned the cap and placed the bottle and glass back in the drawer.

"No."

Apparently, the clear liquid inside the bottle was not water. Good to know.

Lord John—the infamous Lord John—resumed his casual position. Ella didn't know all the facts about Lord Oliver's infamous brother, but she wasn't sure who in the *ton* did. Like everyone else, she'd heard he set sail at sixteen, sporadically visiting his family after that. If she believed some, Lord John owned his own shipping company; if she believed others, he was a nefarious pirate. Sadly, no middle ground had ever been taken.

The taciturn man hadn't spoken to her since he'd thrown her in her seat—and "thrown" was the nicest way she could put it. Clearly, time was of the essence, which made her heart beat faster and harder.

The duke was dying. It was written all over the mysterious man's solemn face, stitched in the lines that fanned out from his eyes and sunk deep in the brackets around his mouth. He wasn't so much scary as intimidating. Although he was dressed like a gentleman and was aware of the social niceties that went along with the garments, he seemed out of his element, uncomfortable in the fine carriage, sharing his air with a viscount's daughter.

But pirates weren't gentle, were they? Lord John's blue eyes may have hinted at ice, but there was a warmth when he'd touched her hands at the house, unfolding her fingers from each other. Ella had spotted his concern when he saw her hands, which had become inflamed and swollen after her time in the lake. He'd taken great care, using just the right amount of pressure and strength to uncoil the panic from her body.

Ella couldn't help but wish that he would do it again. But she couldn't ask him to. She wouldn't demand that he allay her fears, because then she'd actually have to tell him what they were. Yes, of course Ella was worried—beyond worried—that the duke would perish from the accident.

But Lord, she was a selfish, cowardly woman. Because she was more terrified that they all might find out that she wasn't who she said she was.

"Hm."

Ella broke from her inner rambling and eyed Jack. He crossed his arms, the muscles doing their best to situate themselves while straining against the fabric of his jacket. His size was *repressive*. No wonder the man spent his days on the bow of a ship; the ocean was probably the only thing in nature that could trump his brawny presence.

Lord John's expression was marred by a frown that kept coming back to her. Whenever he managed to tear his gaze away, he did it with another "hm." As if Ella were a vexing puzzle. As if Ella were an unsolvable riddle. For a man who'd undoubtedly traveled all over the world, to be so confusing felt almost a little exotic.

But even that little boon wasn't enough to quell Ella's anxiety. Her nerves were frayed to a ridiculous level, and by the tenth "hm," she unleashed.

"You can either stop making that sound or tell me why you're making it. The choice is yours."

Lord John's fathomless gaze fell on her, heavy as the stone they tied to witches right before they threw them in the lake to drown. "Sorry—"

"You're not sorry."

"That's not what I meant—"

"I know what you meant."

Perhaps it was the desertion of her mother, or maybe the untrusting glint in his eye that was even apparent in the moody carriage—or maybe it was the lingering effects of the sherry—but Ella was impelled to regain her voice *and* her backbone. She needed some sense of control in all this mess.

Jack's arms tightened over his broad chest even more. His tongue played with a tooth in the back of his mouth. Ella imagined he rubbed it back and forth like it was a genie's lamp with varying results. His voice reminded her of a knife's edge, sharp and precarious. "I can't get a proper read on you."

Ella steeled herself. His words hit, but she would not grimace. "Is that right?" she returned softly.

The corner of Jack's mouth lifted in a sardonic smile. Because Ella was so used to people always thinking and believing the best in her, the smile almost felt approving, though his next words squashed that hopeful idea soon enough. "It *is* right," he drawled lazily, "because you said you're engaged to my brother. I assume that means you love him, and yet I had to drag you out of your house to see him. In fact"—he leaned forward, resting his forearms on his knees—"why did I even have to come and get you? Why didn't your parents send a letter inquiring about my brother? Why didn't you try to come earlier?"

That was a lot of *whys*.

"Because," Ella replied, knowing that she was blinking too fast to seem normal, "we … we … thought it best to give your family space in this private matter."

Jack nodded as if he'd already known that she would respond

in that way. "But as your mother just said, you're practically family. Or close enough."

Ella pressed her back into the carriage cushion, almost wishing she could sink into it and hide from his inquisition. She didn't have a brother and had always assumed sisters to be the nosiest siblings. She hated being wrong. "As much as I would like to think it is close enough, it is not. I did want to overstep—however much I might have wished to. Do you think I wanted to leave your brother that day? Do you think I wasn't lost as I watched the cart carry his bloodless body away? You weren't there. You don't know what I saw. Don't you dare judge me and how I acted. I only got out of bed this morning. I'm sorry I didn't rush outside and knock on your door—excuse me, your *brother's* door—the instant I could feel my toes again."

That felt bloody good. Perhaps a bit much, but still good.

Ella was inexperienced in defending her character. Everyone liked her—or at least pretended to. For years her brothers-in-law had catered to her feelings, attempting to get on her good side, knowing that if she didn't like them, then they'd have little chance with her older sisters. Yes, it was just flattery at first, but she'd come to recognize them as true brothers who would do anything for her.

Now, this man—this sea dog—thought he could call out her character? Call her a liar?

Well, she was, but she hadn't meant to be! If only he could see that!

A wistful smile crept onto Lord John's face. "And I thought love was the strongest force in the world."

Ella threw up her hands in defeat. "Well then, maybe I am just a weak creature."

His gaze narrowed. Ella felt herself grow warm under it, not knowing how to react to his study of her. He was an odd man who said odd things, not like the dandies of the *ton* who frequented the Westons' household, reciting poetry, declaring their love to her sisters as if by rote. This man—this roguish second son—

said what was on his mind, when it came to his mind, and that unnerved her to no great end.

Jack rubbed underneath his chin, sliding his hand back and forth in a hypnotic fashion, drawing out the raspy sound as if he enjoyed it more than the scratch. "I'd already settled on that thought, but now I'm not so sure."

Ella blew out a blustery breath, slapping her hands down on her lap. "Well, how kind of you."

His teeth were sharp and bright as his lips curled away. "Oh, there's nothing kind about me."

Ella shrugged. "You're here. That says something."

"It says I'm afraid of my mother."

Laughter burst from her mouth before Ella could stifle it. His blue eyes flashed, and Lord John settled back in his seat, a new demeanor overtaking him, one much less combative. The man was still frightening, still large, still mysterious, but for some strange reason, just by making that comment, Ella's confidence fluttered. The thought came to her: *I can handle him.* It would take both hands. But she could do it.

"Should *I* be afraid of your mother?"

He *hmphed*, tearing the shade away to check outside. "Are you daft? She's been trying to marry my brother off for years. She'll love you. The fact that you're not a whore or an opera singer will make her kiss your feet."

Ella watched him jerk when he realized what he'd said. She could feel the color on her face, but she could see it on his. He twirled his hat in his hands.

"My apologies," he grumbled, eyes averted. "As you can tell, I don't spend much time with … *ladies* such as yourself." The stress he put on that word made her want to kick him in the shins. "I forget myself. It won't happen again."

"I didn't mean that," Ella said slowly, waiting for him to get over his embarrassment. "I meant … should I be worried if I can't help your brother?"

Lord John's lips quirked, and he stared at her as if she'd just said something completely nonsensical. "What makes you think you won't?"

She shook her head, her frustration with the night beginning to take root and sprout inside her. "I'm sure you grew up listening to fairytales like all the rest of us, so you know that it's the man who saves the sleeping maiden. In no story is it the woman."

"Are you sure about that?"

"I am."

Jack continued to contemplate her, again with that arresting way that made it hard for her to breathe and think at the same time. Ella's heart pumped so hard against her ribcage that she reminded herself to check it tomorrow for bruises. She barely knew him but was certain that he was the type of man who could make something like that happen, for better or worse.

"Well, that's fine, Miss Ella, because we don't need a fairytale."

"What do you need?"

"We need a miracle."

Chapter Five

THE CARRIAGE LURCHED to a stop, and Lord John wasted little time ushering Ella out the door and toward the steps to the residence. Her feet stalled halfway up. The duke's townhouse loomed large and forbidding in front of her, but before Ella could identify a foolproof escape plan, the door swung open, magically pulling her inside. The butler must have been waiting for them.

The atmosphere struck Ella at once, put her back on her heels. It was quiet and morose, still and hauntingly acrid. Ella had usually been the sick person in her household, so she had little experience dealing with somber realities from the outside vantage point. But this sensation was immutable, sticky, and cloying to the touch. Death wasn't the only thing in the air. Fear was taking up its fair share as well.

"Oh, thank the Lord, she's here!"

Ella followed the exuberance up the veiny marble staircase to where a tall, fleshy woman held on to the shiny walnut banister with both hands. Ella had seen Lady Evelyn, the Duchess of Winchester, at a few balls and had even stood off to the side while her mother and she engaged in inane pleasantries, but she never had reason to speak to her before. Known for her cutting tongue and dry wit, the duchess rarely suffered fools, and, to be perfectly frank, since Ella couldn't be sure if she was one or not, she'd preferred to stay out of her way.

But that luxury was long gone. Ella couldn't possibly slink into oblivion with the lady flying down the stairs like a hawk zeroed in on its prey. The lady overwhelmed her with a hug that smacked of pure desperation.

"Thank you. Thank you," the duchess cried, sinking her hands into Ella's back. She swayed them back and forth until it felt like they were in the middle of a melancholic dance. Ella was like a doll, her arms hanging listlessly at her sides, waiting for her owner to do with her what she would. *Please, Lord, don't let her smell the sherry.*

Ella lifted her eyes and scanned for Lord John, finding him leaning casually against the door. She wasn't fooled. His gaze was focused on his mother, his body rigid and ready for anything she might need.

If he seemed out of place in the carriage, he was positively lost in this grand foyer, indicative of the very best breeding and a line that could be traced back to the Conqueror. The entire entryway was housed in a giant glass dome that served to invite the heavens into their home. On both sides of the staircase, three mammoth pillars surrounded the space in a semicircle, making guests feel at once protected and welcomed. This was a palace. A fortress. A home for dukes.

Not for pirates.

"Mother, let the woman breathe."

Lady Evelyn's hand fisted along Ella's back, and she tensed before finally dragging herself away. "Oh, of course. Of course, yes, I'm sorry, my dear. I don't know what came over me." She held a white lace handkerchief in one hand and held it up to her nose. "I've just been waiting. For you."

Ella's conscience felt like it had been kicked and beaten and was now being gagged and held hostage somewhere in the depths of her sorry soul. How could she stand here in front of this woman and maintain this charade?

The duchess's eyes were red-rimmed and expectant, underscored with jewel-colored bags. Her black hair was brushed away off her face, leaving her skin bare and open. There was no doubt that she hadn't slept in days. She wore a simple gray dress—not quite in mourning—as if she was approaching the inevitable in stages.

"I'm so sorry for everything, Your Grace—"

The woman snatched Ella's hands back, not able to stay away. "You? What do you have to be sorry about, my beautiful girl? Ella, darling, the only reason my Oliver is still with us is because of you. I told him not to race those silly horses. I told him it was dangerous, but he would not listen to me." Again, she held the handkerchief to her mouth, stifling a sob. When she'd contained her emotions, she continued. "When your son is born, you will understand how difficult it is to harness a Winchester boy."

Ella's smile was weak. *Everything* about her suddenly felt weak. "Of course, Your Grace."

"Mother …" Lord John said.

"Oh, yes, yes!" the duchess cried, corralling Ella toward the stairs. Ella glanced over her shoulder to see Lord John following only a few steps behind, as if to make sure she made it up in one piece. He caught her stare and smirked, mouthing, *Don't trip.*

Ella glared at him because she was scared and frustrated and he seemed to be the only person she could take it all out on. He was the wall she could punch and kick, knowing she would do no damage.

Lord John dismissed her, turning his head away. His expression returned to its baseline—blank and unflappable. Ella turned away with an unmistakable reality. This lavish townhome may have been built centuries before, but it was only standing now by the will of Lord John. His staid and severe presence was the glue holding everything together for his brother.

Ella found herself on the second floor, where a host of men stood milling around outside a room at the very end of the wide corridor. Faces and expressions contorted as soon as the duchess was spotted, undoubtedly in an effort to spare her more anxiety. Lady Evelyn shooed them out of the way as if they were nothing more than bothersome pigeons.

She lightly tapped on the door, opening it an inch before speaking in a motherly, singsong tone. "My love. I have someone special here for you. Someone I know you've been waiting for."

The lady smiled at Ella then, giving her an encouraging nod. She opened the door all the way, motioning for Ella to go inside.

Alone? Already? Ella didn't know what was on the other side of that door, but she did know she didn't want to experience it by herself.

Her smile faltering, the duchess flicked her head toward the dark room, harsher this time.

Ella gulped. She'd had the impression they'd go in together, and perhaps the older woman would sit at her son's side while Ella lurked in a deep corner.

Apparently, she'd been wrong.

She felt a body come up behind her. Lord John.

"Mother." He placed his hands on Ella's shoulders, and this time she did not flinch at his touch. Nor did she jerk away. If anything, she had to restrain herself from grabbing those heavy palms and pulling him tighter around her. "Perhaps this isn't the time—"

"This is the only time!" the older woman snapped. She attempted to swallow her outburst. Regaining her calm, she tried again. "My son is inside that room. And I don't know how much longer he will be there. She is our only hope."

A tall man made up of sharp angles and pocked skin stepped forward tentatively, coughing into his delicate fist. "Lady Evelyn, that is not the case. We've spoken to you about the surgery." He turned to Lord John. "My lord, I've had some success in this area. Your brother has a large bruise on the back of his head along with an alarming protrusion. We assume His Grace struck his head against a rock after falling in the lake. If you allow us to open it up, relieve some of the pressure, we think the duke might have a better chance of waking."

Lord John stared at the doctor, implacable as always. A grand-father clock stood stoically across the corridor. Seconds ticked by as Lord John contemplated the doctor's words. "I am well acquainted with trepanning, doctor. Tell me, what is your success rate with the procedure?"

Ella surmised that most men would have grown flustered when Lord John bore down on them with that steely voice, but the doctor was in a league of his own, as sweat began to slide down his temples. "T-ten percent, my lord."

Lord John's brow rose. "Ten percent?" he replied. "Ten per-cent of men lived after you drilled holes into their skulls?"

The good doctor shook his head raggedly. "No, my lord, ten percent survived the surgery. Only two percent lived."

Ella's stomach dropped.

"How long did they live … the two percent?" Lord John asked. His tone was more frightening than the odds.

The doctor's Adam's apple jumped. "None longer than a few months."

Lord John lunged. Gripping the tall man's lapels, he lifted him off his toes, slamming him into the wall. Face to face with the doctor, Lord John finally showed the turmoil, anger, and, yes, fear that he'd been suffering through over the last forty-eight hours.

"That was years ago," the doctor rambled, hurrying to make his case. "The surgery has evolved, become more precise."

"More precise?" Lord John growled, baring his teeth as if he were about to begin his own surgery on the doctor. "I've been on one ship after another for the past fifteen years and seen my share of learned men like yourself only too ready to open up a man's skull. And every last one of those cases has come to naught. Do you think I would actually set you and your curiosity on my brother?" Slow and menacing, he shook his head. "You will not touch him."

"B-b-b-but," the doctor stammered, spittle flying from his lips, "there is nothing else to be done." He dropped his voice to a whisper, and Ella leaned forward to catch his words. "He will die. If he doesn't eat or drink soon, he will die. You have to know this. It's his only hope."

Deliberately, Lord John backed away, releasing the doctor enough so that the man could finally put his feet back on firm ground. Ella watched as he contemplated what the doctor said, running a hand over his face again and again, as if one of those passes might inform him of the right decision. The doctor was right. Ella hated to admit it. Desperate times made desperate people. A risky surgery had only one thing going for it—hope.

Ella closed her eyes, sending up a quick prayer that Lord John would heed the doctor's words. It was the only rational decision.

"It's not his only hope," a fragile, gravelly voice rang out, pulling all eyes down the corridor. A frightfully old woman limped toward them, her cane punctuating the seconds as faithfully as that grandfather clock. Her face was riddled with wrinkles.

Ella wanted to sink into the carpet when she noticed the woman's gimlet eye was solely on her. She raised her cane directed at Ella as steady as a hunter aims his gun. "We have her."

Chapter Six

ELLA HAD SAT quietly beside the bed for close to an hour. Words were lost to her. She didn't know what Lord Oliver wanted to hear. *If* he could hear.

Guilt coated her like thick honey because she knew she was wasting valuable time, but it had taken her longer than anticipated to even leave the safety of the door and venture into the room. This was not the Lord Oliver she remembered.

His breathing was shallow, and his skin was pale and waxy, lips and eyes coated in a light-bluish tint, giving him a ghostly pallor. He wore a simple dressing gown under piles of blankets and lay supine, remarkably relaxed, on the massive four-poster bed as if he were just taking a restorative afternoon nap before tearing out on the town. Ella could have believed the fantasy if they hadn't shaved his head.

The doctors had obviously attempted to be tidy, but patches of his silky black hair remained, some sections longer than others. The back-left side of Lord Oliver's head was truly made bald, highlighting the contusion spoken about. A few seconds was all she could give the vicious wound, which appeared to pulsate. A craggy fissure cut through the middle like a poorly thought-out country road, the dried magenta blood gluing the two sides together.

Ella thought back to the accident. She hadn't known Oliver had hit his head. Had she made it worse with all the jostling and yanking?

She stared at the fresh handkerchief the dowager had stuffed into her hand before she entered the room. It was still dry. Ella was too numb to cry, too lost to pull herself out of her guilt-ridden mind.

Love him.

Her mother's words plucked her inside as if she were an instrument, growing dust and needing to be played. But the more Ella fixated on Lord Oliver, the more she questioned that love. Being here, in this place, only served to remind her that she knew next to nothing about him.

She looked about the room. Clearly, the man had an affinity for navy blue, since one version or another of it covered anything that would stand still in the luxurious quarters. From the curtains to his bed covers, to the round rug to the Asian-inspired wallpaper, everything was splattered in blue. Which truly wasn't saying much. Most men would have done the same. It wasn't as if Ella had expected pink or orange.

The room was tidy, if a little bit cold, without knickknacks or bric-a-brac littering the bureau or dresser. There was no book, dog-eared and waiting for him on his bedside table, no journal opened with an unfinished sentence at the small desk against the covered window. All in all, she felt like she knew even less about Lord Oliver after seeing where he spent his nights. And sadly, he knew even less about her.

And Ella couldn't do anything more about that—not unless the duke decided to open his eyes.

Or was she wrong?

She cleared her throat, feeling foolish, because her initial thought was not to wake him from his sleep. "Um … hello," she started, squashing down the silliness that threatened to stop this endeavor before it even began. She scooted herself to the edge of her seat. "You don't know me, Your Grace. At least, I'm almost sure you don't. If you saw me, maybe you'd think that you'd seen me once before at some ball or Society event, but I doubt it. We've never even been introduced."

Ella's words flowed more freely. She imagined granting the duke a perfect curtsey while he bowed. "Let me just say first that I'm terribly sorry about this. Yes, the accident, but also the fact that I'm here talking to you. I would love to explain the whole thing—and I *can* explain it—but it would take too long now, and it's really not worth it at this point. Let's just agree that it's awkward all around." She frowned, placing her hand on his lifeless arm. "That's not to say I don't want to be here. I do. I mean, I suppose I do, I just wish it was under more *truthful* circumstances."

Ella paused, waiting for him to speak, and then shook her head. "I feel ridiculous," she said, mostly to herself. "I don't know what they want me to do. You see, I've never considered myself a talker. I know what it feels like to be where you are now, Your Grace. I spent a great part of my childhood in my room, suffering from various complications and illnesses. My sisters—I have four of them—were a great comfort, but they all had lives to lead, and left me to myself most of the time." She angled her ear toward the bed. "What's that, you ask? No, I don't blame them. No one wants to be stuck inside when the sun is shining. Besides, my mother and father always made sure I had plenty of books to keep me company. So … so there's that."

She laughed softly, patting the duke's arm in a playful rebuke. "That is so lovely of you to say, Your Grace. I'm flattered that you don't think I look sickly. I'm not. A little skinny, yes, but not sickly. I still have flare-ups every once in a while"—she shook out her pink hands—"in fact, I'm having a small one right now, but I've learned to manage them. Just as you will when you come out of this. No, no don't argue with me. You *will* come out of this and do everything your doctors tell you so you can be good and healthy again in no time."

Her smile turned wan. "Yes, yes, I think you're right. It's

difficult to come out of something like this and be the same as before. These kinds of events change a person, whether you want them to or not. Perhaps they even make one feel more cautious. I love my sisters, but I've always envied their ability to jump into things. Almost as if they never experience fear or worry about any outcome. They're quick to fight, quick to laugh, and even quicker to dance and smile. I love that about them. Sometimes I think that maybe if I hadn't been sick so often, I would have been more like that … more like you."

Ella sighed, stacking her arms on the bed and resting her chin on top. "Can you actually believe Cordelia was angry when I told her that I'd grown an attachment to you? She thought your reputation would be too much for me. *You* would be too much. They're always thinking that about me. I know my family is only trying to protect me, but sometimes I think they really believe I'm still a sickly child who needs their help to get out of bed in the morning. I can handle a man like you. My life can take adventure, and my body will not tire from it. I promise you that. So please, don't worry. If you want to dance with me three times at a ball instead of one or two, rest assured that it will not be too much."

She laughed quietly, rolling her eyes, and lowered her voice to a whisper. "No one's ever asked me that before." She paused to think. "I want to travel and talk to interesting people and run down long green hills, and sleep under the small yellow stars. I want it all. And the moment I saw you in that ballroom, I knew that you would be the one who would do it all with me. Every day with you would be something new and exciting."

Before Ella could stop them, tears burned the back of her eyes, and the tip of her nose itched with heat. She straightened away from the bed, tilting her face toward the ceiling. "No, no, no, Your Grace, I'm not crying. No, it's just a little dust, I think. Nothing to worry about. I'm sure you're sick of crying, sick of people worrying over you. Your brother does. Did you know that? He doesn't say much, does he? A bit of an enigma. But I can see it, every time I look at him … the concern. The fear. It's off-putting seeing fear in a man like that, so large and intimidating. He could do with some of your manners, that's the truth, though I hazard he wouldn't know what to do with them."

Tears under control, Ella shrugged, staring pitifully at her palms in her lap. What was she doing here, yapping on?

Making a fool out of myself.

Perhaps a real love was powerful enough to pull a man away from an eternal sleep, but not a simple infatuation.

Ella rose from her chair, turning toward the door. The prince didn't revive Snow White by talking his head off and divulging his inner secrets. In fact, the prince didn't wake Snow White at all. One of his men dropped Snow White's coffin, dislodging the poisonous apple from her throat, bringing her back to life.

Well, Ella had jostled the duke enough for a lifetime; she wasn't about to roll him off his bed and dump him on the floor to see what might happen next.

She would say goodnight … say goodbye. That was all that was left for her to do. Ella had come here as his family asked. She'd talked to the poor man. They would be disappointed—heartbroken. No doubt everyone would be. The Duke of Winchester would be greatly missed. But Ella was at a loss.

She crept back to the bed. Before she could stop herself, she stretched out her arm and cupped the side of the duke's face. His bristles scratched her, and she smiled. He was warm. Peaceful. Balancing on the precipice of life and death.

Slowly, she leaned over the bed, lowering her head to his. She closed her eyes, losing her nerve by the second. His breath was weak and fleeting as it brushed against her lips.

One quick kiss on his cheek and then she would leave.

Ella continued to hover when an odd sensation unfurled itself, like she was being watched. She punched her hands on either side of the duke, holding herself up and away from his face.

Where his dark green eyes were now open and fastened on hers.

Staring. And very much alive.

Ella couldn't move. She dared not to even flex a muscle.

Until he blinked.

And then she gasped.

Lord Oliver clapped his eyes shut, and his hand swept to his face. Lurching to his side, he let out a gut-wrenching roar and began to tremble spasmodically.

"Help! Please, help us!" Ella screamed, turning toward the door, but no one came. Where could they be?

She faced Oliver once more, alarmed by his jerking movements. Hunched over him, Ella held his shoulder as he continued to heave back and forth. The anguished sounds coming from the base of his throat tore at her center, bringing more tears forth. They launched from her eyes while she issued all the inane words that came to her.

"Shh," she murmured. "It will be all right. I promise."

Lord Oliver slammed his back onto the bed, still covering his face with his hand. "The light! The light!" he growled.

Instantly, Ella turned down the light on the oil lamp next to the bed. It had barely thrown off enough light to illuminate the room; how could it cause him any pain?

She was about to ask him if she could do anything else when the door finally banged open, and Lord John and the duchess flew inside.

Pure, unmitigated relief covered Lady Evelyn's face. She fell to her knees at her son's bedside, taking his hand in hers, holding it to her lips. "Thank you, Lord," she whispered in between kisses. "I knew you would answer my prayers. Thank you."

One by one, the doctors and other men that Ella hadn't been introduced to crept into the room, quiet and almost timid. To her, they appeared awestruck, beyond surprised at the duke's recovery, as if not a single one had been expecting it.

Ella refocused on the bed. She couldn't be sure if Lord Oliver's groans were weakening or if the duchess's cries were strengthening.

"Can you talk, my son?" she asked, standing to place her palm on Lord Oliver's forehead. "Can you tell us how you feel?"

The duke could only utter muffled words behind his hand, shaking his head back and forth. Every few seconds another shudder would run through his entire body.

But his mother was not to be deterred. The duchess reached back and found Ella, grabbing her arm. "Don't worry about anything, my love," she said, dragging Ella forward until she stood right next to her. "We're going to do everything to help you recover as quickly as possible. We're all here. Everyone that loves you."

The duchess's grasp intensified on her fragile fingers, and Ella had to bite her lip from squeaking from the pain. Sensing what the older woman was asking her, she leaned over the bed, patting the duke's arm once more. "We're here for you," she repeated weakly, her voice losing its steam now that others were in the room.

Her startled gaze found its way to Lord John, who stood on the other side of the bed, his hands locked in fists at his sides as if he were holding himself back. He was like a wild animal to her, all instinct and emotion, barely keeping himself in check. Ella wanted to tell him to touch his brother, to hold him, because it was obvious to her that that was what he wanted to do.

Lord John lifted his shiny eyes to her, and Ella quickly averted her own. This entire moment was too overwhelming, too intimate. She didn't belong here, but even when she tried to back away the tiniest distance, the duchess was there to stop her.

"Please, Olly," Lady Evelyn cried as she attempted to pull his hand away from his face, "talk to us. Say anything! I need to hear your voice."

Lord Oliver groaned in answer, the sound reminding Ella of a creature in the kind of wretched pain that would make one wish to be put out of one's misery.

But a mother's dictate was difficult to ignore, even in agony such as the duke's. Reluctantly, he lowered his hand, then blinked rapidly, adjusting to the added light in the room filtering in from the corridor. Shadows flitted along his high cheekbones, highlighting tiny, thin tears. The muscles around his eyes tightened as he attempted to fix on his mother and then his brother. When his eyes eventually narrowed on Ella, she felt her stomach knot. Once more, she tried to fade into the background, and once more the duchess thwarted her efforts.

Lord Oliver opened his mouth and closed it. His eyelids drooped. Even the few minutes he'd been awake had drained him.

"We should leave," Lord John announced.

"No!" his mother replied. "He wants to say something. I know it. Let him speak, and then we will let him rest."

The duke opened his mouth again. It stayed that way for so long that Ella thought he'd fallen asleep that way. Her stomach eased, the viselike grip relaxing enough that she could finally take a shaky breath.

And then the duke's eyes snapped back to her.

He frowned, from pain or her presence, Ella could only guess.

And then he spoke. "Who *are* you?"

Chapter Seven

"MOTHER, STOP IT! If you toss another item out of my bag, I'll toss *you* out the window!"

Lady Evelyn's eyes twinkled at Jack, her ebullient smile splitting her face from ear to ear. It had only been one day since Oliver miraculously awoke from his coma, and Jack didn't think his mother had stopped grinning once. The doctors—all five of them—had cautioned against the duchess's optimism, warning her that Oliver had a long way to go before he'd be fully recovered, but that hadn't stopped the woman from flitting around the house like she was twenty years younger, completely devoid of worry.

A mother knows, was all she'd told them. *A mother knows.*

Her confidence was good enough for Jack, which was why he'd started packing.

Unfortunately, his mother had had different plans.

Lady Evelyn giggled in his stern face and continued to rifle through the leather valise on top of his bed. "Oh, I would love to see you try it, Jackie. You think just because you've grown so tall and so big that you can lord over your own mother? You are sadly mistaken." With an impish smile, she seized a linen shirt from the bag and chucked it over her shoulder. Jack's valet stood in the corner, the tortured man's shoulders slumping in defeat as the once-crisp garment drifted to the floor.

Glaring at the half-crazed woman, Jack snatched up the shirt and shoved it back in the bag. "Goddammit, Mother!"

The duchess stopped twirling around the room like a devilish sprite to shoot him a withering look. "Don't you use that voice with me! And stop thinking you're going to desert your brother in his time of need. Just because he's awake, doesn't mean you can just hop back on one of your little boats. You will stay here. End of story."

Jack lowered his head, his jaw clenched so tight he thought it might break. *Little boats.*

Over the years he'd attempted to explain his shipping business to his mother, and had left a few times thinking she'd actually heard and understood the words that had come from his mouth. Apparently not. Because the Sutton Shipping Company was anything but little. With fifteen clippers under his command—and plans to add steamers to the mix—Jack had created a viable business from nothing more than his unflappable will.

Less than nothing, actually. Even when his father had offered to purchase the first ship for him, Jack had different ideas. He'd never wanted to hear anyone say that someone had given him a leg up, that he was only successful because of his lofty background. So, in the beginning, his blood, sweat, and tears had been the only capital at his disposal. And he'd made good.

And if he played his cards right, his growth would continue. With the Navigation Acts repealed, competition was at an all-time high, but so were lucrative contracts. Jack wouldn't land them if he whiled away the hours in his brother's comfy home, shuffling his feet. He'd been stuck under this roof for one week and already his palms itched, his clothes too tight and scratchy. London always stifled him. It threatened to put him in a box and make him sing for his supper like all the other second sons.

Lord John might have had to do that.

But Jack Sutton would never.

"Mother," he sighed, already exhausted by the argument he

was sure was coming, "I can't stay. I have to get back. I know you hate hearing this, but I have to work. I have a job, a company—"

"You have a duty first," Lady Evelyn snapped, her expression leaving no room for argument. In her haste, her tenacious mask slipped, and Jack saw the fragile cracks in his mother's morale. He clapped his mouth shut. He was a man. A grown man. He was certainly not afraid of his genteel mother. But he wasn't not *not* afraid of her either, especially when her nerves were as pulled as tight as they were.

There was a reason the *ton* kowtowed to the duchess, turning to her for guidance and navigation in the choppy, turbulent waters of Society. The woman's spine was made of steel; her aptitude for recognizing which way the wind was blowing (usually the direction serving her best) was uncanny. Jack had always assumed that he'd received his adeptness for leadership from his father. He might have been mistaken.

But everyone had their limits, and Jack surmised that his mother was reaching hers.

Lady Evelyn patted the sides of her head, as if checking to see that her outburst hadn't upset her demure hairstyle. She'd had her maid do it differently today, Jack noticed. Her black hair was pulled back softly, allowing for a couple of hanging curls at each ear. "It's not just you, Jackie," she explained patiently. "We all have a duty to your brother, to the dukedom. And we will see it through."

"Oh, yes, the dukedom," Jack drawled like he'd heard this story before. The delicate dukedom and its constant need to squeeze blood from stone. "It's a well-oiled ship. It hardly needs both of us. You are perfectly capable of handling everything while Ollie mends."

His insufferable mother was already shaking her head before he'd finished his sentence. "No. I have too many responsibilities, on top of helping your brother." Lady Evelyn raised her hands, ticking items off on her fingers. "This will be a three-pronged approach. I will see that his house is settled; you will keep his affairs in order; and the girl will see to his heart. Nothing will be left behind. Now, the only way I will leave this room and allow you to pack is if you tell me that you are packing for Sutton Park. Because that is the only place you are going. Surely you can operate your little business from there."

Little business. Jack growled, shoving his hands in his pockets. They could go at it all day long, and it would amount to nothing. There was simply no getting through to his mother when she put on her grande dame voice. Jack was no better than the simpering debutantes that trembled in his mother's wake.

Which reminded him …

"Is the girl really coming with us? Certainly, you don't mean to drag her from her home to play nursemaid in the country for God knows how long."

Lady Evelyn flashed another winning smile. Clearly, she approved of the "we" in his pathetically defeatist sentence. She spun back to his valise and took out the linen shirt once more, folding it as well as any valet Jack had ever seen. All these years, and the woman still surprised him.

"Of course she will come. I've already spoken to her mother. Lady Weston is a very smart woman—she called my idea genius," the duchess declared, albeit a tad defensively. "Ella can use the time to become acquainted with the house …" She shoved the shirt back inside a little too harshly. "And why wouldn't she want to play nursemaid to your brother? He will be her husband, her life now … It is the way it should be."

Jack raked a hand through his hair, apprehensive at how to form his next argument. His mother thought she had everything figured out, and she couldn't be more wrong. "Don't you think there's something a little odd about the girl? You haven't even said anything about what happened in the room."

"Miss Ella. Address your future sister-in-law with respect, please."

Jack came up to her side. She avoided his gaze, continuing to rifle through the bag. "He remembered everyone but her."

The duchess's voice grew higher, her hands working faster. "That's not true. He couldn't remember all of the doctors' names either. They didn't think much of it, and neither should you."

Jack's exasperation could not be contained any longer. "But at least Ollie knew they were doctors! He had no *clue* who that girl was."

Lady Evelyn huffed and turned to face her son, her head tilted in irritation. "What is your point?"

"My point is that …" Jack's mind went blank. *Fuck.* "My point is that I don't trust Miss Ella as far as I can throw her."

"Why on earth would you want to throw her?"

"You know what I mean," he growled. "Don't you think there's something *off* about her? Be honest, she's not the woman you'd expect Olly to settle on."

The tension around Lady Evelyn's eyes eased. She looked at her son as if someone had just turned on the lights. "Oh, I see what this is about. You don't like her," she accused. "You don't think she's good enough for your brother. Do all your fellow sailors know you're such a snob?"

"I didn't say I didn't like her! I just …" Jack trailed off. He wasn't sure what he was trying to say, nor could he put words to the uncertainty that nagged at him regarding Ella. But something wasn't right; he was sure of that. Jack had been trained to read the stars and track the weather. He could hear, see, and even feel a storm in the air from the slightest change of wind. And the second Miss Ella stepped inside the same room as him, everything had shifted. The earth had tilted. Nothing had felt right. And he was damned if he wasn't going to find out why.

Lady Evelyn placed her hand on Jack's cheek, dragging him from his thoughts. "Jackie, I understand your concern," she said softly. "I know Miss Ella is different than"—her expression clouded—"before. But we have to trust Oliver. He loves her; I am sure of it. And now I'm asking you to love her too. Can you do that?"

JACK ABSOLUTELY HATED when Jeremiah Sinclair looked at him like that. His ridiculous spectacles made his disapproving eyes appear two times their normal size. It made a simple frown more like a glare. And Jack had disappointed enough people for one day—namely, himself.

"A month? An entire month?" Sinclair kept repeating like one of those colorful talking birds from the West Indies. The businessman actually looked like one too, with the sides of his light brown hair standing on end, no doubt from all the pulling he'd done to it ever since Jack entered the office that afternoon.

Jack sat across from his business manager, resting his long legs on the desk between them, his ankles crossed in a devil-may-care fashion that belied his own gnawing vexation. Whistles, shouts, and a wide variety of colorful curses wafted in the open window. Located on the second floor of a newly built warehouse just off the docks, Sutton Shipping Company may have been a growing enterprise, but one would be hard-pressed to tell from the spartan office space. Sinclar obviously wasn't one for decorating. The walls were empty, the floorboards bare. Neither chair held a whiff of padding or comfort. The only accoutrements were the piles of papers and folders littering the giant, cheap desk. And, to Jack, there was nothing inviting about them.

The men had known each other for years, starting off as able-bodied seamen together on Louis Cannahan's crew, running cotton and sugar on the Barbados-to-Liverpool route. Like Jack, Jeremiah had had dreams of making a name for himself at sea—until he ultimately realized his stomach wasn't made for the water. Luckily for them both, his brain for numbers more than made up for that, as well as his appreciation for floors that didn't sway when he scribbled in his ledgers.

"I said a month *at most*," Jack replied evenly, hoping his calm veneer would help settle his anxious partner. "I'm sure I can wheedle it down by a few weeks. No doubt my brother will be begging me to stop hovering once he's … well, once he's better."

Jack had been about to say *once he stops being sick every other hour and can keep his eyes open for longer than five minutes at a time.* He'd headed straight to the office after his conversation with his mother, but not before stopping in to check on Oliver. His brother had been in the middle of another of his violent episodes, retching uncontrollably into a bucket beside his bed while the doctors circled him with disconcerting expressions. They'd attempted to reassure Jack, explaining that this terrible effect was normal for head injuries and all everyone could do was wait for it to pass. Jack put very little stock in those doctors, but he sure as hell hoped they were right this time.

"My brother is strong," he added, almost to himself.

Sinclair slipped off his glasses, plopping them on a stack of papers. He rubbed at his eyes until Jack winced. "What will we do about the *Siren*? She'll be full and ready to go by then." Sinclair replaced his glasses and answered his own question. "I suppose Darby can run it. He's the only one with the experience that I trust."

Everything in Jack's body screamed at him to revolt at Sinclair's suggestion. The *Siren* was *his* ship—his very first one—and nobody captained it except him.

That had been the hardest thing about owning Sutton Shipping. Thinking like a captain had always come naturally to Jack. Leading men was second nature. But his current situation was forcing him to act like a businessman. Which was tedious, to say the least.

And Sinclair was right. Every day the *Siren* sat moored was a missed opportunity. It needed to get out into the water. Where it belonged. Where Jack belonged.

"Fine, tell Darby," he said, moderating his tone. "He'll do well. Just make sure he knows that it's just this once."

"Of course," Sinclair conceded as he began scratching his pencil on the paper in front of him. Needless to say, the strength of those two basic words did little to curb Jack's uneasy feeling. The feeling that, yet again, everything was changing, and he couldn't do anything about it.

"You know," the manager said, peeking up from under his glasses while his hand kept moving, "this might be a blessing in disguise. The contract for Caddell Tinplate Works is up for bid. We've been waiting for this for a long time. With you home … especially with your connections …" He shrugged.

Jack yanked his legs off the desk. He leaned forward, propping his forearms on his knees. "Contracts are your job."

Sinclair lifted his hands before letting them fall back to the desktop with an audible *plunk*. "Can you not see I'm drowning here? I've got paperwork coming out of my ears. I barely have enough time to sleep as it is, and you want me to spend my nights hobnobbing for contracts. If we want to stay competitive, we're going to have to fight."

Fight. At balls. At musicals. At bloody lazy clubs.

"But you like hobnobbing," Jack replied, at a complete loss.

Sinclair scoffed, his huge eyes narrowing. "No, I don't. I just don't hate it as much as you do. Besides, I've heard Caddell is a bit of a snob. Looking to elevate his choice of friends. Who do you think he'd rather talk to"—he shoved his thumb into his chest—"the son of a lowly grocer, or the hoity-toity son of a duke?"

Jack glowered. He fisted his hands, afraid that if he stretched them out, fire might start sparking from his fingertips. "I hate that kind of shite."

Sinclair's smile only added to Jack's annoyance. "That's the price you pay for being cheap. You refuse to allow me to hire an assistant. I *need* a clerk. Hell, I need two. So this is your penance."

Fuck! Jack shook his head. "I'd rather be in the middle of a squall or dodging icebergs."

Sinclair *tsked*, showing not one shred of sympathy. "Well, Captain Sutton can do that when he's on the water. On land, he's needed for more dangerous assignments. Like mingling."

Chapter Eight

FOR A SECOND time, Ella stood in the Winchester townhome foyer, preparing for the absolute worst.

She was going to do it.

She was.

Now. While she still had the nerve.

Ella was going to tell the truth.

And then run.

Where? She had no clue.

Her mother had just spent the morning overseeing the packing of her bags for the journey to Sutton Park, explicitly telling her that she would disown Ella if she did that very thing. Ella was certain her mother had been exaggerating, though.

Or, at least, she was *almost* certain.

As Ella twisted her hands into a mangled mess, trying to motivate her feet into moving, the butler did what quality butlers did best—stare at her out of the corner of his eye. "The family is in the drawing room, miss," he remarked, even though he'd told Ella that when he first encouraged her inside.

Ella nodded. "Yes, thank you," she replied, smiling weakly. The house was like a museum, so large and vast that she could hear her racing heartbeat bouncing off the pristine marble walls. She'd used the entire carriage ride over bolstering her confidence to do the deed. Unfortunately, she hadn't come up with a plan for *how*. She couldn't possibly announce it to the whole room, could she? To the doctors and other mysterious men who seemed to meander about the corridors like mice searching for crumbs? No. She needed to speak to the duchess alone. That was the only proper way to do it. The duchess was only a woman. A very terrifying one ... but surely, she would understand the mix-up? They might even laugh about it.

Maybe.

One day.

Probably not today.

Fear seized Ella's insides. She couldn't do this. Not now. Not ever. She would just leave. Explain everything later. Maybe she'd run to the docks and hop on a ship. She'd travel to one of those islands in the Pacific that she'd read about, join a tribe and learn their ways and be a functioning member of their society—and maybe years from now, when she was strong and courageous, she would return and have that conversation with the duchess. *Then* they might share a laugh about it all.

Maybe.

One day.

Though probably not that day, either.

Nevertheless, turning tail and fleeing did seem like the better option.

The decision was made. Ella spun on her heel. Just as she was about to step toward the door, it swung open. She jerked back, narrowly avoiding having her nose broken as Lord John charged inside.

His eyes flared at the sight of her, though a welcome was not in the cards. If anything, the man's insolent mouth pinched even tighter as he took her in.

"Excuse me, Lord John," Ella said, courage thinning by the second. "I was just leaving."

He widened his stance, blocking her from the entrance. "Leaving? I was ordered to be here so we could all go to Sutton

Park together."

"Ordered?" Ella laughed but instantly cringed, as it sounded hysterical to her ears. "Oh, by your mother ... Do you always do everything she tells you to do?"

Lord John didn't appreciate that question one bit. Ella didn't care. Once he shoved out of the way, she would never have to think about him again. Island life was in front of her.

"When I can," he replied tersely.

More of her hyena-like laughing. Why couldn't she control herself? "Please, move."

"Why?"

"Because I'm trying to get out the door."

"Why?"

Ella inflated her lungs. "Because I'm trying to leave. Why do you think?"

The ridiculous man actually crossed his arms, widening his shoulders even more. Would he tackle her if she tried to ram through her? Was it worth finding out?

He lowered his head to her level. At any other time, Ella might have focused on the blueness of his eyes, the way they reminded her of glaciers or some other impenetrable object. But now she only saw exhaustion, the way the lines at the corners felt deeper, more set, as if he'd finally come to terms with something that had been clawing at the recesses of his mind. Resigned.

She also noticed the earring.

"Is that...?" Ella pointed at the small, round golden ball situated in Lord John's left ear. "Is that what I think it is?"

Instinctively, he reached for his lobe, his frown melting as he spun the jewelry around in its hole. "It's an earring."

"I know that."

His confounded stare convinced Ella that she was one more non sequitur away from Bedlam. "Then why did you ask?"

Good question. Ella retreated, tearing her gaze away from the glinting ball. Staying on task, remembering what she was here to do, was becoming more and more difficult. It didn't help that this pirate smelled like fresh air and salt water. Sunshine on her skin. But that was impossible. How could anyone smell like sunshine?

It was official. She was insane. She'd finally cracked under the pressure of her lies.

"Lord John, will you kindly move—"

"Jack."

Ella blinked. "I'm sorry?"

"Stop calling me Lord John. I can't stand it."

Ella huffed in exasperation. "But it's your name."

"I don't give a shite."

That was it. Now the barbarian was cursing at her like she was some lowly thief and not the woman who'd saved his brother's life!

"Fine, *Jack*. I don't want to be standing here, and I don't want to be talking to you, and I definitely don't want to be wondering what you smell like."

Jack may have blanched, but Ella didn't notice. She was too far gone. Her nerves had been pulled and prodded and stretched too thin.

"I just want to go home," she said, her voice wavering, "but I can't do that, so I'll have to settle for an island—a peaceful one, hopefully. I've read about cannibals; I don't want anyone to eat me." She rambled on, "I just want to live simply, maybe pick seashells on the beach, sing songs, read books, those sorts of things. Do they have books on those islands? I hadn't thought about that. Maybe I will have to stop at home and pack some. Maybe if I wait until my mother has gone out, I can do it without her knowing. She can't see me. Because then she'll know that I told you, and then she'll probably march me right back here or send me to a nunnery. Can you go to a nunnery if you're not Catholic? Will they accept me? Why are there so many things that I've never thought of before this day—"

Warm, large hands clasped her shoulders. "Stop. Just stop."

Everything was blurry. Ella shook her head, and slowly but surely the world pieced itself back together into one coherent picture. Jack and his concern were right in the center of it. With that damn earring.

His blue eyes held hers, capturing her anxiety before it could do more harm. "Breathe, just breathe," he said softly. Ella did what she was told, sucking in great gulps of air, trying not to think about the way his thumbs traced little circles over her shoulders.

"Now," he said when she had calmed, "what were you going to tell me?"

Ella swallowed. Why did he have to seem so caring? Why did his expression have to be so soft, so understanding, so nonjudgmental? Because it made her want to open up and tell him everything. It made her want to believe that someone like him— no, not like him, *Jack*—could actually deliver her from this cataclysmic situation.

Or, at the very least, provide a ship and safe passage for her exile.

"I-I …" Ella stammered, willing her tongue to unfreeze. Perhaps it would have had a chance if he would stop staring at her mouth. No one other than her parents or sisters had ever held her like this before. And Jack's hold was nothing like theirs. It was possessive in a way that made her question if she'd ever belonged to her family at all.

She licked her lips, trying again. "I … Jack, I …"

The butt of a cane stamped into the marble. "There you are! We've been waiting for you, my dear. It looks like Jack has found you."

Jack released her like she was a red-hot poker, and Ella stumbled back before locking eyes with the elderly woman she'd seen outside Lord Oliver's bedroom the previous night. The one who'd brandished her cane like it was Excalibur. "I'm sorry—"

"Don't be." Her smile was kind, though Ella couldn't surmise if it was genuine. Up close, the woman appeared even older than Ella had thought. There didn't seem to be a square centimeter of her face without a line on it, but her eyes were shrewd, forthright, giving the impression that she could see right through any and everyone. Her hair was a brilliant silver, and her back had withstood time by her maintaining the posture and strength of a woman half her age. Try as she might, Ella could find nothing soft about this woman, nor motherly.

And despite all this, Ella couldn't help but instantly like her—and desperately wanted the woman to like her in return.

The lady jabbed her cane into Jack's side. "Introduce me, boy," she ordered him.

Jack snorted. "Miss Ella, this is my formidable grandmother, Lady Amelia. She lives here. Along with everyone else," he added in a strangled voice.

Ella curtseyed, but Lady Amelia waved her off. "I don't have time for that sort of nonsense," she scoffed. "I'm old and I have things I need to get done before I meet my maker at the pearly gates."

"Pearly gates? You're feeling rather sure of yourself today," Jack teased.

The woman glared at her grandson, fighting back a smile. "Be quiet, boy, before I send you to meet him first."

Ella muffled a gasp. She'd only known one grandmother, who'd died when Ella was ten. The woman barely spoke above a whisper and spent ninety percent of her days at her needlepoint. Lady Amelia was nothing like her—she was a revelation.

Before Jack could offer another biting retort, Lady Amelia wrapped her arm around Ella's and directed her down the hall without anything resembling a goodbye. Ella's nerves relaxed when she realized it was not the same hall that led to the drawing room, meaning she still had time to make her exit.

But if Ella thought that Lady Amelia's clutches would be weaker than Lady Evelyn's, she was mistaken. She couldn't get out of the older woman's hold until they entered the library, and the lady deigned to set her free.

Though perhaps she should have asked the lady to prop her up once more, because the sight of the room was almost too much to take. Ella's jaw dropped as she lost herself in the grandeur of the library, in complete awe of the books hemming her in on all sides. How many hours she would love to spend in this room, wandering through the titles, getting lost in all the worlds they represented.

But not today. Not ever.

And especially not now, while Lady Amelia's brow was sinking lower and lower on her forehead the longer Ella stayed quiet.

Ella remembered herself. "Should we sit—?"

"Quiet," the older lady barked. "I'll let you speak, but you will listen first."

The hair on the back of Ella's neck stood to attention, and she had the odd sensation to steal Lady Amelia's cane. Protection seemed mighty important at the moment.

"I heard you last night," Lady Amelia began. "I heard everything you told my grandson in his room. Oh, don't worry. I pushed the others away, wanting to give you privacy. No one else heard your little confession." She bobbed her narrow shoulders. "I'm old. I can listen to anything I want to. And my ears have never been better."

Despite the alarm pounding between Ella's own ears, she smiled wanly. "So then you know—"

"I'm not done!" the lady snapped. "And yes, I know everything. And what's worse, I know what you were babbling on to my other grandson about just now. Of all the stupid ..."

Ella's temper ignited. "I don't understand. You don't want me to tell them?"

The lady threw up her hand. "Of course I don't! You're the best thing to happen to this family in years. Misguided, perhaps, but still good."

Dumbfounded, Ella felt her legs almost give out. "I don't understand," she replied, wobbling on her feet.

"Stop saying that!"

"I can't help it!" Ella flopped onto the nearest couch, folding her arms like a sullen child. "I lied to you. I lied to this family. I didn't *mean* to lie. It was all a misunderstanding. I never meant for this to happen."

Lady Amelia's eyes were glassy and opaque, eerily unreadable. Ella couldn't decide if she was an ally or not. "And yet it did happen. So let's keep it that way."

Ella's spirits sank. Just when she'd thought she had pulled herself out of this mess, someone just had to come along to yank her back in. And now she had a partner in crime!

Lady Amelia's cane thumped over to the couch as she carefully took a seat next to Ella. "You can't hear it now, my dear, but there's laughter in this house. In the drawing room. My daughter is laughing again. Those men," she grumbled, "my nephews' uncles … They're actually behaving like real people and not the vultures they are."

So that was who all those odd men were … Jack's uncles? Or, rather, Lord Oliver's uncles.

The lady's hand was tiny and dry, riddled with veins and dark age spots. She placed it over Ella's. It was an awkward movement, certainly lacking warmth; however, Ella appreciated the effort. "This house has been a tomb ever since my daughter's husband died. We thought Ollie could revive it, but then his engagement went sour and …" Lady Amelia gave her an apologetic look. "All that's the past. The second you walked in here, everything changed. And everyone felt it. *Change.* A new future for this old, tired house."

"But he doesn't know who I am."

The lady shrugged. "He also has a pretty sizeable bump on his head. Give him time."

Lady Amelia wasn't getting the point—or maybe she just didn't want to. "But time won't help him remember me," Ella insisted. "He still won't know me."

The lady squeezed Ella's hand, and what the woman lacked in compassion, she made up for with pure strength. "Then *make* him know you. My grandson has led a very silly life these past few years. I allowed it because he's been nursing a great hurt. But that's all over now. Ollie is not a fool. He will see the accident as a sign to take his life more seriously. To make better decisions. To start fresh."

Ella sighed. The weight that she'd rid herself of on the way to the house restacked itself on her shoulders. "But what if I don't want to be someone's good decision? I want to be someone's love."

Lady Amelia rolled her eyes, muttering something that sounded awfully like a filthy curse. "Sometimes, I actually hate young people," she said, releasing a put-upon breath. "All right, fine. You want love, then make him love you. The man has just looked death in the face. For the next month, everything he looks at will be the brightest, most beautiful, and earth-shattering thing he's ever seen."

"And?" Ella asked helplessly. "What should I do?"

"Make him see you."

Chapter Nine

ON A GOOD day, the journey from Town to Sutton Park took a little over an hour. As a child, Jack had grumbled about the shortness, envying his friends whose country houses took various stops and horse changes to get to. As he believed that good things always came to those who waited, the adventure of the long pilgrimage seemed exotic and wholesome.

However, at thirty-one years of age, practicality won out, and he counted himself lucky. Even decamped at Sutton Park, he would be able to get back to town with ease, keeping an eye on Sinclair and the business as well as doing as his manager had asked … attending a few events in the Season. Just the thought of it made his stomach curdle, and his mother—in her way—made the matter worse by encouraging all of it. He'd made the mistake of informing his mother why he would have to split his time some nights, and she'd been positively delighted, saying the family must keep up appearances, lest the *ton* believe Oliver's situation was dire.

Heaven forbid people think that. Apparently, his mother didn't mind when the *ton* gossiped about Oliver's whoring and drinking. That was perfectly respectable. Being close to death's door was beyond the pale of propriety. Nobody's business but their own.

By midafternoon, the party was firmly ensconced in their new habitat. After Jack had trailed behind all five doctors, making sure Oliver was set up in his room with everything he needed, he made himself scarce until dinner. A pile of correspondence sat on Oliver's desk, waiting for Jack's attention, but the idea of rifling through it without a few brandies in him felt unconscionable.

Besides, his mind was elsewhere, had been elsewhere since he encountered Ella in the foyer that morning. Jack had planned to question her further. Her erratic behavior had been bewildering, to say the least. What had been even more perplexing was his irrational desire to fix it. Seeing her that way, so discombobulated, so panicky, had affected Jack in ways he didn't wish to read into.

If Ella were a man, he would have pressed that moment of weakness, squeezed her until she betrayed herself and handed him the truth. But Ella wasn't a man. And the notion of causing her more pain and anxiety was anathema to him. He'd only wanted to hold her. Comfort her. Brush the frown lines from her mottled face.

And *then* yank the truth out of her.

But his grandmother had beaten him to it.

When Jack encountered Ella after, she'd been composed and relaxed, one with the party as it prepared to leave. All signs of agitation had disappeared with the morning fog.

And with that, all of Jack's resolve to go easy on her had also vanished. He would get to the bottom of her subterfuge. If it was the last thing he did.

Dinner proved to be the perfect place to start.

Jack didn't miss the horror flooding Ella's face when she noticed herself seated next to him at the monstrously long table. Lips pursed, she allowed him to pull out the chair for her. If she detected that Jack pushed her in with a little more force than necessary, she didn't say anything.

In fact, not saying anything appeared to be her new defensive tactic of choice. Which only made Jack even more determined to sniff out what she was hiding under that attractive, poised, enigmatic visage.

Nevertheless, ever the gentleman, he waited for her to get halfway through her soup to strike.

"So, are you going to pretend that what occurred earlier between us didn't happen?" He threw out the words under his breath, making sure only Ella could hear him.

And she heard him, all right. Ella's spoon froze halfway to her mouth. With a finesse that Jack couldn't help but admire, she returned it to her bowl and sat, straight-backed, in her chair. "Honestly, my lord, you make the short time we were alone together sound rather clandestine. It was only a few little minutes."

Jack smiled. He'd never give haughty women the time of day; however, he found that he liked when her voice took on that icy tone and her straight nose crept higher in the air. It was damn near erotic. A challenge.

"A lot can happen in a few little minutes."

Ella angled to him, her brown eyes narrowing to slits. "I doubt that."

A bark of a laugh escaped him, and Jack quickly worked to muffle the sound, lest the rest of the party feel left out of their conversation. He would always be a second son—when he wanted something, he wanted it all to himself.

"You know … I'll stop talking if you just tell me what you wanted to say earlier." He lowered his head closer to her. She smelled like lilacs. Springtime. Youth. Fighting to concentrate, he had to feel the words in his mouth before he could get them out. "I know you're hiding something. Tell me. I can help you."

Ella held his gaze for a long, disconcerting beat. Slowly, she mimicked him, lowering her head as well. "I'm not hiding a thing. I'm here for your brother. The second you come to terms with that, the happier you'll be."

Jack wrenched away, unleashing a silent groan, expelling all the air he was holding out of his nose. "And you want me to be happy? You don't even know me." He swept a hand in front of them, just narrowly avoiding a tapered candle. "You don't know anything about what you've just walked into."

Ella cocked her head. "Perhaps." Her chocolatey eyes glinted, pulling a smile from Jack despite his frustration. Once more, she reminded him of a mischievous elf, hellbent on trouble. Sure enough, she looked the part of a lady well enough, with her high-necked silk gown and ruffled pagoda sleeves, but that was just a ruse—another attempt at hiding. There was more to Miss Ella. She was like sand in the palm of his hand, difficult to hold on to, and vexingly mesmerizing.

She widened her shoulders, hiding the intensity of their conversation with a pleasant smile. "Why don't you enlighten me—if you can, that is. I may be a stranger to everyone, but from what I hear, you aren't much different."

Jack let that little comment slide. She'd obviously been talking to his mother. He wouldn't allow anyone at this table to make him regret or even question his path in life. Did his mother truly want him to be like his uncles?

Ha! His uncles.

Jack took a long drink of his red wine and placed it back on the table with a demonstrable *thud*. "Well, I'm sure my mother introduced you to all the doctors. Don't bother trying to remember all of their names. I like to number them one through five and call it a day." Next, he jutted his chin across the table at the three gentlemen who'd been present all his entire life. Like wallpaper, they were always around but could never be remembered with accuracy. Just there. Bland. "And then there's my uncles. You've met them, yes?"

Ella's mouth twisted. "Yes, they were … nice."

Jack chortled. *Nice*. Was there anything worse? If a beautiful woman ever called Jack *nice* in that particular way, he would have to rethink his life decisions.

Not that Ella was beautiful.

Oh, who was he kidding? Of course she was. In that Ella way, which he would be hard-pressed to describe to anyone. Probably because her particular brand of beauty was so distinctly fitting to him. With her disapproving glares and impish smiles; her hair that wasn't blonde and not quite brown; her husky voice that lingered in his mind as he fell asleep at night.

Jack shifted in disgust. He could feel himself growing hard under the table. Now was not the time. Actually, it would never be the right time for his brother's fiancée. If that was what she was. Regardless, the best way to deflate a hard-on was thinking of his uncles.

Yes, that did the trick.

"*Nice,*" he murmured. "Hardly. Degenerates, all of them. Just do yourself a favor—don't get too close to Uncle Christopher. He's the one on the right." Jack waited until Ella surreptitiously followed his line of sight as she used her napkin to wipe her mouth. "He can be a bit handsy. Bloody good with numbers, though. Brilliant, actually. For a crude bastard."

Ella's chest bobbed as she fought off a laugh. Jack's heart hammered from the sight. "And the next one?" she asked, sotto voce. "Uncle Edward, I believe."

Jack tore his gaze from her face, landing on his middle uncle. "You don't have to shield yourself from that one. Big drinker, bit of a hermit. Likes to read and draw, if I recall."

"That hardly sounds like a degenerate."

Jack laughed. "I didn't tell you *what* he likes to read and draw."

Ella couldn't disguise it that time. Her giggle rang out along the table. Luckily, the servants were busy taking away the soup and crystal glasses, diffusing most of the lovely sound.

Desperately, Jack wanted to make her laugh again. "And then there's Uncle Andrew." His voice dropped off and his expression froze as he watched the uncle at his mother's right speaking in hushed tones, not at all dissimilar to the way Jack was speaking to Ella.

"Well … what about Uncle Andrew?" Ella encouraged him,

her cheeks flushed. "I'm waiting for your pithy warning."

Jack fiddled with the tines of his fork. "Um …" He closed his eyes, shaking his head. "No warning there. Uncle Andrew is too busy spending his nights with my mother to be much of a bother to anyone other than her."

Ella had been in the process of reaching for her glass. At his words, she flinched, knocking the crystal over, spilling the wine. Silently, they both watched it bleed a thin river into the white tablecloth.

"Fuck, I apologize. I shouldn't have said that." Jack ran his hand through his prickly hair. "And fuck, I shouldn't have said *fuck* just then."

Fuck. Sometimes, Jack forgot just how much sea life had shaped him. He'd thought wading back into his old world would be seamless. Judging by the pink creeping up Ella's neck, he could see it was not.

"Please forgive me—"

"How do you know?" Ella asked, cutting him off. She tugged on her lower lip, and while admiring that little habit, it hit Jack— she wasn't offended. She was curious. And embarrassed by her own curiosity.

"I noticed a while ago," he admitted gruffly. "Once, when I was visiting, I saw him go into her room in the middle of the night. After my father died, of course."

Ella's eyes jumped all over his face. It wasn't a caress, but Jack could feel her all the same as she searched him. "Do you mind their …"

"That my uncle is sleeping with his dead brother's wife?" Jack flexed his jaw and watched his mother. Always aware of appearances, the duchess never slipped. Her smiles were never too wide, her laughter never too loud. But her eyes always made their way back to Uncle Andrew as if there were an imaginary string between them. His uncle was a soft-spoken, unassuming man. Weak, Jack's father had called him, but not with malice. He'd said it the same way a man would say it was cold outside. It was fact.

But facts could mean different things to different people. And it was obvious that the duchess didn't share her late husband's judgment.

"No," Jack replied plaintively, finally answering a question he'd asked himself over the years. "He makes her happy."

They fell into another silence. A companionable one.

Jack took another drink of wine. His mouth was parched. Everything about him felt parched. He wasn't the one who was supposed to be divulging. But there was something about Ella, something that made him want to tell her things.

And she wasn't done with him. Unlike Jack, she waited until the roasted chicken, sauteed carrots, and roasted potatoes were in front of them before she struck.

"I will give you that your uncles are a little … eccentric, but even that's hardly unusual in families like ours," Ella began diplomatically, pausing to load her fork with food. Jack watched in rapt attention as she stacked a small piece of dark chicken, a bit of carrot, and a splash of potato before inserting it in her mouth. She closed her eyes as she chewed. Jack fisted his hand in his lap, just waiting for her to moan. She didn't. It was for the best. Ella opened her eyes to find him staring at her. Eyelashes flickering, she hurried to finish her thought. "Why do you loathe them so much?"

Jack's throat tightened as she began to load her fork once more. She was such a tiny thing. He'd assumed she ate like a bird, but this blatant passion for food confused him. *And* charmed him.

His Adam's apple bobbed over his necktie. "I, ah, hardly loathe them. To be honest, I don't have much feeling for them either way."

"That's not true," she countered. "Their presence seems to upset you. Why?"

"Because they've always been here," he spat. "Always. My father felt guilty that their father never gave them anything, so he allowed them to stay when he became duke. They never pushed themselves, never wanted more than my father's handouts.

Living off another's generosity and benevolence ..." He sneered down at his untouched plate.

"Hm."

Jack glanced up to see Ella piling her fork again, this time wearing a smug, self-satisfied expression.

"*Hm?*" he asked.

She shrugged.

He wouldn't let it go. "Why *hm?*"

She chewed thoughtfully. "Just explains a lot, that's all."

"A lot of what?"

Pointing her fork at him, she drew a small circle in the air. "A lot of you." She went back to cutting her meat. Jack racked his brain, and he couldn't remember anyone putting so much thought and attention into eating before.

Ella went on. "You know, not everyone has a voracious need to conquer the world. Not everyone is like you."

"Damn right they're not."

She rolled her eyes. "Most people don't have your ambition."

"What do you know about most people?" Jack asked, slightly taken aback by the vehemence in his tone. "You're a viscount's daughter. And you're barely out of the nursery. What the hell do you know about anything?"

That comment got another eye roll—a slower one this time—as well as an icy glare. "I know things ... I read."

Jack guffawed, though he stopped when she saw the hurt flit across her face. It was there and gone, but he caught it all the same. She'd mentioned reading before. Adventure stories, wasn't it? Tales about shipwrecks and ... and cannibals.

He eyed Ella's hands as she tried for another bite. They were still splattered with pink splotches, but not nearly as red and swollen as before. He hadn't gotten around to asking her about them, if they were a constant source of pain. He'd have to add it to his ever-growing list of what he didn't know about this woman. For another day.

Ella's fork trembled as she raised it to her mouth. Her chewing had lost its zeal. Because of him.

Jack sighed, forcing the irritation to drain out of him. "Oh, I, ah, well, I thought you should know," he started conversationally, pausing for her to look up. She didn't. Served him right. "If cannibals are keeping you from exploring the West Indies, you shouldn't let them. I've sailed there more times than I can count, and I've never come across any. That's not to say there aren't cannibals but ..." He bobbed his shoulders. "I wouldn't let it worry me if I were you."

Ella's eyes remained down at her plate. "That's good to know," she said quietly. "I suppose you thought my worries childish."

"Not at all. I've known many men with the same concerns before venturing out." Jack admired the color that crept back into her cheeks. The shape of her lips as she released a silent, steadying breath.

Once more, he caught himself speaking after he'd told himself to quit. "I don't know anything about nunneries, so I can't help you on that front; however, books shouldn't be an issue either."

Finally, her eyes collided with his. Jack offered a shy smile. "So, no need to worry on that account. Sailors are always leaving books and picking up new ones. I once found a copy of *Dante's Inferno* when visiting the Sandwich Islands. Stumbled upon it while I was hiking to a waterfall I'd heard about. And there it was. On the other side of the world."

Ella's lips parted into a smile that made Jack miserably warm. "Did you take it?"

"Fuck no, I hate that bloody book. I left it for the next miserable bastard."

There it was. That giggle again.

It made the whole bloody night worth it.

It also served as a warning: rough waters ahead.

Jack's favorite.

Chapter Ten

I T WAS AN undeniable fact that time ran slower in the country. Ella had already known this from all the months her family spent at their estate in Norwich throughout the year. But at least there she was acquainted with the staff and had friends. Most importantly, she'd had her sisters (before their inconvenient marriages). All this to say that, however glamorous and awe-inspiring Sutton Park was from the outside, the inside was intolerably lonely those first few days.

Lady Evelyn and her mother tried to help. They gave up their hours, showcasing the grand house, giving Ella tours and backstories of the mammoth rooms—which king slept in that bed, which painting had crossed the Channel with the Conqueror. But the ladies had their own routines and schedules and settled into them seamlessly, leaving Ella to her own devices. It didn't take long for the innumerable gold chandeliers to lose their luster and the countless marble busts of dead dukes to lose their shine.

Too much time on anyone's hands was never a good thing, and soon Ella was wondering why she'd been brought along to begin with. She'd assumed her job was to be helpful, to spend time with Lord Oliver. However, that was proving not to be the case.

She tried not to take it to heart. The doctors were merely overprotective, and the duchess accepted everything they advised. Lord Oliver needed sleep, they said. He needed quiet and darkness, they said.

He didn't need anyone except them, they said.

For now, they said.

By the third day, Ella was at her wits' end. She'd already considered herself a liar; now she was an interloper as well.

If it wasn't for the library, she'd have gone stir crazy. When she wasn't eating or sleeping, Ella decamped to the cavernous space (which put the townhouse's library to shame), stretching out lazily in the tufted leather chairs like a cat in a patch of sunlight.

But something caught her fancy that afternoon, and it wasn't *Robinson Crusoe*, which she'd already read four times anyway. Staring out the tall, mullioned windows, she noticed Uncle Edward setting up an easel outside in the middle of the garden that stretched out, long and rectangular, in the back of the house.

Remembering what Jack had told her at dinner, Ella frowned at the stately man, carefully lining up his paints and materials in just the right way. Obviously, the gentleman didn't *only* paint scandalous things, she concluded. Landscapes must be another passion. Perhaps Jack, in all his insufferable wisdom, didn't know his uncle as well as he thought he did.

And she couldn't wait to tell him that. Whenever the opinionated pirate emerged from whatever hole he'd hidden himself in.

Ella chided herself for the ungracious thought. It wasn't like she hadn't seen Jack over these last days. She'd grown quite accustomed to his back, since he always seemed to be walking as far away from her as possible whenever they happened upon the same place. But the fact that he'd refused to join the family for dinner since the first night rankled her. She couldn't help but take it personally. Ella had always considered herself a rather lively dinner companion. A proper conversationalist.

Perhaps she'd been wrong.

No.

No. No. No.

She slapped her book closed and launched herself from her chair. She refused to doubt herself because of that man. She was a bloody *great* conversationalist—instructed by her mother, and the viscountess never failed.

Ella would prove it.

The light was already violent and blinding by midmorning, and Ella cursed herself for not grabbing her bonnet before marching into the garden. She'd be sweating in no time in the summer heat.

But no matter. She was on a mission. And a few freckles never hurt anyone. Especially if her mother wasn't here to see them.

Not wanting to disturb Uncle Edward, Ella eschewed the pebbled path that led to the manicured hedgerow garden. She kept to the lawn that eventually sloped down to the green and murky pond, which sat placid and calm in the windless expanse. Framed by long, willowy grass, and a cloudless sky, the scene evoked peace and tranquility, and it was no wonder the uncle had chosen to paint it. Ella would start the conversation by admiring his choice. That bit of approval would be sure to break the man from his shell.

When they'd first been introduced, Uncle Edward merely bowed and gave Ella a shy, panicky smile before scuttering away. She was determined to start a conversation that lasted longer than a minute this time around.

Naturally, she would get him talking about painting. Everyone loved talking about their hobbies. Ella knew nothing about it—had never shown aptitude, her mother had announced when she was seven. She would be a blank slate for the man and prove that she could be trusted with his time.

Maybe Uncle Edward could even give her lessons. He could teach her about mixing colors and instruct her on how to create a bucolic scene with the sun reflecting off water, and maybe even a frog chirping merrily from its lily—

Breasts!

Breasts …

Good Lord, were those *flippers*?

"Oh!" Ella tripped, catching herself just before she fell face first into a hedge.

Uncle Edward spun around to face her. "What are you …? Who? What?" He spread his arms out like a horrified eagle, blocking his canvas.

Ella wanted to tell him there was no need. Her neck would not lift her head until she was safely out of range.

Had he been drawing a busty, naked woman with flippers instead of legs? A mermaid? Yes, that was it. Uncle Edward had been drawing a very, very naked mermaid.

"I'm so sorry," Ella exclaimed, holding her hand over her forehead, shielding her eyes from the sun. *And other things.* "I didn't mean to startle you. I wasn't sneaking. I just didn't want to disturb your"—she gulped—"art."

Uncle Edward's feet shuffled back and forth on the pebbles. He was tall. All the Sutton men were. But none of the uncles had the bulk of Oliver or Jack, and Edward was the skinniest of the bunch. Reedy and pale, he seemed incredibly delicate to Ella, like he might break if anyone spoke too harshly to him.

"Oh, it's fine. It's fine. I was just … adding," he sputtered. Ella lifted her head to catch his blush, wondering if clothes would be among the additions. "No one ever bothers me out here. You just surprised me, is all."

"Of course."

Uncle Edward took the canvas off the easel and placed it face down on the ground. "I don't like people to see anything before it's done."

"Of course," she said once more. So much for being a great conversationalist.

The silence dragged on.

"How are you enjoying Sutton Park?" the gentleman asked. "It's quite lovely this time of year."

Ella smiled, grateful that someone remembered how to engage in polite dialogue. "It's like a dream," she replied truthfully. "But I have a feeling that Sutton Park is lovely throughout the year."

Uncle Edward nodded. "It is that."

Another silence. For the life of her, Ella didn't know what to talk about. She'd planned to ask him about his painting, but there was no way she was ever going to broach that subject. Ever. She had to pivot.

"I don't wish to bother you any further. I think I'll just go for a walk around the pond. I always find it fun to peer around the edges and see what life I can find there just under my nose."

"Care if I join you?

Ella squinted through the sun, finding the lord to be genuine. "If you'd like."

Uncle Edward nodded, his nose glowing red with pride. "I would. It's not every day that I get a chance to join a pretty woman on a stroll."

Ella smiled shyly before hesitating. She glanced at the lord's hands, remembering too late that it was the other uncle's wandering touches that Jack had warned her about.

"Is something wrong, Miss Ella?"

"No." She shook her head, feeling a hot flush climb onto her cheeks. "I just remembered something."

"Something important?"

Ella accepted his arm and started down the path. "No, nothing important at all."

HOURS LATER, SURROUNDED by the London Ladies Cricket Club in the corner of the Flying Batsman tavern, Ella could finally let out a hearty belly laugh.

"And he didn't mention it? Not at all?" Lady Anna asked, concern etched into her kind face. "He must have known you'd seen it."

Ella lifted her shoulders. "Not one time. He was more interested in telling me about the gardens and the pond. It was … nice, if a little odd."

Mrs. Myfanwy Everett scoffed, placing a hand on her large, pregnant belly. Rearranging herself in her seat, she grimaced. "They all sound odd. Why didn't any of the uncles ever move out? Didn't this Edward consider joining a regiment?"

Ella hid a smile behind her teacup. "He did. But then he realized he didn't like running."

"What about the church?" Anna tried.

Ella raised a brow. "He found he didn't like people all that much either."

"And the other brothers are the same?" Anna asked.

"I'm not sure," Ella replied slowly. "From what I gather, I don't think their father was very encouraging. All I know is they are perfectly content to live simple, quiet lives, and the duke allows them to."

"Why is it that when ladies of a certain age want to live simple, quiet lives, we're labeled spinsters?" Myfanwy asked.

The club answered with chuckles and laughs, nodding in accord. Ella hadn't thought of that, but the term perfectly encapsulated the brothers. They were spinsters, and happily so, not lazy, as Jack concluded.

Anna's sister, Beatrice, leaned forward and cupped her head in her palm. Her smile wide, her face took on a dreamlike quality. "Enough about the uncles—tell us all about the duke."

Ella smiled at the young woman. Everyone in the club knew that Beatrice, although a competent cricket player, had only joined because they were low on members and Anna forced her to. She was a sweet, lovely girl, but was much more interested in the gossip the ladies shared than the tactics of the game.

Before Ella could open her mouth to respond, Myfanwy beat her to it. "Yes, please, Ella, tell us why you decided to miss our last practice and move into the duke's country house. We'd all like to know when cricket became just a passing fancy that you could so carelessly throw aside."

Ella tapped her teeth together, knowing that her reprieve was over. Ever since she'd walked into the tavern, she'd been waiting for Myfanwy to confront her over missing the previous practice. A year ago, Ella would have been mortified to be called out like that in front of the team, and by the captain, no less. But knowing Myfanwy—and her unmitigated zealousness for the sport—better now, she understood that the captain couldn't help herself, nor did she want to.

"I'm sorry," Ella said, meeting Myfanwy's eyes. "It all happened so fast. I should have written a note. I apologize. It won't happen again."

Seeming to accept that, Myfanwy leaned back in her chair, once more adjusting her growing body to a more comfortable position. According to Ella's mother, Myfanwy shouldn't be there, but Ella wasn't about to tell her captain that. Per the viscountess, it was mortifying that Myfanwy kept creeping out into Society while she was so far along in her confinement.

Ella had told her mother that Myfanwy's husband, Samuel Everett, didn't mind that his wife didn't want to be cooped up in their home, but the woman had refused to believe it. Ella supposed that it wasn't entirely accurate anyway. Most likely, Samuel would have preferred that his wife stay at home, but she had other ideas. And to Myfanwy Everett, her ideas were usually the right ones.

"Please don't let it happen again," Myfanwy replied wearily. She rubbed her eyes, and Ella noticed the bags lagging joylessly underneath. "Our match against the Matrons is coming up fast. We have to be vigilant. I won't let them think we're resting on our laurels. I'd like to beat them soundly, so no one thinks last year was a fluke."

"Of course," Ella replied. "I'm sure we will."

Myfanwy went on, her tone low, like she was having a conversation with herself. "Everyone's just dropping like flies," she muttered irritably. "First me and Jennifer. No offense, Anna, but you're going to be useless to us soon too."

Anna smiled, placing a hand on her own ripening stomach. "No offense taken, captain. I can't wait to be useless to you."

"And then there's Maggie," Myfanwy continued, "who swears that she's going to be back in time for the game, although I don't know if I believe her. Who goes on their honeymoon in the middle of the summer?"

Beatrice shrugged. "Probably someone who just got married."

Myfanwy swept her hand in the air like a knife. "Normally I would agree with you, but this was her second wedding to the same man. I will allow a honeymoon after the first union, but the second time ..." She pinched her lips together, obviously thinking it too difficult to finish her train of thought.

Ella reached over to pat Myfanwy's hand, but could only do it twice because it felt so odd to her. The only cricket member blunt and courageous enough to calm Myfanwy's theatrics, to talk sense to her, was Lady Jo Everly, and she was noticeably missing.

"Where is Jo?" Ella asked, hoping the change of subject might lessen the flush in the captain's cheeks.

Myfanwy groaned.

Obviously not.

"She wasn't at the last practice either," Anna answered tentatively. She gazed at Myfanwy like the woman was a wild animal, not wanting to speak in a loud voice or make any sudden movements. "She wrote a note saying she wasn't feeling well. I assumed she would be back today, but ..." Anna shrugged.

"Has anyone talked to her?" Ella asked. Everyone around the circle shook their heads. "That's odd. I wonder what could be the matter. I'd hate to think it's something serious."

Over the summer, Ella and Jo had formed an unlikely friendship as they inserted themselves into the love life of their teammate, Lady Maggie. Their meddling had drawn to a close when Maggie married gambling den owner Harry Holmes, and so had their time together.

Now, sitting amongst the club, Ella noticed how much that bothered her. Perhaps she would stop in on Jo before traveling back to Sutton Park, be the friend she thought she was.

And it dawned on Ella that Jo had a history with Lord Oliver. It wasn't something she was particularly forthcoming about, but Ella learned that they had grown up together. If anyone could tell her more about the man—what he liked and disliked—it was Jo.

Ella just hoped that she fell into the former category and not the latter.

Chapter Eleven

JACK SHOVED HIS hands in his pockets, releasing a long breath while eyeing the daunting pile of correspondence crowding his brother's large, mahogany desk.

"Why is it so quiet today, Carlisle?" he asked the butler, who stood a polite few feet away along the bookcase that lined the wall of the duke's study.

"Quiet, my lord?" As usual, Carlisle's voice came out passive and unaffected. Jack could have told the unbothered man that his jacket was on fire and his voice would have sounded exactly the same.

Jack cocked his head, one side of his mouth twitching up in a wry half-smile. "You know what I mean."

The butler returned a barely there nod. "Miss Ella ventured to town today. She informed your mother that she had a meeting."

"A meeting?"

"A meeting, my lord," Carlisle repeated. "So, that must be the reason you think it's quieter."

"Hmm," Jack answered, trying (and failing) to sound as indifferent as his brother's loyal man. His father's loyal man as well. Carlisle had the good fortune to be one of those people who never seemed to age. Jack had known him since he was a boy and didn't notice a difference in the butler between now and then. It had to be the hair. Carlisle's was white, snow white, and it had always been that way. Scrutinizing a man's advancing age was difficult when he'd always seemed old.

Carlisle nodded to the correspondence. "Should we get to it, my lord?"

Jack squinted, painfully inspecting the unopened letters with one eye. There was no telling what was in that pile. This was what Sinclair was for, damn it! The last thing Jack wanted to do was dip his toe into his brother's ducal affairs—and *not*-so-ducal affairs.

"Do I have to read all of them, Carlisle?" Jack asked. "Surely all the important letters are sent to his business manager?"

"Some, my lord, but not all," the butler responded evenly. "Your brother likes to stay on top of things. He is incredibly vigilant when it comes to the title and its responsibilities." He paused, his calm veneer finally cracking. "Despite what some people say."

Yes, what people said. About Oliver's drinking, whoring, and the myriad other vices that Jack didn't know about but assumed he had. But, damn it, that was his brother's business. Jack had no right to pry, and yet here he was in Oliver's office, doing just that. But every ship needed steering, even one as trained and well looked after as the duke's.

"Fine," Jack said grimly. He rounded the desk and took a seat, rifling through the letters with an impatient hand. "But I'm only opening the ones that seem pressing. The rest can wait for Oliver."

"Of course, my lord."

Over the next fifteen minutes, Jack came to the annoying realization that everyone who sent a letter to a duke thought it was pressing. Bills, bills, bills. From the tailor, the modiste, the jeweler, the flower shop … Oliver led a merry life, there was no question, but Jack couldn't help being a little disgusted by the profligate spending.

Sinclair could have five new clerks from the money Oliver spent in one month at the flower shop alone.

And if people weren't demanding that the duke settle his debts, they were accosting him for handouts. Charity after charity begged for donations, most asking that Oliver continue the generosity that he'd doled out the previous year. Jack's ire was tempered a little at this. His brother may be a cad and a rogue, maybe even a libertine, but his heart was always in the right place.

His heart.

Jack tapped the sharp edge of a manilla envelope against the shiny, polished desk, letting his mind wander. Had the flowers Oliver ordered been delivered to Ella's residence? What about the jewelry? Had Oliver purchased a ring for his soon-to-be duchess?

What about the modiste? Ella's parents would hardly allow the duke to send her clothing. Were they a surprise for a later date, or were they intended for some other lucky woman?

Jack didn't know what he hated more, the idea of Oliver buying delicate bits of lace for Ella or doing it for someone else behind her back.

And this was the problem. The woman wasn't even standing in the same vicinity as him, and she still plagued him. The house wasn't quieter with her gone; it was louder. Because it left a vacuum for his ungainly thoughts to grow and fester, always, always, always coming back to Ella.

"My lord?"

Jack blinked, realizing that the crisp letter in his hand had been demolished into a crinkly ball. "Shite, sorry, Carlisle. I got lost there for a moment." He took his time smoothing the envelope back into a respectable shape until he could read the address on the back. "St Bridget's Orphanage," he mused, tossing it to the side. *Asking for another donation, no doubt.*

But when Jack reached for the next envelope on the stack, he saw that it was also from the same orphanage. As was the one under it. And the one after that.

He lifted his brows at the butler. "Demanding nuns, aren't they?"

Carlisle didn't laugh. Which wasn't unusual, but it still gave Jack pause. As did the butler's starched demeanor. He didn't know if the man's spine could snap any straighter—but it did.

Jack held the envelope up toward the butler. "What's this about?"

"I am not aware of its contents, my lord."

Jack frowned. That was a tight go-around if he'd ever heard one. He tried again. "Have you been aware of its contents before?"

"Perhaps, my lord. A long time ago."

Jack's shoulders slumped. He was not in the mood for a mystery, especially one that made his unflappable butler … well, flap.

Muttering, he tore open the envelope and ripped out its contents. It was only a matter of seconds before Jack's frown morphed into a glower. And only a minute before the cursing began to trip from his furious tongue.

"Fuck!" he hollered, erupting from the chair. He pointed a finger at the butler. "You and I are going to talk when I get back."

The butler nodded as Jack marched out of the room, his "Of course, my lord," as calm and unconcerned as ever.

⸻⁂⸻

IT REEKED OF soap—and not the good kind. Not the heady, soft, flowery aroma that followed Ella around wherever she went and lingered for long, tantalizing minutes after. This smell was caustic, acidic, the kind that made your eyes water and your nose burn.

St. Bridget's Orphanage also held the unappealing aroma of sad, unwanted children. Jack had never considered that something like that could give off a scent. Now he knew differently.

"Many brats have black hair," he declared, standing in the

middle of a large, colorless room made small by the ridiculous number of beds crammed in rows on either side of him. He angled his head to the nun standing at his right. "It doesn't mean anything."

Mother Agnes's eyes narrowed slightly. It was expertly done. Somehow, the nun managed to convey utter disdain for Jack's apparent stupidity while also pitying him for it.

"That's true," she replied coolly, turning her attention to the child in question. The little girl sat on her thin, little bed in the far corner, ostensibly combing a tattered doll's few remaining hairs with her fingers. "But most children don't come to us with notes saying they're the Duke of Winchester's bastards."

Jack clenched his jaw. Hearing his brother's name used in such a crude manner was intolerable, especially when Oliver wasn't there to defend himself. "Still," he remarked, desperately trying to keep his frustration in check, "it's hardly proof."

"You're absolutely right, my lord," Mother Agnes said, her voice taking on a defeatist quality that immediately put Jack on edge. "All I have is a piece of paper that the girl held in her hand when she was placed in our care. I chose to believe it, because I had no reason not to. I would never say that St. Bridget's Orphanage is an expert on handling children born on the wrong side of the blanket; however, we do have great experience, as I'm sure you can understand."

Jack nodded curtly.

The nun went on. "And I believe the letter to be credible."

Jack glanced down at the letter in his hand. The nun had foisted it upon him the second he stormed into the orphanage asking for answers. It wasn't so much that Jack didn't believe it. He just didn't want to.

"I hear the mother was quite good at her craft," the nun said. "I'll have to take other people's word for it. I don't have much of an ear for opera." She leaned over the letter, nearly poking Jack's eye with her wide, winglike cornette. "Apparently, after she died, friends watched over the little girl, but that only lasted a year before the money ran out. The money the duke had initially settled on the mother."

This was the second letter of the day that Jack nearly gripped to death. Taking a deep breath, he relinquished his hold. "My brother would never do that. He would never willingly give up a child. I don't care if it was a mistake. I don't care who or what the mother was."

For the first time since they'd met, the nun's tone became wistful, plaintive. "Perhaps you didn't know your brother as well as you thought you did."

"No." Jack's fury collided with the woman's pragmatism. But it was like hitting a steel wall—nothing would dent her opinion. "No," he repeated. "My brother would never be ashamed of a child. He's many things, but he's … he's not that."

Mother Agnes backed away, once more leveling Jack with an expression filled with disappointment and compassion. "I'm sorry. I don't know what to tell you. I only know what's in your hand. After the child was born, the mother went to the duke asking for money and help, and he settled her with a tidy sum. Apparently, it did not last, and the friend of the mother's couldn't keep the child any longer. Now, she's here."

A tight band of tension crowded around Jack's head. Nothing the nun was telling him was unusual. Men from his circle did things like this all the time. Unwanted children were taken care of and rarely heard from again. But Oliver wasn't like most men. He wasn't like *those men*. He was a fucking duke.

He was … not a duke ten years ago.

Jack flipped the paper over in vain, hoping that the answer to the mystery was hidden on the opposite side. No such luck. "It says the mother went to the duke," he muttered to himself. "Not Oliver. *The duke.*"

Could the woman have gone to Jack's father for help? And if that was the case, could Oliver still not know that there was a young girl in this world who was thought to be his daughter?

"This is all beside the point," Mother Agnes announced. Gone was the empathy, replaced with a businesslike, cold demeanor. "Will you be taking her today? Or, at the very least, leaving a donation?"

A quick look at the nun's hands showed that her nails were short and clean, stumpy. So why did it feel like she'd just clawed Jack's chest, opening up skin?

Mother Agnes took his arm and guided him from the room, toward a dark corridor that led back to her office. One last glance showed the girl still on the bed, holding her hand out, blocking a taller, heavier girl from trying to take the doll. Jack rounded the corner before he saw the shite situation play out.

The chattering and limp laughter of children stretched away the more they walked, their footsteps filling the vacuum of the lonely, dimly lit hall. "I can see this is all new to you, my lord," the nun said, keeping her steady hand on his. "But, again, let me remind you that it's not new to us. If you don't know how much of a donation to leave, we would be happy to guide your conscience in this time."

Jack searched the nun's face. Her expression was placid yet assured, buoyed by experience in these situations, dealing with men such as himself. Men with guilty consciences. Men who lived lives where right and wrong were mere suggestions, something nebulous and blurry along the horizon.

As Jack sat in the seat offered to him in the office, it became clear that Mother Agnes had known from the beginning that he would not be bringing the girl home with him. It didn't matter how many years he'd spent at sea—the stench of being highborn still stuck to him. The rancid smell of money and lack of accountability. Just another lord dealing with another bastard.

What would Oliver do? Jack asked himself, racking his brain for the right answer. The only true answer. But this whole episode had shaken him to his core, shattered what he thought he knew about his older brother, *and* his father. And Jack was not his brother's keeper, no matter what his mother declared.

He cleared his throat. "Thank you, Mother Agnes," he said,

avoiding the knowing look she returned. "That would be very kind of you."

A grim smile was his answer. It offered no comfort. The smile was like one between co-conspirators, a verbal handshake between partners in crime, making the best of a bad situation. Jack wondered if the job had done that to the nun, or if she had always been this utilitarian.

"That's what we're here for," she said. "Some secrets are best kept hidden."

Chapter Twelve

"WELL, LADIES, MY husband is giving me that look that means I've overstayed my welcome." Myfanwy gingerly lifted herself from her chair. Ella couldn't complain. This late in the afternoon, the tavern was filling up with men making their nightly stops before returning home for the day. She'd stretched her time with the club as long as she could, but she had to leave if she was going to make it back to Sutton Park for dinner, as she'd promised.

Myfanwy leveled her with a hard look. "We'll see you next week, yes?" she said, arching a sharp brow.

Ella laughed. "Absolutely. I will be at practice. I promise."

Beatrice stood up as well, smoothing down her skirts. "And be sure to come prepared with more stories about the duke. You were much too tight-lipped today."

Anna rolled her eyes, placing a hand on her sister's shoulder. "What my little sister means to say is that we all want to make sure that he's on the mend."

"And," Beatrice interjected, "we want to know what it is you two talk about, and what makes him laugh, and what he likes to get up to in the middle of the night when no one's watching."

Ella snorted. "The man can't even get out of bed on his own steam, and you want to know his nighttime proclivities?"

Beatrice's eyes sparked. "Yes, please."

"All right now," Anna said, pointing her sister toward the exit. "That's our cue to go. It was lovely seeing you all. Ella, please forget everything Bea just asked and remember that we're not all sinful voyeurs."

Myfanwy scoffed. "Speak for yourself." Ella's shock stopped her. "What? The meeting is over. I don't mind gossiping about rakish dukes when the cricket is out of the way."

The rest of the ladies said their goodbyes, each giving Myfanwy commiserating pats on the arm as they filed past.

Ella swiveled her head around the tavern, her eyes watering from the pungent sting of smoke and hops. "Is Samuel there?" she asked. "I don't want to leave you alone."

"Thank you, dear, but he's right over there," Myfanwy said, pointing at the far side of the bar where the cricket star stood wearing a bored, dejected expression, sandwiched between two younger men who were obviously rabid fans. In the short time Ella watched, the young men hadn't stopped talking once, their ruddy faces bright with amazement and the effects of too much alcohol. "The man has become my shadow. He's never far," Myfanwy added.

Ella noticed that Myfanwy didn't sound remotely upset about this fact of married life. In fact, her tone was almost shyly proud. Ella wondered what it must feel like to have someone so attuned to her, someone who wanted to know where she was and whom she was with. It didn't seem at all suffocating, like the way Ella's mother always manufactured her schedule. Quite the opposite— it seemed sweet and beautiful.

"Well, then take care." Ella smiled to herself, gathering her reticule. She maneuvered around the round, unfinished tables, apologizing whenever her voluminous skirts knocked against an elbow or a thigh.

She was almost in the clear when a hand lashed out, clutching her elbow in a soft, forceful manner.

"I'm sorry—" she began before her stomach leapt up into her throat.

Jack Sutton stared up at her from his seat, his expression blank. He tilted his head, his blue eyes studying her as if she were an artifact in a museum. And then his jaw clenched, and his face wasn't so unreadable anymore.

He took a pull of his drink and slowly stood, keeping his hand on Ella so she couldn't run away. "If you had a hankering for more sherry, Miss Ella, I'm sure you didn't have to come all the way to London to get it."

⇌⇌⇌✳⇇⇇⇇

WHEN JACK'S GRIP relented, Ella took her opening. Yanking her arm free, she spun on her heels straight for the door, praying the man wouldn't cause a scene. He might. She didn't know him well enough to say otherwise. The man wore a gold earring, was roguishly good looking, and had no manners. She didn't care what he said—that meant pirate. And didn't pirates spend their afternoons drinking in taverns before demolishing them with silly brawls?

Ella hit the sticky summer air and could finally take a breath. She inflated her lungs, her feet never stopping. The carriage was only a few yards down the path, and she gazed upon it like it was nothing short of salvation. If she could just get inside, she could use the next hour or so formulating a way to explain why she'd been in the Flying Batsman surrounded by day laborers and ordinary, everyday men.

A more courageous woman might have halted and just told Jack about the cricket club and Myfanwy's condition and Samuel's sweet deference, but that woman didn't know him. Jack needed the hour to cool off. They both did.

However, the moment Ella heard the telltale slap of determined footsteps behind her, she knew salvation would not be hers that afternoon.

"Where are you going in such a hurry?" Jack's voice wafted

over her shoulder, polite and casual. Ella shuddered.

Two could play that game. "I have to get back," she replied, proud that her voice didn't fall off until the very end. "I promised your mother."

Jack was closer now. His scent captured her before his hands could. Spicy with a tangy hint of pine. Ella was amazed at how quickly she'd become accustomed to it. Jack always smelled like he'd just finished sanding or polishing wood. Even with her nerves as frayed as they were, Ella could appreciate that.

"Did you also tell my mother that you were spending your afternoon in a tavern?"

Ella's skirts flared as she twirled to face him. For a swift second, Jack gave her pause. He wasn't as indifferent as he'd tried to sound. A far cry from how he appeared inside the dark tavern, there was now an intensity to his form, a hardness to his mouth. He reminded Ella of an animal who'd been biting his tether, with only inches remaining until freedom.

"I was not drinking. Or I *was*. Tea. Tea. We only drink tea," she stammered, attempting to snatch one thought in her whirling mind and make it make sense.

Jack stretched his neck to each side, once more gently taking her arm. Four long strides were all it took to reach the carriage, and in something that was becoming a habit, he whipped open the door and dropped her inside.

Grumbling, Ella straightened her skirts and made herself presentable while she heard him holler at another carriage, instructing it to follow behind. What was he doing in London? When she'd left this morning, she'd been under the impression that he was staying in, ignoring her from afar, as he always did. In all the taverns in all of London, how in the world had he ended up at this one?

Unfortunately, Ella's questions would have to wait. When Jack settled in his seat, bearing down on her with yet another disappointing glower, she understood that she would not be the one making inquiries anytime soon.

"Well?" he asked, crossing his arms.

Ella pushed her spine up against the back of her seat. As was his custom, Jack splayed his thighs wide; he took up most of the room between them, and something deep inside Ella desperately warned her not to touch him.

Nevertheless, his knee still skimmed hers, forcing Ella to jerk away. The more room she gave up, the more he decided to take.

She lifted her chin in the air. "I've done nothing wrong. I was at a cricket club meeting—"

Jack snorted. "I don't know much about ladies and their little clubs, but I do know they don't usually host them in taverns."

Little clubs. Ella seethed.

"*Shockingly*, there's much you don't know, my lord," Ella said, enjoying the way her words caused his brows to slash across his forehead like knives. "If you knew anything about me, you would know that my cricket club coach is Mr. Samuel Everett." She tore the shade back from the window and pointed outside to the tavern fading into the distance. "He is the owner of the Flying Batsman. Ordinarily, we meet elsewhere, but seeing as his wife is in a delicate condition, he wouldn't allow her to go anywhere without him today. He needed to be at the tavern, which meant that *she* needed to be at the tavern, which meant that *we* needed to be at the tavern. I'm sorry to disappoint you, but it's hardly the nefarious interlude you think it is. I know you're desperate to catch me out in something, but this isn't it."

Daintily, and with great care, Ella stacked her prim, kid-gloved hands on her lap, batting her eyes in a demure, patronizing fashion. "Now, if I may ask, what were *you* doing at the Flying Batsman? It hardly seems like the type of establishment that you would frequent. I thought with your line of work you'd only deign to drink at the taverns along the docks with the rest of your kind."

"My kind? Hmm." Jack's laugh was joyless. "You think I should be with the rest of the good-for-nothing sea dogs down by the docks?"

Ella shook her head. "That's not what I meant. Forget I said anything—"

"No, keep going, please," he urged, sinker farther into his seat. "Thieves and murders, men running away from things, criminals hiding from their pasts. That's what the docks mean to you, am I right? Low-life men who don't have two coins to rub together—"

"Actually," Ella cut in, "I meant cricket."

"What?"

Ella threw up her hands. "The Flying Batsman is primarily a cricket bar. Only men who want to spend their afternoons, and nights—*and* sometimes mornings—discussing the game in avid, minute detail go there." She paused, peering up at the stumped man from under her lashes. "Do you … you enjoy cricket, my lord?"

"Fuck no, I don't enjoy cricket," he said gruffly, running a hand over his face.

"Why not?"

He regarded Ella balefully. "All those rules … The gentlemen stopping play to drink tea in between innings. Hitting a small ball with a ridiculous-looking stick …"

"Well, I enjoy it," Ella said, slightly miffed. How dare he diminish the sport with his petulant comments! And why did he make her want to defend it to the death? "I think it's good fun."

His smile morphed into a grimace. "I'm not surprised by that at all."

She'd had enough.

"Why are you so angry all the time?" Ella lashed out. "What did I do besides save your brother's life and, now, waste away the hours reading in your family's library when I'm not attempting to start conversation with your uncles?"

Jack cocked his head. "Which one did you talk to?"

Ella closed her eyes and sighed. "Edward. I … I surprised him while he was painting outside."

Jack scrunched his nose, rubbing the bottom of his chin with the back of his hand. "Did you see what he was painting?"

Ella stared up at the pleated ceiling, ignoring his sanctimonious expression. "I don't want to talk about it."

"I warned you—"

"I know!"

Seconds passed as Ella attempted to contain the blush scaling her neck and cheeks like an unstoppable weed. Jack's gaze never wavered from her. He watched her like he was trying to read her thoughts. Ella desperately hoped that he wouldn't realize that he was the center of all of them.

When his expression began to soften, when something akin to exhaustion crept deeper into the lines branching out from his eyes, Ella tried again.

"Are you going to tell me?"

"What?" It was a bark, but devoid of bite.

"Why are you so upset?"

Again, Jack studied her, but Ella didn't believe he was trying to reach inside her anymore, mining for information. Instead, she wondered if he was sandbagging the perimeter of his own soul, guarding it from her invasion.

He bobbed his shoulders, breaking away to peer out the window, his voice deep, casual, and hopelessly drained. "I'm just so fucking tired of secrets," he started wearily. "This is why I don't come home. This is the reason I stay away from the mess of London and all its endless complications." He leaned forward, resting his forearms on his knees.

Ella tucked her hand under her thighs. She had to quell the urge to take his head in her hands and hold him. "What happened? What did you learn?"

"Nothing."

"Now who's keeping secrets?"

Jack's head fell as he let out a mirthless chuckle. "What is it about my brother?" he asked, surprising her with the non sequitur. He lifted his head, his expression serious and daunting, as if he'd just asked Ella to explain the effect of the moon on the tides. "Why do you love him so much?" His eyes were open and clear, and Ella didn't think that anyone had ever wanted to hear what she had to say more than him at that moment.

A week ago, Ella would have had a rough-and-ready answer. It would have flown from her lips without a second thought. But now it was different. Maybe it was because she knew the duke better now (albeit barely), or maybe she had learned more about herself.

"I …" Her lashes flickered as she searched for the right words, the ones that used to come straight from her heart. But she couldn't find them. Instead, she settled for the ready-made answer already planted in her brain. "It's easy to love him. I remember the first time I saw him. He was … light. Pure light and excitement and"—a loopy smile formed on her face—"fun. Lord Oliver is the ideal for the women in the *ton*: handsome and polished and courageous—"

"Courageous? In his starched cravat and spit-shined dress shoes?"

Ella's brow furrowed. "*A little* courageous, I'm sure. It helps that when you squint at him, Lord Oliver looks a lot like the princes in the stories. I suppose we all grow up reading the fairytales. We all want the dashing prince who's fearless enough to face the dragon but also refined enough to dance the waltz."

Jack's response was soft and careful, as if Ella had just built a sandcastle and he was desperate not to wreck it. "And Oliver is that ideal for you?"

Was he?

"Not just me," Ella replied, straightening her shoulders. "Your mother as well. He's been placed on a pedestal by so many. Yes, he acts in a certain way, a rakish way, but I think most people overlook that because his character is sound."

"You know my brother's character?"

A knot formed in Ella's stomach formed. "I do." *In theory.*

Jack leaned forward. "How well?"

"As well as I can."

His face was drawn. When he chuckled, Ella felt a stab in her chest from the sorrow. "What about *my* character? Or does it not matter?"

"Of course it matters!" Ella exclaimed. What was all this? What had gotten into him? "Your mother adores you. Have you heard the servants talk about? They think you hung the moon." She laughed, but the sound quickly faded away as she gave his question more thought. "But you can scare people. You're rougher around the edges. And you're quiet, so you leave so much space for people to wonder what you're thinking, and that can be a frightening thing." Ella stared at her lap, wondering why she kept going when she'd answered the question enough. "I've never met anyone like you before, which is probably why I always act so out of sorts when I'm around you. Not many people would have stayed and helped like you did—"

"My mother ordered it," he said.

"Your mother asked because she knew you would stay. She knew you had a good heart. Even though she secretly thinks you might be a pirate."

Jack's chest bubbled with laughter. "I try to tell her what I do, but she never listens."

"She listens," Ella said. "She listens more than you think. I think she's just scared. The ocean is dangerous … unpredictable. Ships go missing all the time. Even for pirates."

Jack looked up at her from beneath heavy lids, his earring glinting, his short hair unfashionable. It left nothing to hide behind. Jack was exactly whom he showed himself to be, and was not afraid to let people know it. "Do *you* think I'm a pirate?"

It was a funny question, meant to alleviate the airless space, but Ella couldn't find the energy to laugh. "I don't have to squint when I look at you. I see you. And you're nothing like the pirates in the books."

"Uglier?"

"No!" Ella finally clamped her mouth shut. Saying anything more would be risky. Not only would it confuse the situation, but it would also confuse her, and her mind was muddled enough. What good what it be to tell him that all the princes and heroes she read about were two-dimensional, stuck forever on the page? She'd used them to help fill in all the romantic holes Oliver represented to her. Or, at least, she'd tried to.

But Jack … With every day he became more real, more fully formed in her consciousness. He was not a character. He was not black or white. Jack was complicated. Jack was dangerous, but not a danger. Jack was entirely inappropriate for someone like Ella.

And yet she craved him all the same.

Ella could feel the blood drain from her face. Her hands became clammy; the knot in her stomach tightened even more.

"What's wrong?" Jack reached for her hand, but she jerked away. Again, something deep inside warned her not to touch him. Even someone as innocent as her was aware that there would be no going back from that.

"I shouldn't have said anything," she clipped out. "I don't even know how we got to this topic."

Jack's expression turned wary as Ella floundered in her seat like a freshly caught trout. "I was asking about my brother—"

"Yes, you were," she said, her words thinning out as she took a massive breath. It did nothing to relieve her anxiousness. "Your brother is a wonderful man. I'm grateful to have met him."

"And he will make you happy."

Ella considered him. It wasn't a question or a statement. The words hung between them, waiting for someone to claim them for their own purposes. She grabbed them like they were a gift. "Yes, he will. Very happy. I never expected to have something so wonderful in my life." Her mouth went dry, her body hollow. "A dream come true."

"Hm." Jack angled his head, his lips curved to a winsome curl. "I want you to be happy, Ella."

The gentleness in his voice made her want to cry. She fiddled with her fingers. "Thank you. I want you to be happy as well." Finally, she lifted her gaze. He was waiting for her. Those glacial blues found her eyes with a jolt that left her dazed. "You deserve it … even if you don't think you do."

"Even pirates deserve a happy ending, is that right?"

"You're not a pirate."

"No," he said quietly. "Just a man."

Suddenly, Jack shot up, knocking the carriage ceiling with his knuckles. He called out for the driver to stop.

"What are you doing?"

Jack moved toward her. In an instant, he reached out and cupped the back of her neck. Ella gasped as he drew her to him. Only one thought landed in her head: why wasn't she resisting?

His hold was gentle. His strength was a question, not a demand, and when he continued to pull her to the edge of her seat, Ella did not hesitate to follow.

He stopped just as the tip of her nose was about to graze his own. "Promise me something," he said. His voice was ragged, breathless. Ella stared at his lips, wondering at his intentions, hoping—yes, hoping—that it was what she thought it was.

"Wh-what?"

Jack's eyes dropped to her mouth, and something odd scorched along Ella's inner thighs, pooling at the very bottom of her belly. Reluctantly, he found her gaze once more. "Promise me that when you see me again, you won't forget everything you told me today."

Ella tried to shake her head, but his hold was too strong. "Why would I—?"

"And don't forget the way you're looking at me right now."

Ella opened her mouth, but it was too late. Jack swept in, crushing her lips with a kiss, silencing all questions and thoughts. It was a hard kiss, punishing in its intensity. Having never been kissed before, Ella kept her lips closed, unsure of what to do.

Jack's fingers mellowed, his grip lessened, as the severity of his kiss abated. His lips melted into hers, teasing and controlling. Ella felt as if lightning had struck. She felt like she was being devoured, tasted, and, most importantly, savored. Her chest fluttered with anticipation, and slowly, her body relented, the tension siphoned away bit by bit.

Jack opened his mouth, parting Ella's lips, spiraling her tongue with his. He came back to her again and again, fusing their mouths in a whirlwind of opportunity and desire. Of pure wanting and eagerness.

A wave of excitement coiled deep within Ella, and she gave herself up to it. She pressed her body into Jack's, gasping at the way her breasts ignited from the added friction. She held his head and felt his earring scratch against her palm. That little nugget of gold incited her even more, and when his tongue swirled inside her again, she sucked on it. She captured his moan and gifted him with one of her own.

She'd never felt so alive before. Feverish with no fever. Pink and swollen with no pain.

But then Jack pulled away, leaving Ella suspended in the aisle of the carriage in disbelief.

Catching her breath, she watched as he fled the carriage, her hands still up in the air where his head had been. Ella's ears rang and pulsed, but she managed to hear Jack order the driver to take her home. He, on the other hand, would be returning to London in the other carriage.

All she could do was collapse back in her seat, trailing her fingers over her bemused and newly awakened lips.

She'd learned so much in those few minutes, but one thing stood out.

Jack couldn't possibly be a pirate.

Pirates stole. And Ella had just given him everything.

Chapter Thirteen

"YOU DIDN'T TELL me you lived in a castle." The little girl glowered at Jack as she made that remark, as if he'd been withholding the information on purpose just to spite her.

The carriage dropped them off in front of Sutton Park with the sun gasping its last breath, falling lazily beneath the horizon. Jack hadn't planned it, but coming upon the giant house with its ancient stone and endless glass sparkling against the waning burnt-orange sun was magical even to him. It was something to truly admire.

Or, in the girl's case, reproach.

Jack exited the conveyance swiftly, offering to help the ten-year-old, but he was too slow. Bypassing the steps, she hopped down to the gravel, her dirty brown boots staking claim like she were a conquering hero.

If only, Jack thought.

"It's hardly a castle," he muttered, brow furrowed at the front door. Despite his earlier talk with Ella, Jack put little stock in fairytales; however, the entrance felt charmed, like if he didn't answer a certain question right then, he and the girl would be devoured before making it through.

Sonia. Her name was Sonia.

Jack placed his hand on her tiny shoulder, pressing her forward.

"This is my home now?" Sonia asked. For the first time, something like awe could be detected in her voice. Her feet—which had been steady when Jack took her from the orphanage—finally betrayed her cool façade, and she skipped.

"It is."

"And you're my father?"

That was the second time she'd asked that pertinent question. Jack answered it the only way he knew how. "I am now."

From the corner of his eye, he saw her nod. And then take a giant, torso-shuddering breath.

Jack paused at the door, hating what he was about to do and especially hating what he was about to say. "This is your home *for now*," he said, softening the words with a tiny squeeze. "We will be leaving soon, after my brother is better."

"Is he sick?"

"Yes."

She scrunched her little nose. The same pert nose Oliver shared with their mother. "Sick like my mother was sick?"

Jack glanced at the girl, hoping his face gave every impression of confidence. But Sonia, as he was learning, was wary by nature, and as she twisted her lips to the side, he understood he had a long way to go before winning her trust.

"No, not like your mother."

Sonia averted her eyes, using the time to dust her hands over the poor, shabby orphanage uniform that was made for a girl two years younger. "Well, that's good, isn't it?"

"It is." Jack, knowing he couldn't stand out there all night, despite wanting to, reached for the door, but stopped himself. "When we get in there … You shouldn't talk. I mean, let me do the talking," he said.

Sonia's little voice raised to a high pitched lilt when she asked, "Why?"

Jack whipped off his hat, running a hand through his hair. "Just trust me. It will be easier this way."

He faced the door again, but could feel her eyes on him, scrutinizing him, sizing him up. Jack was woefully unprepared and promised himself that he would never ask her what she'd thought of him on this first day. He was afraid his ego wouldn't be able to take it.

"I like your earring," she said, placing her tiny hand in his. Like a nesting doll, it fit inside perfectly. Like they were made from the same cloth. The same people. The same family. Which they were.

Jack exhaled and stepped forward. Perhaps he *would* ask her about today. In the far, far future.

The family hadn't gone in for dinner yet. Towing Sonia behind him, Jack ventured into the drawing room, hooking everyone's attention the second he crossed the threshold.

He'd debated sending her to the nursery. Jack had no idea the kind of welcome his mother would give. Calling her a loose cannon was simply too kind. Nevertheless, the thought of leaving Sonia alone felt wrong. If they were going to start a life together, it was important that they begin as they intended to proceed.

"I was wondering if we were going to see you tonight—" The duchess's words were cut off as Sonia came up beside him. She was tall for her age; the top of her head reached Jack's belly button, and the intense pride that hit him when he noticed Sonia stretch her neck even longer in the face of his mother's owl-like eyes was startling and fast.

"Mother, I have something I want to tell you. Someone you should meet."

Lady Evelyn didn't hesitate. Setting her glass on the table next to her, she stood, wiping her hands together like she was washing them of this muddy conversation before it even began. "Later," she said, plastering a stiff smile on her face. "We're all about to go into dinner, and I'd hate for our guests to go hungry."

Jack swiped his tongue over his front teeth as he took in the *guests* pretending to hide their morbid curiosity—the five doctors, whose entire livelihoods depended on this family, and his uncles, who could barely contain their interest in the obvious drama Jack was about to rain down on them all. He had spent his life disregarding his father's brothers, considering them cautionary tales. But any indiscretions they might have had were dealt with the *proper*, quiet way. Jack could read them easily: *Say what you want about us, boy, but at least we didn't bring our problems home.*

Because his grandmother was snoring in her chair next to the fire, the only expression Jack couldn't decipher was Ella's. Her face was blank though increasingly alert. But Jack knew it was only a matter of time before her disappointment and censure were made known.

So be it. He knew damn well this wasn't going to be easy, and certainly not comfortable.

Placing his arm around Sonia's shoulder, Jack straightened. "Mother, I'd like to introduce you to Sonia," he said. "Your granddaughter."

The duchess giggled nervously, looking at all the others as if Jack were playing a trick on them. "Honestly, Jack … the stories you tell. Now, send the child to the kitchens to eat with the servants and let's go in to dinner."

"Sonia will be eating with us."

Lady Evelyn lurched to standing. "I don't know what you're doing, Jack, but I do not like it—"

"She will also be staying here. I'm sure there's more than enough room for her in the nursery."

"No." His mother shook her head, back and forth, back and forth, as if trying to rid herself of something stuck in her ears. "This will not happen. This is not how things work. You might spend most of your time with thieves and savages, but you can't have forgotten the rules we all live by."

Jack tousled the little girl's black curls, trying to distract her. That elicited a baleful glance that struck his conscience, giving him the strength to do what he had to do, even if it meant breaking his mother's heart and fracturing her good opinion of him. "Those aren't my rules. And I won't blindly obey them. If you won't let my daughter stay here—"

Lady Evelyn gasped, slapping both hands against her mouth. "She can stay, just not in the nursery—"

"If you won't let my daughter stay here," Jack continued, never raising his voice, "then I will not stay here either. I will respect your decision. I have many ships at my disposal; I can have us on one by tomorrow."

"Jack!" his mother cried. She wobbled on her feet, and he stepped forward, afraid she might fall. However, the instant she saw him move, her red-rimmed eyes went dangerously wide. Jack's instincts told him to stand in front of Sonia, covering her from whatever hurt and pain his mother couldn't contain.

But Ella did it first. Sliding in front of the duchess, she grasped her hands, whispering words that Jack couldn't hear. His mother released a plaintive sob and rushed from the room, taking great pains to give Jack and the skinny little girl a wide berth.

Ella hurried after her.

Just as she was about to pass him, Jack reached for her arm, pulling their heads together. Ignoring the way her closeness affected him, the way the scent of her lavender soap squeezed his chest, he lowered his lips to her ear.

"It seems I don't always do what my mother says."

ELLA TOSSED IN her bed, switching to lie on her opposite side. Sleep remained elusive. Despite using all her energy and ploys to help the duchess nod off, she still had too much life coursing through her. As well as so many mixed emotions.

Ella didn't know what to think or whom to feel sorry for. What Jack had done was inexcusable—not the part about the little girl. Ella was naïve, but she wasn't deaf. She'd heard her fair share of similar stories, some even about her own brothers-in-law. No, her issue with Jack stemmed from how he'd presented the little girl to his mother. In front of all those people. That audience of gawkers. How could he do that to his mother or the girl?

Sonia.

A beautiful name for a beautiful girl. Jack's girl. Or so he said.

Fine. If she couldn't sleep, she'd get answers instead.

Exasperated, Ella escaped the comfortable confines of her bed and found her robe. She peeked out the door, hoping that none of the uncles were late-night walkers. It was difficult enough attempting to find common ground with them during the day—doing it with only a few layers of flimsy muslin between them would be soul scarring.

Ella had never ventured to the upper floors before. Only the servants' quarters and the nursery were housed upstairs, and with no children in the house, the nursery was an unnecessary stop even in her bored wanderings.

Tiptoeing down the corridor, she saw a light slanting sharp and stretched along the floor, escaping from a partially opened door.

Jack's deep, resonant voice floated down the hallway, dragging a smile from her.

Because she'd known he would be there. If she were being honest with herself, she'd acknowledge it was the reason she was there.

"… the sea monsters were vicious," she heard Jack say. His no-nonsense demeanor and matter-of-fact way of speaking touched her from the distance. The man wasn't a natural storyteller; nevertheless, he was effective, and Ella found herself hanging on every word. "Anyone that ventured to drive a ship there was immediately pulled into the whirlpool by Charybdis or pulled apart and devoured by Scylla."

Ella grimaced, gluing her back to the wall outside the door. Was this gruesome tale supposed to put the girl to a blissful sleep?

"But then why did Odysseus go near them? Why didn't he steer through the Moving Rocks?" Sonia asked, no hint of sleep in her voice.

"Because that meant certain death," he explained. "The captain had to make the best decision for his men. And that meant facing the monsters."

"Doesn't sound like that good of a decision, if sea monsters ended up eating them."

Ella planted a hand over her mouth, stifling a giggle.

"Are you going to listen to the story or not?" Jack grumbled. "Odysseus had to make a choice. He could go through the Moving Rocks, knowing he and his men would probably all perish, or risk the monsters and only lose some. He chose to sacrifice some of the men for the greater good."

"*His* greater good." Sonia *humphed*. "Will we face monsters like that when we go on your ship?"

Ella wrapped her hands around her midsection, warding off a chill.

"No," Jack replied. His voice was solemn, concrete, and Ella hoped it comforted the child as much as it comforted her. "My ship is the safest place you'll ever be. You'll never have to worry when you're with me."

"Do you promise?" Sonia asked. "Don't make a promise if you can't keep it."

"I promise," Jack said. "Now, you've kept me up long enough. No more stories. We have an early day tomorrow, so time for bed."

"I don't want to go to bed," she whined. "One more story."

"No more."

"Then what if I tell you one?" Sonia asked. "Has anyone ever told you about Orpheus and Euridice? That's my favorite. It doesn't have a cyclops or sea monsters, but it has three-headed dogs and wood nymphs and Hades. I much prefer Hades to Poseidon. You see, Orpheus's wife died, and he missed her so much that he went all the way to the underworld to see her. You'll like this part—he had to travel over the River Styx, which is filled with dead bodies and haunted souls, and dismembered limbs—"

Ella's face contorted in horror. She peeled herself off the wall and flew into the room. "All right, I think we've had enough of the Greeks for one night."

Father and daughter stared at her with matching irritated expressions, mouths agape. Apparently, Jack had become just as enthralled in Sonia's story as she'd been in his.

Hands on her hips, Ella tried to appear as stern as her old Nanny Goodbody used to be, which would be difficult, because Ella didn't have a hunchback and random, dark black hairs protruding from her chin. "Like your father said, it's time for bed. Actually, it was time for bed two hours ago."

Sonia cocked her head, her shiny black hair falling over her shoulder to the bed like a waterfall. "Are you my new nanny?"

"Ah, no," Jack answered with a shy smile. "That's Ella."

The little girl shot him a censorious look. "You didn't tell me you were married."

"I'm not." He straightened in his seat on the edge of the bed, stretching his neck from side to side. "Ella is my brother's fiancée. She's staying here while he recovers."

The words, said so blandly and casually, hit Ella square in the chest. She'd never heard him say it in that way, without a hint of irony or disbelief. It made it feel oddly real, oddly true. And yet it had never felt more wrong.

Ella hurried toward the bed. "Never mind all that," she said, prodding Sonia to recline on the mattress. Ella threw the covers over her, tucking them deep under the child's sides just as Nanny Goodbody used to do to her. Ella had loved that feeling, like she was a caterpillar in a cocoon, safe and warm where no one could hurt her—not even her fevers.

Sonia reached for Ella's hand, stopping her from moving away. "Tell me a story," she said.

Ella scoffed, trying not to show how much the little girl's touch affected her. She made her tone as gruff as possible. "You've heard enough stories." She glared at Jack from the corner of her eye. "The *wrong* kinds of stories."

"What are the right kinds?" Sonia asked.

Ella chewed on the inside of her cheek. "You know, happy stories. Fairytales. Ones that don't end in loss of limbs and decapitation."

Sonia's brows drew together. "Sounds boring."

"Boring is good," Ella countered. "Boring helps you sleep."

"All right, then." Sonia wiggled in her cocoon. "Tell me one of these stories. And then we'll see if they make me tired."

Ella narrowed her gaze as she sized up her little adversary. She knew exactly what the girl was doing. Hadn't she done it herself countess times in her childhood? But even knowing Sonia's aim couldn't keep Ella from caving. The girl had had a hard enough day as it was, and saying no (even though it was the responsible thing to do) felt unfair. What was one more story?

"Fine," Ella said. She got comfortable on the edge of the bed. Jack mirrored her on the other side, his arm stretched out as he leaned on his palm. Ella ignored his questioning look. She'd grown used to his quiet nature, but it didn't make it any less discomfiting.

Ella launched into "Snow White," the tale of the princess who'd been driven from her house by a jealous stepmother and forced to seek refuge with the seven little people in the forest.

With no younger siblings or nieces and nephews yet, Ella had little experience telling stories. She was surprised by how much fun it was. Watching Sonia's sweet, expressive face as Ella described the magic mirror and the evil witch was addictive. Ella lost herself so completely, she didn't notice that Sonia wasn't getting more tired the longer the story went on. Quite the opposite. She was getting confused.

"I don't understand," she cut in, biting her bottom lip pensively. "The prince just saw her and fell in love?" She snapped her fingers. "Just like that."

The question rattled Ella. "Yes. Just like that. It was love at first sight."

Sonia pulled a face. "But he didn't know her. He knew nothing about her."

Confused, Ella looked to Jack, but his face was blank. *No help there.* "The prince thought she was beautiful."

"Many people are beautiful. I'm beautiful. My mother was beautiful."

Ella admired the girl's confidence, but she wouldn't have minded being included in that little list as well. "Well," she began, "the prince must have sensed an inner beauty in the princess too."

"How?"

"Yes, how?" Jack said, causing Ella to flinch.

"I don't know exactly. He just did."

"It just doesn't make any sense," Sonia continued. She ticked off the fingers of her hand one by one. "He doesn't know her; has never even talked to her; she's almost dead and sleeping in a glass coffin. Why did he take her from the little men? How could he be so sure he loved her?"

"Because love makes you sure," Ella cried, shocked at how shrill the words came out. She pressed her lips together, finding composure. "And Snow White must have looked very peaceful and loving in her coffin."

Sonia scoffed. "I lived with my mother's friend, Mrs. Stalrope. And Mrs. Stalrope was a beautiful woman—everyone was always saying so. Her voice was *almost* as good as my mother's— everyone always said that, which never failed to make her upset. Anyway, she looked mighty peaceful when she slept too, but the moment she would wake up, all that would be thrown out the window. She always woke with headaches, you know." She nodded knowingly at Jack. "Too much wine. And I learned very quickly to be out of her reach until she'd had her morning glass."

Ella massaged her temples. "What does all that mean? What are you trying to say?"

Sonia rolled her eyes. "It *means* that one shouldn't fall in love with someone while they're sleeping. A man is setting himself for a lifetime of strife when he does that."

"Who told you those things?" Ella asked. "You grew up surrounded by opera, yes? How could someone your age have such a jaded view of love already?"

Once more Sonia regarded Ella like *she* was the only child in the room. "Have you ever been to the opera? People cry at them for a reason."

Ella unleashed an unladylike grunt. The girl had her there. "Well," she countered, lifting her chin in defiance, "I believe that"—she searched her brain, lighting up when it came to her—*"true love always makes a man better, no matter who the woman is that inspires it."*

Sonia scrunched up her nose. "Who said that?"

Ella puffed out her chest triumphantly. "Alexandre Dumas. And before you ask, no, he did not write operas."

Sonia snorted, once more exchanging a patronizing look with Jack. "I can tell."

Chapter Fourteen

JACK CLOSED THE nursery door quietly, wincing when the latch made its tiny click. Retreating a step, he finally allowed his shoulders to slump.

A breath was released behind him, and he knew that he wasn't the only one with steam to let out.

He turned to face Ella, regretting the way she instinctively moved back, creating more room between them.

It was an action determined by propriety, but also ... perhaps self-preservation? Jack told himself not to wonder, but could Ella possibly want him the way that he wanted her?

Was it as all-encompassing and ever-growing as his need? Because if so, then God help them both. All Jack needed was one little encouraging look, one hopeful glance, and he would lose himself to the deep. Like the poor bastards in the whirlpool, never to be seen again.

Jack stared at her, watching myriad emotions dance across her face in the shadowy corridor. She was tired, overwhelmed, superior, plaintive, shy.

But not the emotion that Jack had been worried about, not the sentiment that he'd guarded himself from. Ella's brown eyes were liquid in the moonlight, full of compassion, with not one drop of disillusionment.

She searched for her blonde braid resting on her shoulder, running her fingers up and down the plaits as if needing an excuse to move. This was the first time Jack had seen her hair out of the perfunctory bun. It hung, hauntingly long and thick, its ends reaching well past the swell of her hips. At once, Jack regretted letting his gaze venture that low. He had no choice now but to take in her lack of attire (as prim as it was) and admire the way the thin, flimsy fabrics skimmed along her lithe body, highlighting the curves that were only meant for a lover's eyes.

Jack was not that lover. And would never be. He'd allowed himself to kiss her this afternoon—he hadn't been able to help it. But that had to be it. Feeling her passion again, knowing that it was for him, might break him.

Ella's smile was hesitant and wry. "Sonia is probably the most interesting child I've ever met. It will … be nothing short of entertaining to watch her grow into a woman."

Jack nodded.

Her gaze was expectant; however, when nothing more came from him, she nodded to the stairwell. "I suppose I should go to bed." She raised a brow. "Are you …"

Jack was no better than Snow White, lost in a stupor. He shook himself out of his muteness, throwing a glance at the door next to the nursery. "I'll stay here tonight in Nanny's room. I remember finding it a comfort when she was close."

The corners of Ella's mouth lifted, and Jack's heart thumped soundly against his ribcage. It did that every time she was about to tease him. "You didn't feel safe even with your older brother in the nursery with you?"

Jack's laugh was rueful. "I didn't feel safe *because* my older brother was in the nursery with me. He used to keep me up at night, telling me the most frightening tales. Now that I think of it, I probably gravitated toward the sea because I liked the close quarters. Even alone in my bed on the ship, I'm never far from other people."

"Unlike here," Ella replied, lifting her head to scan the enormity of the house.

"Unlike here."

Seconds passed. It was like an awkward dance, both of them swaying slightly, fidgeting with fingers and hair, shifting their weight to opposite legs.

Jack didn't know what she was waiting for, but he couldn't hold out for much longer. Having Ella here, alone, close enough to be kissed and held. Close enough for him to want to tell her everything and anything. It was untenable.

A small patch of pink simmered on the tops of her cheeks. She was such an innocent; Ella was the perfect mold for the naïve, elegant, stainless girls that the *ton* routinely created. The kind that had never appealed to him before. But that was because he was oversimplifying her. Ella was more than a production of a time and place. Her quality was on a different level, meant to stick in his heart and last for all eternity.

And Jack's hero's quest would be to bear it. *If* he was considering himself a hero—which he wasn't. There was hardly anything heroic about the way he wanted to strip her down to nothing and lick the cleft between her legs.

"So that's why you did it?" she asked sharply, dropping her braid to her shoulder. "That's why you kept Sonia beside you when you told your mother?"

Jack was taken aback by her tone. "Do you think I should have hidden her away?"

"I think you should have protected her."

"I *was* protecting her!" Jack said, forcing Ella to take another step back. "Fuck, I'm sorry," he added, swiping his hand over his face. Weariness seeped into his bones. The effects of all the decisions he'd made today rushed at him all at once. And now the inevitable: her disappointment. And Jack wasn't as prepared for it as he'd thought.

"I *was* protecting her," he repeated, softer this time, giving every word the effort it deserved. "I could have tossed her upstairs, could have fostered her off to the kitchens, but I wouldn't do that. It was important she know …" He swallowed the lump in his throat, warding off the anger attempting to break through. "Sonia needed to know that I wasn't ashamed of her, that I wouldn't allow anyone to ever be ashamed of her."

"But your mother—"

"My mother needed to hear that most of all."

Ella crossed her arms; the curious way she regarded Jack made him feel like an animal in a zoo, which was almost right. There was always something feral in him when she was near, something primitive that made him want to take and then take some more.

"So that's it, then?" Ella asked suddenly. She sniffed. "I should have known you wouldn't ease the poor girl into her new life. Hammering her in is more your style."

"The fastest method is usually the most painless."

"Hmm," was all she said, letting that inane sound that meant so many things and nothing at all stretch between them. Then she bobbed her shoulders. "Good."

Jack arched a brow. "Good?"

"Good," Ella repeated sternly. With a pert nod, she took the first few steps down the corridor.

Jack told himself to let her go. No good would come from speaking to her—ever. But Ella, it seemed, was the only one with a sense of self-preservation that night. Jack's had vanished along with his solitary life.

"You don't despise me?" he asked, inwardly cringing at the desperate crack in his voice.

Ella stopped, hesitating for a heartbeat before coming back to face him. Her steps were slow but sure, and her ambiguous expression frightened him more than any of the tales his brother ever could have conceived of.

When the toes of her slippers kissed his, she finally stopped. Ella remained quiet. Her eyes traveled back and forth between his own, and an unbearable lightness bore down on Jack, as if she were drinking the very essence of him, stealing all the thoughts and fears he held inside for his misery alone.

He almost came undone when Ella lifted her hand. He shuddered as she slid the tips of her fingers down the side of his face, from the edge of his hairline to the side of his jaw. It wasn't just a simple touch. It was a knowing that Jack had never experienced before. A knowing that he'd never thought he needed.

His eyes were heavy. He ached to close them and imagine Ella with him in his room on his ship, their undressing each other with the nonchalant reverence of a married couple, both habitual and exotic.

But her gaze clung to his, ordering him to stay with her, condemning him to feel and to understand what she was trying to convey.

Jack's hunger drew her closer. He switched his focus to her lips. Her breath scalded his chin, making him so very thirsty. The desire reminded him of men floating on detritus in the middle of the ocean, baking under the hot sun, being surrounded by limitless water and yet unable to drink it.

That was Ella to him. She surrounded him always: her scent, her laughter, the sounds of her skirts as they swished against corners and table legs. She was the only thing that could satisfy him, but one drop of her and he would be burned from the inside out.

And standing there in the empty corridor filled with such desperate yearning, Jack thought it might just be worth it.

"What do you want, Ella?" he murmured. He skimmed his hands against her gossamer robe and held on to a piece of the garment, pinching it between his fingers, satisfied with this one gluttonous allowance.

Ella's mouth opened, and he saw her two front teeth peek through, the tip of her pink tongue. The tongue that had tasted his this afternoon.

"I don't know," she rushed out in a whisper.

Jack fisted the fabric, burning his knuckles white. "Tell me what you want, and I'll do it. You have to know that. Anything."

Her eyes were shiny, glassy in the cloudy moonlight streaming through the windows. Ella's face became determined. "I want you to tell me the truth," she said. "Tell me that Oliver is Sonia's father."

Jack flinched, but Ella followed, not letting him out of her grasp. The lie came to him, but he couldn't say what she asked. The lie was meant to protect his brother—protect the love *she* held for his brother.

But Jack was lost to that good intention.

Because *he* wanted her to love him, he realized.

Ella caressed his jaw with her thumb, sweeping a path along the corner of his lips. Jack grabbed her wrist, just holding her, feeling the insistent thump of her heartbeat through his fingertips.

Her expression fell, overladen with too much sympathy. "You can't, can you?"

Jack remained firm. Silent.

Ella's hand dropped back to her side, forcing him to let her go. "Then do something else for me," she whispered. "See the way that I'm looking at you now. And know that it hasn't changed. It never will."

⤜⟫⟫⟫⟨⟨⟨⤛

WITH ONE HOUR left before sunrise, Jack sat next to his brother's bed. He couldn't remember being more exhausted than he was then. Or more confused. Or angrier, for that matter. Nothing was right. Nothing had felt right in a long time.

He rubbed his hands over his face and leaned toward his brother, who'd spent the last few hours snoring and grumbling through a restless sleep. Oliver's skin was ghostlike and waxy, his body a shadow of its once-indomitable self, lying limp under the avalanche of covers. His prickly black hair was doing its best to grow back after being shaved, but it was at an unfortunate length, sticking out at all angles, reminding Jack of an angry hedgehog.

Jack hadn't spoken since he'd entered the room. He never did when he visited his brother. It felt unnecessary.

But maybe it was the lack of sleep, or the way his heart felt like it was snapping into millions of tiny, sharp pieces that were taking turns ripping him apart from the inside, but Jack eventually broke through the silence.

With laughter. Sardonic, miserable laughter. "I was never jealous of you. I never lied about that." The words tripped out of his mouth, stumbling as if he'd emptied a whiskey bottle down his throat. "I never cared about the way people walked past me to get to you. I never wondered if Mother and Father loved you more. And I certainly never gave a shite about all the women and their come-hither looks." He snorted at his ridiculous speech, resting his head in one palm as he imagined a roguish smile on his brother's classical face.

Jack took his brother's hand, holding it like they did whenever they would jump into the pond together, making sure the other didn't experience the first splash before the other. "Do you hear me? I was never jealous of you, brother. Until now."

Chapter Fifteen

FROM HER BEDROOM, Ella peered out the window and saw two skinny little legs disappear into the carriage. She stormed into the hallway, down the stairs. Carlisle heard her coming and opened the front door in preparation.

"Wait! Please wait!" she called out, getting to the carriage just as the footman was folding up its stairs. At the same time, Sonia and Jack popped their heads out into the open space, looking at her like she had two heads.

"We're leaving," he said grumpily, and Ella could guess why. The man looked like hell warmed over. With two sets of purple and blue bags under each eye, it was evident that sleep had not come easy after she'd left him the night before.

"I can see you're leaving," she replied testily, annoyed and not a little hurt by his tone. Hadn't they shared a moment outside Sonia's bedroom? Or had that just been her overactive imagination? "Where are you going?"

"I have a ship scheduled to come into port," he answered like he hadn't just allowed Ella to peer into his soul hours before. "My partner can't do it all himself. I have to be there."

Ella thought that was perfectly reasonable. What wasn't so apparent was why he thought a ten-year-old girl should accompany him.

"Why are you bringing Sonia?"

"Because I'll be there."

Did it always have to be so difficult getting more than a few words out of the man at one time? "Do you honestly believe the docks are a safe place for a little girl?"

Sonia had reclined back in her seat, and her voice rang out from inside the carriage. "I'll be fine!"

Ella ignored her, dubiously lifting her brow at Jack as she waited for his answer.

His wide shoulders rolled off a shrug. "She'll be fine. She'll be with me."

Jack reached for the door and tried to shut it, but Ella blocked him with her arm. "I understand that," she began, "but I must repeat myself and say the docks are not an appropriate place for a little girl."

Jack lowered his chin, leveling Ella with a withering glower. "What do you want me to do? Find a woman there and ask her to watch Sonia while I'm busy inspecting cargo? Fine, then. Wonderful idea. I'll get to it the second we arrive."

Ella's eyes felt like they were bulging out of her head. "You will *not* ask a woman at the docks to watch this child. Do you hear me?"

"What's wrong with women at the docks?" Sonia's voice was alarmingly curious.

"Nothing," Ella snapped.

"Nothing at all!" Jack snapped back. He shot her another baleful glare. "What do you want me—"

"She's staying with me," Ella announced. Before either of them could argue, she reached inside the carriage, waving her fingers. "Come on, you," she said, pulling the girl from her seat. "You can have fun with your father on his ship later. For now, you're spending the day with me."

"Ella," Jack warned, but she wasn't having it. She was aware that he had only been a father for a day, but someone needed to put him in his place. Since no one else seemed to care, that person was going to be her.

Ella turned Sonia to face Jack and hugged her shoulders, planting a cheerful smile on her face. "Have a wonderful day at work, my lord. We'll see you when you get back!"

Hearing Sonia sulk, Ella picked up the child's arm and waved it for Jack's benefit.

In turn, both father and daughter regaled her with matching groans. But that was as far as it went. Jack caved. Tousling Sonia's hair, he told the driver to get on with it. Ella and Sonia watched in silence as the carriage faded away into a tiny dot down the dusty path.

Sonia's shoulders hunched over as she followed Ella back inside the house. "What are we going to do?" she whined. "There's no toys here. This house is so *boring* and *old*. I want to be with Jack."

Ella had to stop herself from agreeing with the child. The house *was* boring *and* old. And she had an insatiable desire to spend all her time with Jack as well. But she wasn't about to admit to any of that—especially to his daughter.

Once more, Ella skimmed through her memories of her nanny, Goodbody. They might not have been particularly enjoyable times, but they were productive. And rigorously scheduled.

And then it came to her.

Sweet relief filled Ella as Carlisle opened the door for them to retreat back inside. She gazed down at the little one, who wore the same shabby, dull-colored dress from the day before. And since Sonia's hair hadn't been braided before bed, it haloed around her in an oily rat's nest.

Ella wouldn't be reading alone in the library today. And she certainly wouldn't be bored. Nor, she considered, would her mind wander aimlessly back to Jack again and again.

She placed her hands on her hips, perfecting her authoritative expression on her new charge. "You, my little girl, are about to start the first day of the rest of your life."

Sonia pouted. "Do I have to?"

Ella nodded with a smile. "Don't worry. It will be so much fun!"

⟫⟫⟩✳⟨⟪⟪

IT WAS NOT fun. Not even a little bit. Keeping a child engaged and on task was the single most difficult thing Ella had ever done in her life. Surviving scarlet fever? Blissfully easy compared to watching a ten-year-old.

It didn't help that Sonia wasn't an ordinary ten-year-old. Hardheaded, canny, and wise beyond her years, she threatened to thwart Ella at every turn.

For starters, she refused to read in the nursery longer than five minutes because she said the dust in the books was making her eyes itchy. When Ella suggested they take the book outside, Sonia declared the sun was too distracting.

She didn't last on their walk because she complained that her shoes pinched.

The house was too quiet; she couldn't concentrate on geography.

She hadn't eaten enough at breakfast, and her stomach growled too loudly for her to pay attention to history.

Her hands hurt too much from when the nuns slapped her, so she couldn't possibly hold a pencil to practice her penmanship.

Ella hadn't the heart to rebuke that excuse. She'd noticed the little red welts when she gave Sonia a bath. Handwriting could wait for another day.

Art had been the only subject that piqued the girl's interest, and naturally, it hadn't been Ella's idea. As Sonia had been staring out the nursery window, blatantly ignoring Ella's lecture on the Battle of Hastings (all two minutes of what Ella could remember), she'd hopped up and down. "He's painting," she cried out. "Let's go out and see it!"

Ella didn't have to ask whom the girl was referring to, and her heart immediately seized. "Oh, I think not." She lunged for the child, but couldn't tackle her in time. Slipperier than an eel, Sonia was out of the room in seconds, skipping down the hallway, laughter trailing behind her.

Ella was quick, but with all her petticoats, she was no match for the ten-year-old. She cried out for the girl to stop, but Sonia was not in a listening mood that day (or probably any day) and paid her no mind.

Ella could only pray as the child reached the outdoors. *Please, Lord, let Uncle Edward have moved on to a more tasteful subject! Or, at the very least, let him hear the little footsteps coming and hide his work quicker than he did before.*

But, like Sonia, the Almighty wasn't in the listening mood. As Ella scurried out to the back lawn, she could only watch in horror as the girl bounded up behind Uncle Edward. The man must have been lost in his art, because he didn't jump out of his skin until Sonia was already peering around his body, inspecting the canvas.

"Sorry, so sorry, my lord" Ella called out, running toward them, hoping to distract the girl long enough for the lord to react. Alas, despite having the attention of a gnat whenever Ella attempted to teach her something, Sonia's current focus was not to be lured away.

And Edward was too slow. Even as he threw his arms out wide, great patches of the piece were more than available for Sonia's frank perusal.

As well as Ella's. Disappointingly, the lord had not finished his previous work. She reached them and placed her hands on the girl's shoulders, pulling her back. But Sonia was stubborn ... and fixated.

She cocked her head. "Her hair's not red enough. You've painted it almost brown," she commented. Sonia glanced over her shoulder, giving Ella a questioning look. "Don't you agree?"

Ella was out of her depth—and, apparently, uncultured. Her hair. *Her hair?* Color was the only issue the child had with the painting?

"I don't know," Ella replied slowly, forcing herself to give the picture her full attention. Edward had made some changes since her last brief, unfortunate viewing. The woman's arm shielded one breast, though the other still left nothing to the imagination. The long hair (which was supposedly too brown) covered her other intimate area. Where was the mermaid? Had there even been one, or had Ella's imagination added the flippers in its state of shock?

She peered closer. The picture *was* vaguely familiar. Ella was sure that she should know it, especially since Sonia's frown turned fiercer at her vague response.

Edward tossed his paintbrush onto his tray in a decided huff. "It's not brown. It's clearly auburn."

Sonia matched his huff with her own. "Not auburn enough. Botticelli's Venus was almost orange. Yours is a bland brown."

Botticelli! That was it! Ella was a philistine. How had she not known Uncle Edward was painting *The Birth of Venus*? Most likely because she'd seen pointed nipples and spun away like a prudish miss. Ella had judged the man poorly. Although she *had* to point out that he had painted Venus completely nude before he decided to cover her up. She wasn't sure if that step was completely necessary to achieve the desired effect.

Edward faced the canvas. "Her hair *is* red."

Sonia snorted.

"What do *you* think?" he asked Ella. He picked up his paintbrush and tapped its end against his cheek. "What does a child know about Botticelli, anyway?"

The comment was soft and fleeting, but it still managed to light Sonia's indignance. She jammed her little hands on her narrow hips. "I know he painted Venus with red hair. I saw it myself!"

Edward rolled his eyes, giving the child a patronizing smile that infuriated Ella as much as it did Sonia. "You? You saw it? In person?"

Ella had to give her credit—when Sonia chose to be patronizing, she gave as good as she got. "Yes. Me. Me. I saw it. In person. At the Uffizi." She shrugged. "My mother and her friends said it helped inspire their performances. Have you been there?"

Edward's jaw appeared to vanish as his mouth twisted in consternation. "Not … not in person."

"Well then, that's why," Sonia replied matter-of-factly, losing her condescension, which Ella thought might have made it even worse. In her experience, sons of dukes didn't usually appreciate being placated by children. "You should go," Sonia continued. "It's good fun. Loads to see. Especially for beginners. You'll learn so much."

Poor Edward. Ella covered her grin with her palm. She'd never seen a heart or an ego break but was quite certain both had just happened in front of her.

He sighed, tossing his paintbrush once more to the ground. This time, Ella surmised, he would not be picking it back up. "Beginner, huh?"

Sonia stepped forward, patting him on the arm. He flinched from the touch, but didn't move away. "Don't worry, you'll get there one day. How long have you been practicing?"

Edward squinted up at the blue sky. "Ah … thirty-five years, give or take a few."

Ella chortled. Instead of scowling at her outburst, Edward saw the humor in the moment and granted her a half-smile. Sonia was the only one who didn't hear the despair in his answer. If anything, it only made her more optimistic. "I'm sure many great painters didn't get started until later in life." Her brow scrunched together. "Not Michelangelo, mind you. Did you know he created the statue of David when he was in his twenties? My mother and her friends always loved staring at it, said it was marvelous. I never understood the appeal myself."

Edward looked at Ella, his eyes impossibly tired. "Please make her stop talking."

"Yes, right," Ella replied, taking the girl's shoulders once more. "Time for us to go back inside and continue our lesson on the Battle of Hastings …"

Sonia allowed Ella to guide her a few steps away, but not before releasing a plaintive whine. "Do we have to? It's so boring. This is so much better." She wiggled out of Ella's hands, marching up to Edward. "Would you teach me?"

The man could have been knocked over with a feather. "Teach you?" Edward scoffed. "Why would you possibly want such a mediocre teacher?"

Oh, but he wasn't fooling Ella. There was a sprinkle of hope at the end of his question.

"You're not mediocre," Sonia argued, "just inexperienced."

"Oh, thank you so much," he replied dryly.

The girl went on. "And you can teach me the basics, can't you? I'll eventually outgrow you, of course, but you'll do for now. Don't you think, Ella?"

Ella had no idea what to think. She'd never seen anyone— man, woman, or child—cut a person to the quick as Sonia had just done. Ella wished her mother had been there to see it. She would have been impressed.

"I … um …" Ella glanced at Edward, hoping he would fill in the rest of her sentence, but he was doing the same to her … with just enough longing to help her make her decision. "Yes, yes, I think that would be a sound idea," she said, punctuating it with a stiff nod. "All young girls should have a sound understanding of art."

Sonia clapped as Edward puffed his chest like a bird ready to strut. "Good. We'll start tomorrow. At this time," he said. "Do not be late."

"She won't be," Ella answered, feeling like a proud parent. A proud, *protective* parent. "But we'll start with the basic things," she cautioned sternly. "Pretty landscapes, adorable animals. Women wearing clothes …"

Edward's cheeks became blotchy, his eyes a little shifty. "O-of course," he stammered, angling away from Ella's discerning face.

But Ella wasn't the only one with conditions. Sonia flicked her head toward the house. "And can we make sure your brother isn't playing this ghastly music during the lessons? I won't be able to concentrate with his banging on."

Ella and Edward exchanged matching frowns. She hadn't noticed it, but jutting her ear to the house, she managed to pick up the faint sound of piano playing. Uncle Andrew. The only brother she hadn't spoken to since she'd been at Sutton Park, besides a polite hello. He spent most of his time lost in conversations with the duchess.

"That's not very kind," Ella began.

Sonia cut her off. *"He's* not being very kind, ruining Beethoven like that."

Edward chuckled. "My brother is quite proficient."

Sonia shrugged again. "If you say so."

Because the girl wasn't calling *his* talent into question this time, Edward wasn't nearly as put out. On the contrary—the man was almost giddy. "What's he doing wrong?"

Sonia took a moment. She stuck her nose in the air and closed her eyes. Ella did the same, noticing how much clearer the notes came to her. To her mind, Lord Andrew wasn't proficient; he was remarkable.

But, like with painting, Ella apparently knew nothing about music.

"His rhythm is off," Sonia replied. There wasn't one ounce of restraint in her remark. She was so bloody sure of herself and her knowledge. Ella wondered if she should have been mortified, if she should have rebuked the girl for behaving in such a manner. But she couldn't. Ella liked the girl's assurance and wanted no part in limiting it.

"He is *a little* proficient," Sonia continued, but Ella didn't believe her. She could sense the girl was attempting to mitigate her criticism for the art teacher's benefit. "However, he lacks the passion needed for the piece."

"Passion?" Edward asked.

"Yes, passion. It's not his fault," Sonia said. "He's English, after all. My mother always said that the English lacked the ability for it." She frowned. "But that never affected me, even though I'm half English."

Edward eyed her for a long pause. Ella wasn't sure if he was concentrating on his brother's music or debating strangling the child.

Finally, he broke. "Can you play that song?"

Sonia nodded at once.

One brow angled above Edward's glistening eye. "Show me."

Chapter Sixteen

THE DOCKS HAD been busy and hellish. Ordinarily, Jack loved being there when a boat came in, distributing the cargo, completing the sales in the lucrative exchange. But concentration had been difficult. His mind kept crawling back to Sutton Park and the troublesome people in it. In the end, Sinclair had ordered him home—disgust evident on his face and in his tone after Jack had narrowly avoided a crane to the head. The docks were no place for a wandering mind.

Now, cranky and hungry and dismally disappointed in his woeful discipline, all Jack wanted was a stiff drink, a warm pillow, and a quiet house.

But as Carlisle welcomed him in, Jack wondered if he hadn't avoided that steel crane after all. The walls appeared to vibrate; the floor seemed to shake. And loud, energetic, expertly played music hit him from all sides.

"What the hell is going on?" he shouted as Carlisle slipped his coat from his shoulders along with his hat. Ella's laughter sprang up in tandem with the sprightly melody, irking Jack instantly. Was it because he was tired, or was it because it was happening without him?

"They've been at it for some time now," the butler answered stiffly. The men still hadn't talked since Jack had stormed out of

141

the house, bringing a motherless child back with him. No doubt the air would remain thick between them until that discussion was had. But Jack couldn't consider that talk now. Not when the house was so damned lively.

"At what? Who?" he asked, pausing in his steps.

"Playing, my lord," Carlisle replied. "Your mother and your"—he coughed politely in his gloved hand—"your daughter."

Jack eyed the butler. That cough said more than words could. "Wait, who?"

He slowly made his way to the source of the music, pausing in the doorframe as the new world opened up before him.

It could have been a dream, if ever Jack had thought to dream that big.

His mother and his daughter sat side by side at the piano, their fingers tripping over the ivory keys with the determination and elegance of an afternoon rain shower.

Jack hadn't heard his mother play in years. When he was a child, she would entertain the family most nights after dinner because his father had loved it. Jack could still remember the look on his father's face as he sat in his favorite seat near the fire, glass of brandy in his hand as he gazed upon his wife. Such love, such adoration, such … surprise. As if after all those years together he was still caught off guard by her extraordinary talent.

Jack had never taken to the instrument, never being able to sit and focus on it for longer than a few minutes at a time. But even in his ignorance, he could see that his mother—for all her skill— wasn't the best player in that room.

Sonia held that honor.

And a quick scan of the space told Jack that everyone knew it. All five of the doctors were scattered about, actively enjoying the performance, attentions masterfully caught. The uncles were no different. Christopher and Edward shared the settee, completely absorbed, while Sonia's fingers stormed over the keys with astonishing speed. Andrew stood off to the side, his expression painted in wonder—and slight pique, which gave Jack his first smile of the day. *Good.* Let them know that Sonia was better than all of them put together. Let them know that the same blood that ran in their veins also ran in hers, and she wasn't about to spoil it with ineptitude or laziness. Jack would never let that happen. Whatever that little girl wanted to be or do, he would see to it.

Though, by the sounds of things, it didn't seem like she would need much of his help.

On the outskirts of it all, Ella leaned against his grandmother's high-back chair while the older woman dozed with a contented smile on her face. Out of everyone in the drawing room, Ella was the only person not fixated on the accomplished duo.

She moved cautiously across the room, avoiding taking any attention away from the performance. When she reached his side, she stood shoulder to shoulder with him, returning her gaze to the piano.

Maybe it was the swell of the music, or maybe it was the profound relief and contentedness coursing through his veins, but Jack couldn't allow Ella to be near him without touching her. Closing the gap, he shifted his weight to the right, slanting his body against hers like it was the most natural thing in the world. The only thing that was missing was her head propped along his shoulder, the curve of her breast resting along his side.

A noise came from Ella, soft and sweet, as fragile as a whisper. Jack turned to take in her face. Her cheeks were pink, her lips a dusty rose. Music—great music—could be the source of the blood rushing to her, but Jack allowed himself to dream big this time. He allowed himself to know it was because of him.

He allowed himself one other indulgence. Like their moment outside Sonia's bedroom, he dropped his arm, letting it slide along her skirt, where he pinched the fabric in between his fingers, holding it like it was a talisman, or a portal to another life.

The tendons of her bare neck flared as Ella sucked in a breath. "Your daughter has more talent in her little finger than most people have in their entire bodies," she said. Jack liked the way she said it, as if she were as proud as he was.

"I can see that," he said, keeping himself from following those long tendons down to the base of her neck. Jack could forget himself in the mysterious abyss of her creamy skin.

"Did you know she lived in Italy?" Ella asked. "Your daughter is fluent in Italian and French. She also has a passing fluency in German."

"Hmm."

"Hmm, indeed," she returned, slicing him with a sly grin.

"You learned all this today?" he asked.

"I learned all this, and more, today."

Jack let out a soundless laugh. For every single minute of this cursed day, he'd been wrecked with worry over leaving Sonia behind. He should have known the girl would be fine. He should have known Ella would make sure of it.

He nodded toward the black-haired females at the piano who were blissfully lost in their own little world. "When did my mother decide to enter this picture?"

Ella's smile widened. "The moment she heard Sonia play. She came down from her room to inspect and hasn't left yet."

"And she's … been kind?"

Ella chuckled. She tipped her head toward him, and for a wondrous second, Jack believed that she might lay it on his shoulder. She caught herself at the last second, and his stomach squeezed in disappointment. "I don't think you'll have to worry about your mother anymore. I heard her say that 'Only a grandchild of mine could play like that.' They've been thick as thieves ever since. Your mother has only stopped playing long enough to instruct Carlisle to put out a request for a nanny and governess and to purchase Sonia a new wardrobe. 'One befitting a lady.'"

"Hmm."

"Hmm, indeed."

Together they continued to listen to the music. The tranquility of the scene mixed with the warm body pressed against his side made Jack's legs grow heavy. His lids felt weighted even as he was filled with the sensation of floating. He never felt this way on land. The rolling of the sea, the limitless expanse, was usually the only thing that could gift him with that out-of-body experience. The sense that he was not merely living in the world but *of* the world. Like every living thing and every emotion ever experienced were one with him.

And instead of fearing that abundance of time and place and feeling, Jack accepted it, understanding that everything was exactly as it should be.

Ella by his side. Sonia next to his mother. No fighting. Jack gave himself up to this brief period, and it was perfect and right.

He unfurled his fingers from Ella's dress, relinquishing his desperate hold. She took another deep breath, her body canting to his. Jack knew she could feel his subtle movements. He also knew that she was aware of his intention.

Because when his hand crept along the ocean of silk, it didn't have to search far. Ella's hand met his. And with heads forward, breaths paused, eyes shuttered, their fingers wrapped around one another's, sliding into place.

Jack's chest trembled from the touch as Ella's palm pressed against his. The acceptance and perfect fit of skin against skin was sinfully innocent and easily the most intimate moment of his life.

And, selfish bastard that he was, Jack only wanted more.

Pulling her hand to his chest, Jack twisted her until she was plastered against him. "Ella—"

"What the bloody fucking hell is going on!"

The music broke.

Every head swiveled to the doorway where the booming voice had crashed along the corridor, down from the staircase. Unwilling to relinquish Ella's hand, Jack towed her to the source of the sound, only coming to a stop when he reached the base of the staircase, everyone else following close behind.

It felt like they all looked up at the same time to find Oliver, standing on the second-floor landing, glaring down as if they were as meddlesome and annoying as ants. Dressed in his nightgown, he leaned on the banister, his opposite hand clutching a long black cane. Jack's mind played tricks on him. Pale and skinny, his brother reminded him of an apparition, and Jack wondered if Oliver had died and come back to haunt them.

Ella's hand fell away from his, and he felt her step to her right. It was only an inch or two, but it felt more like a chasm.

The duchess was the first one to snap into action. "Oliver," she cried, her voice breaking. She tackled the stairs, arms outstretched. She tripped on her skirts twice before reaching him. "You should be in bed. You're not strong enough yet."

Even from below, Jack could see the anguish darkening his brother's white face. Oliver pounded the top of the cane into the side of his head. Once. Twice. "I can't sleep. I can't think with all that noise. It hurts," he bellowed. He was like a bear with a foot caught in a trap, tameless and panicked. Oliver regarded his mother helplessly. "I told you not to play. I told you …"

Lady Evelyn sobbed. Her hands were raised around Oliver's face, but each time she got close to touching him, he flinched away. "I'm sorry, my love. We forgot ourselves. Let's get you back to bed. Come now, Ollie."

Resigned and haunted, Oliver looked at his mother and then craned his neck around, not able to settle on anything.

Tears welled up in Jack's eyes. His brother appeared so lost and so scared. So small.

Oliver blinked, smacking his head again. "I don't know how I got here. What am I doing here?"

The duchess managed to hold Oliver, covering his shoulder with her arm. "You're home, Oliver. You're safe. And you're going to get better, I promise."

Jack took the stairs two at a time. Positioning himself behind his brother, he swept his arms underneath and picked him up, holding him like a child. It hurt Jack to treat his older brother this way. And it was made worse by the fact that his brother didn't have the strength to fight him. Oliver would have died rather than let others see him so crippled with injury. But he had no choice now but to accept the help, knowing that he couldn't make it back to his room on his own.

As Jack carried his brother back to his quarters, he felt Oliver grasp at the lapels of his jacket. Jack kept his attention straight ahead. He knew if he looked at his brother, he could fall apart. But Oliver called out to him in a harsh rasp, his energy diminishing by the second. "Jackie. Jackie." His voice was so light, as light as his weight in Jack's arms.

Oliver waited for Jack to look at him. "I saw her," he said. "I saw her, Jackie."

"Saw who, Ollie?"

Oliver's voice became thin, fading the instant it left his mouth. "You can't have her. She's mine."

Chapter Seventeen

"**I** DON'T THINK I should go," Ella said cautiously. "With everything that's happened here lately, I think it's best if I stay."

Side by side, Lady Evelyn and Sonia stood across from Ella, neither of them appreciating her decision. Being on the receiving end of their displeasure, she could only appreciate how quickly things had changed. Ever since their impromptu musicale last week, granddaughter and grandmother had become thick as thieves. Sonia had morphed into the lady's shadow, following her around the great house, interjecting and commenting on a whim.

Sonia was the *only* person the duchess allowed to question her. At present, Ella couldn't help but be a little jealous of that fact.

Lady Evelyn flicked her hand in the air impatiently, her nails reminding Ella of claws just waiting to strike. "Nonsense. Your sister is hosting her first ball. Missing it would be unconscionable. If I were Lady Cordelia, I would never forgive you for the slight."

Sonia nodded firmly.

Ella sighed. It was hardly a slight. Her sister would understand. Their relationship was made of stronger stuff than that. "But what about Lord Oliver?"

A flash of concern passed over the duchess's face before she tucked it away, nice and tidy. "What *about* Oliver?" she asked, her voice a shade deeper. "He's fine. He's getting better every day."

Part of that was true. Yes, the fever that had overtaken the duke so acutely had finally released its hold, but to say the man was on the mend was a gross overstatement. He was still plagued with headaches and dizzy spells, and the doctors continued to shroud him in his bedroom to keep the light and other sensory irritants at bay. Ella must have been labeled as one of those "irritants," because she still hadn't been asked to join him, even though she knew Jack, the duchess, and Lady Amelia routinely spent time in his quarters most days.

For some reason, Oliver was holding Ella at a distance. She could only guess why, and none of those guesses boded well for her. She couldn't fight the overwhelming feeling that she was a lamb biding her time before slaughter. She'd spoken to Lady Amelia twice since their initial discussion, pleading with the woman to let her spill the truth, but the lady wouldn't budge. She insisted Ella continue with the illusion, explaining that it would all work out in the end.

Work out for whom?

Ella couldn't help but think that everything would be different if she didn't love being at Sutton Park so much. Gone were her days of boredom. Spending time with the sweet duchess and her direct mother, not to mention the indomitable Sonia, had been just the balm for her lonely soul. Even the uncles provided sustenance with their quiet, puzzling ways. Although not always willing to break out of their shells, the men were kind to Ella, and she'd enjoyed watching them get to know and appreciate their grand-niece.

Retreating back to London into the safety of her family didn't hold the allure it once had. Those muted halls, reticent dinners with her mother and father, endless hours waiting for letters from her sisters … It only reminded Ella of how desperate she'd been. So desperate she'd walked six miles every Monday to spy on a man racing his horses. A man who had no idea she existed.

He probably *still* didn't know.

So, what would it hurt if Ella went to Cordelia's ball? It wasn't like Lord Oliver would miss her. *He* wasn't the one Ella wanted to miss her, anyway.

The duchess must have spotted Ella wavering. "Go on," she said, poking Ella toward the stairs. "It's time you started getting ready. Your mother sent over a new, lovely gown, and you'll be late if you stand here frowning any longer. Remember, my dear, frowning is how all those old women have wrinkles." She glanced down at Sonia, placing a gentle hand on the side of her head. "You don't want wrinkles, do you?"

"No, Grandmother. Never!"

"Exactly!" the duchess exclaimed, so pleased that she bopped the child's nose with the tip of her finger.

Lady Evelyn returned to Ella, the smile stalling on her face. "What are you still doing here? Go upstairs!" she chided. Her expression became grave. "If you don't go, people will talk. They'll worry and gossip about my son. And we can't have that, can we?"

On cue, Sonia chimed in, "No, we cannot."

The duchess stepped closer to Ella. "They'll see you and Jack, and they'll know that Oliver will be on his feet soon. Your presence will be a message and a relief for them all."

"Jack?" Ella startled. "Jack is going?"

"Of course," the duchess replied, picking a stray piece of lint off the sleeve of her plum gown. "Although, naturally, he's complaining about it just as much as you are."

"You're *forcing* him to go?" Ella asked.

Lady Evelyn snorted, and Sonia joined in with one of her own. They looked at one another and rolled their eyes. An odd fluttering tickled Ella's chest. It *was* adorable how well the two were getting on, but she had the distinct feeling of being the third wheel.

"You know Jack better than that," the duchess replied dryly. "He only listens to me when he wants to. No, he said something about needing to talk to someone who was going to be there, something about gaining contacts. Or was it contracts?" She flicked her hand through the air once more. "Business," she added with a put-upon sigh. "Whatever that means."

ELLA WASN'T SURE how to quantify if a ball was a success, but if not being able to move without elbowing someone in their throat was any indicator, her sister could sleep with ease that night. It seemed like all of London had come out to witness the Marchioness of Tykesbury's foray into hosting, and Cordelia had been nothing if not prepared.

Standing next to her sister and brother-in-law in their glorious ballroom, Ella could feel the nervous pride wafting off them. Cordelia had said that it took her two whole months to decide on the flowers and food, and Ella could concur that, though that sounded excessive, it had been well worth it. If something wasn't shining and sparkling, then it was blooming. Crystals and diamonds mixed with elegant roses and fat peonies created an environment that evoked good taste and high standards. Though it was clear that Cordelia's mission was to impress, she'd used a deft hand, indicating that she didn't want to impress *that much.* Because that would be gauche. That would not be fitting.

And Cordelia fit.

Ella, on the other hand, not so much.

"Why does he keep looking at me?" she asked, edging behind her sister, hoping to lose the miserable scowl directed at her.

"Who?" Cordelia asked.

"Lord Lucas," Ella replied, sneaking furtive glances at the viscount over her sister's puffed-silk-covered shoulder. "He's been doing it all night. It's … vexing."

The Marquis of Tykesbury tapped his teeth together. "It's … well … I think it's my fault."

Ella turned to her newest brother-in-law. "What did you do?"

Ordinarily, she wouldn't accost one of her sister's husbands in public, but the marquis was as close to a real brother as she would ever get. Lord Daniel's father had been great friends with Cordelia and Ella's, and the children spent many summers together. The parents would never admit it, but it had probably always been the plan for Daniel to marry one of the Weston daughters. To Ella, it showed good judgment that he'd eventually come to his senses and settled on Cordelia.

Daniel squirmed under Ella's condemning glare. "I didn't mean it …" he started uneasily. "It's just … The man was asking about you, and I felt terrible because he likes you so much, and he's a good chap and he has that weird eye …" The marquis shrugged his brawny shoulders. "I thought he still had a chance, so I told him so."

"A chance at what?" Ella asked icily, gaining a few odd looks from the crowd closest to them.

Daniel's handsome face fell. "A chance at *you*. Last time I heard, you were practically engaged. I thought that was the plan."

Ella's astonishment could not be contained. "What plan?"

"The plan!" Daniel screeched. "Your mother's plan. I thought he was the man your mother wanted for you. I thought the whole thing was as good as done."

Cordelia groaned. She closed her eyes, hands on her temples, careful not to disturb the diamond diadem her husband had surprised her with before the ball. "But that was before, darling."

"Before what?"

She gave her husband a pitying smile; it was the verbal equivalent of patting a dog's head for trying. "Before the *Lord Oliver* situation."

Daniel threw up his hands in exasperation. If people weren't gawking before, they were definitely doing it now. "You ladies change everything so quickly! *You* told me that the situation with the duke wasn't real. You told me Ella was in love with someone else, so I assumed it was Lord Lucas!"

"There *is* someone else!" Cordelia replied.

Daniel leaned toward his wife, completely eclipsing her tiny frame. The man was as tall as a tree and just as wide. "And that someone else is *not* Lord Lucas?"

Cordelia slapped her palms on her husband's lapels. "No, of course not!"

The marquis had never been more confused in his life. "I still don't understand," he said lamely.

Ella cut in. "Will you two please stop talking about me like I'm not here? And also, be so kind as to inform me *whom* I'm in love with!"

Cordelia cocked her head, assessing her sister to such a degree that Ella couldn't meet her eyes.

"Darling," she started, "I think Lord Lucas might be so … *intense* tonight because you haven't looked at him once, as you've been too busy staring at someone else."

Ella blinked. "Who?"

Cordelia rolled her eyes. "Lord John! You came with him! And I'll tell you if you need me to—you're in love with him."

"Jack?" Ella laughed. "Sister, I don't know what gave you that impression, but you are wrong. Besides, the duchess demanded we come together. It's nothing to read into."

Cordelia arched a brow. "And does she also demand that you write 'Jack this' and 'Jack that' in all your letters to me?"

Ella didn't like the way this line of questioning was going. She felt as uncomfortable as her brother-in-law looked, though he was doing much better now that his wife had moved her focus off him. "He's interesting." Ella shrugged. "That's all."

"Interesting, yes," Cordelia agreed, twisting her lips into a smile. Coyly, she slid her eyes to the opposite side of the room. "But not very *interested* in this ball, is he? Whenever you manage to take your eyes off him, *his* are staring at you."

"That's ridiculous," Ella scoffed. Jack had barely mumbled a complete sentence to her on the long journey here, making the carriage ride awkward and uncomfortable. Not two minutes before she entered the ballroom, she'd considered ignoring the man for the rest of her life. His vertiginous moods were giving her whiplash. One second, he was peering into her soul, conveying feelings that made Ella's toes curl inside her slippers, and the next he was pretending he could see right through her.

"It's not ridiculous," Cordelia countered. "He's stood there all night with that scowl on his face, not talking to anyone. He's as bad as Lord Lucas! And is that an earring? Mother won't like that all."

"I like his earring! And what about Mother? This has nothing to do with her!"

Cordelia didn't bother responding to that rot. Everything *always* had something to do with their mother. Lady Weston made sure of it.

Cordelia dropped her head closer to Ella, lowering her voice to a whisper. "What is happening? What are you doing in that house?"

"I don't know," Ella replied. Which was the truth. She could lie to everyone—even herself—before she could lie to her sister.

"Oh dear," Daniel announced, breaking through their moment. The women turned to find his face getting redder by the moment. "He's coming over here."

"Who?" Ella asked. She spotted Jack at once, but the wallflower hadn't budged an inch from his corner. There was only one other option.

"Go hide," Cordelia ordered her, shoving Ella farther behind her. "We'll hold him off. It's the least *we* can do," she said, glaring at her husband.

Chapter Eighteen

ONE FOOT IN front of the other. That was all Jack had to do. It was such a simple thing, a thing he did every day without even thinking twice about it.

What was it about these claustrophobic ballrooms that made him shrivel up, forgetting everything he'd accomplished or become? He was Jack *fucking* Sutton. A self-made man who was on his way to owning one of the most lucrative shipping companies in the country.

Who just happened to be a duke's son.

Why was the second part always the most significant at these kinds of events? Men nodded to him in deference; women coquettishly batted their eyelashes in his direction—all because of where he came from and what that represented.

Jack hated it.

And the more he ruminated on it, the harder it was for him to act.

But Sinclair was right. If Sutton Shipping was going to break ahead of the competition and plant themselves firmly at the top, it needed the Caddell Tinplate Works contract. America was booming. A gold rush had just been declared in some far-off place called California. The rapidly expanding country needed iron for its railroad and the multitudes of new cities springing up. If ever there was a time to make money, this was it. Jack was standing on the brink of having everything he'd ever wanted.

And he couldn't find the nerve to take one step across a crowded ballroom.

It wasn't like Michael Caddell was avoiding him. Whenever Jack glanced his way, he could see the tycoon stealing looks at him. Waiting for Jack to make his pitch.

Waiting for a duke's son—a duke's brother—to come to the bricklayer's son.

Was Jack proud? He'd never thought so before. Over the past fifteen years at sea, he'd broken bread with natives and slept in hammocks next to all sorts. But he'd been Jack Sutton on those occasions. And now he was forced to be Lord John. And he wasn't sure if he even liked Lord John.

Just as much as he hated that he couldn't take his fucking eyes off Ella.

Looking absolutely fucking perfect and demure. Standing at the right hand of her equally suitable and appropriate sister and gigantic brother-in-law, the Marquis of Tykesbury, who'd been fortunate enough to be told exactly who he would be when he grew up and didn't have the ornery compunction to want anything different. *Good for him.* It was true what people said. *Ignorance is bliss.*

"I was told on good authority that if you don't stop scowling, you'll get wrinkles. You wouldn't want those, would you?"

It took a few seconds, but Jack smiled.

Ella rounded in front of him wearing a daring peach-colored gown and a mischievous smirk.

Jack's head swiveled to Lady Cordelia and her husband, who were both watching him now, curiosity more than evident. "I thought you were over there," he said, feeling dumb the instant he said it.

Ella bobbed her shoulders. The innocent action made Jack's balls tighten. Her gown draped just off those well-formed shoulders, leaving them mostly bare and so inviting. Jack had spent many minutes in his spot tracing the beautiful lines of her clavicles.

"I'm here now," she said. "I needed rescuing. It looks like I'm not the only one."

Jack played with his earring, twisting it round and round in its hole. He smiled wryly. "Is it that obvious?"

Ella's laughter gave him the answer. "Your mother said you didn't come to dance. She said you had some business to handle. Why aren't you handling it?"

With her brown eyes focused squarely on him, Jack was hit by a gust of selfishness. This gentle lady shouldn't be wasting her time on him. This was a ball. Ladies like her lived for these moments. With her new gown, and the hairstyle that had made him pace in the drawing room for thirty minutes as he waited for it to be completed, she should be showering other eligible, *appropriate* men with her attention.

During Jack's darker moments (and the last week had been full of them), he'd told himself that she only dealt with him at the house because she had no one else. Oliver was indisposed half the time, and all the others were too young, too old, or merely repugnant. Jack had been the least of evils.

He only wished he could remind himself of that now. Remind Ella as well. Because the way she was fixed on him, with that innocent delight, that sparkle of teasing, that welling of desire, made him hope that all was not lost.

"Well?" she asked, prodding him out of his stupor.

Jack cleared his throat and took a deep exhale, attempting to clear his mind. But even with a room clouded with smoke and perfume and desperation, he was only filled with Ella.

"I am handling it," he growled.

Her brow pinched together in response to his anger, but how could Jack explain that it wasn't directed at her, but *him*? His feelings for her. He'd been so obvious about it that even Oliver, crazed with a fever dream, saw it. *She's mine.* Those words had echoed over and over again in his mind all week. Jack had been wrong. So very, very wrong. Maybe he'd wanted to be all along. Because Ella hadn't been lying. She hadn't been keeping a deep secret regarding Oliver. She'd been telling the truth. They were engaged!

Jack was better than this. He wasn't the kind of man who would steal his brother's fiancée from under the man's convalescing nose.

And yet here she was, smelling that way, looking that way, speaking that way, and Jack was helpless. He couldn't move from her because he didn't want to. Plain and simple.

"How, exactly, are you handling it?" she asked, biting back laughter. Jack tried not to watch her teeth plunge into that pillowy lip, but once again, he was a selfish bastard.

"I'm waiting for the right moment," he retorted hotly. He flicked his chin toward Caddell, who was standing across the room next to a woman Jack assumed to be his wife, holding court with other scions of industry. Lines had been drawn in the ballroom—titles on one side, and everyone else on the other. Only a brave few ventured into the other's territory, and of those, all were men.

Ella followed his line of sight. "Oh," she remarked casually, "Mrs. and Mr. Caddell? Is that whom you need to speak to?"

"Do you know them?"

She shook her head. "I know *of* them. They have a daughter my age—Louisa. I think I heard my mother say Mrs. Caddell is trying to elevate her, find a good match."

"How does your mother know this?"

Ella clicked her tongue. "My mother knows everyone in the *ton*. She makes it her business to know their business. Maybe you should be talking to her right now instead of me."

"I don't ever want to talk to anyone other than you."

The words flew out of Jack's mouth before he could stop them. He ducked his head, but not before watching Ella's face burn red. An insatiable desire to hold her beckoned him, a desire to press her head against his chest and protect her from his embarrassing ardor.

Ella's giggle surprised him. "I think if you considered it a little more, you would disagree. One word from my mother and she'd have Mr. Caddell eating out of your palm."

Jack smiled, tossing his humiliation to the side. "She's that good?"

"She is. It's undeniable."

Jack narrowed his gaze, letting the moment stretch. "I bet you're just as good."

"Oh, I doubt that." Ella paused, and Jack could see that she was considering the silent invitation. Blowing out an exhale, she widened her shoulders, considering Mr. Caddell and his crowd with a new, shrewder gaze.

"All right, then," she said boldly. "Let's go introduce you to Mr. Caddell. I've always wanted to see if I could do it just as well as my mother."

"Do what?" Jack held out the crook of his arm, his heart jumping when Ella placed her hand upon it. The small motion completed him in some odd way, like he had been a puzzle waiting for its last piece.

Ella stared down at their point of contact. He heard her breath quicken, could see her two top teeth peek out as she licked her lips. Her voice was wobbly as her eyes collided with his. "Bend a man to my will."

Jack laughed, a loud, booming sound that trailed behind them as he guided Ella across the room. Such an innocent. If she only knew what she did to him. She'd never wonder something so ridiculous again.

ELLA LEANED BACK against the carriage seat, a superior quirk curving the side of her mouth. Jack was waiting for her to crow. He was surprised she'd gone this long. Perhaps he was the one in the wrong. The moment he'd helped her into the conveyance, he should have told her that she was a revelation. Jack had spent five years working to make his company a success; she'd managed to do just as much in one night.

"So …" she began shyly, twisting her fingers in her lap. "Do you think you have a chance to win the contract?"

Jack chuckled. At the end of their conversation, Montogomery had been practically begging him to have Sutton Shipping send over a bid for the contract. He couldn't wait to get to the office tomorrow to tell Sinclair. The account manager would still complain about too much work, but at least he'd have a sunnier tone about it.

"Thanks to you … maybe."

Ella beamed, her cheeks rosy and high. "I didn't do much," she added demurely.

Jack sent her an exasperated scowl. "You were fantastic. Don't fool yourself. The way you wrapped the Caddells around your little finger—it was masterful, and you know it."

It was harder and harder for Ella to beat the pride away. "It was hardly masterful," she tried. "I merely spoke to the couple and listened to what they had to say."

But Jack knew it was more than that. There was an art to conversation that he'd never learned or appreciated. People talked to each other all the time. Better people even listened. But to do both while making the other party actually feel heard, like what they said *mattered*, was a true talent. Standing on the sidelines, speaking whenever Ella opened up the perfect place in the exchange for him, Jack had known exactly what the Caddells had been thinking. Because he'd been on the receiving end of Ella's talent before. He'd felt the acceptance and curiosity of her. He knew what it was like to witness her interest and questions and realize that she wasn't asking them only to use his answers as currency against him, but rather because she genuinely wanted to know more about him.

It was a heady feeling, could make a person feel drunk with

promise. It could make a person greedy for more.

Just as Jack was now. He wanted all of Ella. All of the time.

Because she made him *feel* so many things.

But most of all, she made him feel like he was the right man for her. That he was *enough* for her.

And beliefs were a dangerous thing—especially when a person was beginning to believe in himself.

Jack palmed his face, running it down until he was certain that that idea had fled. He needed to get out of his mind. Thinking was doing him no favors. "How did you get to be so good at it?" he asked, needing Ella to whisk him away from the tortures of his hope.

"Talking to people?"

He nodded.

Ella's mouth puckered as she gave the matter some thought. Jack used the time to settle in his seat. He was no better than Sonia, getting comfortable for one of Ella's lofty bedtime tales.

"It's nothing astonishing, really," she began. Her body tensed as she peeked out the sliver of window left uncovered by the shade. "My mother trained all of us to be what Society asked for. My father insisted we had a good education, and she insisted we knew how to put everyone at ease. Be the consummate hostess."

"You're more than that."

Her smile was wistful, and it tugged on something deep and hidden inside him. "I suppose I'm good at listening to people." Ella hesitated as if she was answering the question for herself along with Jack. "After the scarlet fever, my body was weak. I would catch fevers so easily, and it made my parents nervous. My sisters were allowed free rein over the house and estate, but the second I showed signs of a cough or a runny nose, I was sent to my room to recover."

Jack listened quietly. He'd known some of this story, but not the extent of the disease. He couldn't fit what Ella told him with how he saw her. Her powers seemed limitless to him. For fuck's sake, she'd dragged his large brother out of a lake. Her being sickly didn't make sense.

She continued. "I spent so much of my childhood reading and listening to my sisters tell me about their days and adventures. I craved it; I wanted to hear everything. It was like I was living through their exploits. Don't give me that look. I'm not to be pitied. I never envied them … too much. Besides, that was a long time ago. And I'm better now."

Ella was wrong. Jack didn't pity her. He pitied himself. Because he wanted to wrap her in his embrace and keep her safe. If he wanted one job in life, it was that one. "You don't get fevers anymore?"

"No," she said slowly. Ella took off one glove and stretched her fingers. "But I do get these … episodes. It's hard to explain, and the doctors don't truly understand it either. Whenever I overexert myself or feel anxious or full of stress for a significant period of time, my hands will hurt terribly. It happens to my feet, too. My knuckles and ankles will become inflamed and tight and difficult to move. It's like being locked in a little prison, and I'm at its mercy. It doesn't happen too often, but I'm always on the lookout for it."

"And the doctors can't help you?"

"They try," she explained. "Some have said that certain herbs can help, so I try to put them in my tea as much as possible; others have tried massaging techniques to bring the inflammation down, but there's been no cure." She shrugged. "This is just something I'll have to live with."

Before the rational part of Jack's brain could warn him off, he reached across the carriage, taking Ella's naked hand. Scooting to the edge of his seat, he pulled the hand into his lap. Then, with painstaking care and precision, he began to rub in little circles at the base of her palm, working all the way up to the tip of each tapered finger.

"Y-you d-don't have to do that," she whispered.

"Yes, I do." He sent her a warm smile. "For all the stress I've caused you these last few weeks."

Ella's laugh was short and choppy. "You haven't been that bad," she said.

Silence fell over them as she watched him knead her hand. Jack went back and forth between pressure levels, taking her to the edge of pain at moments before returning to a gentle, soothing caress. Blood pumped harsh and loud in between his ears, but he could still hear the erratic pulls and hisses of her breath.

For a solid minute, Jack focused on the meaty section of her palm, at the base of her thumb, grinding with his fingers until she released a gusty moan.

"Hit the spot?" But he'd been wrong to look up. Ruffled and spent, the woman looked one push away from crying out. Lord help him if that happened.

"What about you?" she asked. Apparently, the woman was capable of speech after all. "Why are you so bad at conversation? Forgive me for saying this, but I expected a little more from a duke's son."

Jack made her wait for his answer. He returned Ella's hand to her lap before taking the other. Gently, he peeled the glove off and started all over again. "I never had the talent for it. And it wasn't me that really needed it. Ollie was good at all of that— good enough for the both of us." Using the backs of his fingers, Jack caressed the length of hers, tickling the soft skin, grinning when she shuddered. "My father understood that I had no interest in the *ton* or the limitations it was determined to place on a second son." Emotion welled in Jack's throat. "He was a good man. The best man. He never held me back, despite wanting different things for me."

"He didn't want you to be like his brothers."

"No, he didn't."

"So he let you go?"

"So he let me go."

Ella's fingers curled, capturing Jack's hand. "He'd be so proud of you, Jack."

His mouth screwed up to the side. "Do you think so?"

"I do."

Jack nodded, too overcome to mutter a word. How did she do this to him? Get him talking enough to uncover everything he tried desperately to hide? Could she see how he'd needed her to say those words? Because his father had died before he could. Did she know that the fear of disappointing or failing his father kept him up some nights? That fear was what pushed him to excel, pushed him to sail harder and faster and smarter than everyone else.

"Jack?"

God, how he loved the way she said his name with that husky voice of hers. A little puff of air. So sexy and coaxing. Maybe even a little wanting.

Maybe a lot of it.

"Yes, Ella?"

Her expression was blank, but also unmistakable.

"I don't want to go home tonight."

Home. Funny how she called it that when Jack hadn't for years. They weren't even headed to Sutton Park, anyway. He'd told his mother that they would stay at the townhouse to avoid that long drive that night. But something told him that she wasn't talking about the townhouse either.

"Where do you want to go?" he asked quietly.

"Take me to your ship."

Jack couldn't help himself. He knew his smile was cocky. "Which one?"

Her eyes flickered down to their hands before moving back to him. "The one you love the most."

Chapter Nineteen

T HE LONDON DOCKS were never quiet, but a sense of pride washed over Jack as he helped Ella across the gangplank onto the *Siren*. The desire to share surged within him—parts of the ship he wanted to describe to her, stories of his crewmates he hoped would make her laugh. However, as Ella stepped carefully aboard the strong wooden clipper, that rush vanished. Watching Ella inspect his ship, his home, *his life*, was more than enough. The pensive, admiring look she wore while she traversed the main deck set his heart at such ease that Jack had to place his hand over it, making sure it was still working.

The *Siren* had never had a woman aboard before. And seeing Ella pause near the stern, the moon at her back creating shimmering diamonds off the water, made Jack want to keep her there forever.

"Was it you who named her?" she asked, finally breaking the trance. Her grave expression startled him at first. He'd only wanted her to enjoy herself as he gave her a glimpse into his real life, his true self. But then Jack understood that that was the very reason she *was* so serious. Ella had recognized the importance of this moment better than he had.

Jack's fingers ached. He wanted to touch her in the same soft, exploratory way she swept her hands over his ship. "No, she was named before I bought her. I thought it was appropriate, since she'd called out to me. The moment I saw her cutting so effortlessly across the water, I knew I had to have her."

"She belonged to someone else?"

"She did."

Jack made his way to Ella. His steps felt forced, unsteady. It was like he was being pulled from the inside out without knowing how to make himself right again. At an early age, Jack had understood how to get things, make them his. Hard work and determination were just as important—if not more so—than money. Money made things easier, but hard work made them possible.

But his need for Ella was different. Jack could weave himself in knots for days and still not come up with a scenario where Ella could ever be his. Too many others would be hurt. Too many of the people he loved most in this world.

Ella watched him come to her. He could see the lines of her neck tense, her lips rubbing against each other as she considered her next words. Jack didn't want to talk anymore. It was fruitless, but it was also sensible. Reasonable. Words created the wall between them that they dared not break.

"Did the previous owner want to give her up?"

Jack shook his head. He was a few feet away from her. Ella backed up against the stern, her elbows bent as she clutched the edge.

"Then how did you get her?" she asked. Her voice became deeper, more breathless, as she continued to keep this moment civil and innocent.

Jack couldn't shake the feeling that someone else was controlling his limbs. Because he knew touching Ella was dangerous, but his arm reached out anyway. He captured the side of her face, and his resistance fled. Ella's eyes drifted closed as she gave herself up to it. Jack took the invitation, wrapping his other arm around her waist, pulling her closer until their bodies were flush. Her hesitance came when he tried to coax her head to his chest. Lord, how Jack wanted her to lie against him. He wanted to feel her eyelashes flickering on his skin, feel her breath as it synced with his. Just that, nothing more. Holding her would satisfy him for a lifetime. It would have to.

Her eyes clung to him. Sad and tortured, the brown orbs peered into his soul, telling him that this was futile, that the only place and time she would ever truly belong to him was on this ship, the place where he was a different man, a man who could steer to the horizon and hope.

"Jack." It wasn't a question, nor an invitation. Perhaps it was a plea, begging him to stop, to drop his hand to his side and give her back her freedom. But Jack didn't hear it that way.

He caressed the soft spot just under her cheekbone, imagining that he and only he could coax a smile from her.

But Ella did not smile.

Her head fell, but she lifted her hands to him, gripping the sides of his jacket. Tension seized him as he waited for her next move. Would she shove him away or pull him closer? Both decisions were the right one.

"We can't keep doing this," Ella said. A breeze came off the water, teasing the curls hanging along the sides of her face.

"We're not doing anything." Oh, but that was a lie, and Jack was almost ashamed he'd said it. These small looks, the barely there touches, the intimate, fleeting moments, meant more, said more, than anything that Jack had ever experienced with a woman.

Ella's laughter was biting. She was angry. At herself. At him too, probably. Raising her head, she contemplated the ship once more. "You're going to leave."

Again, not a question. Jack answered it anyway. "Yes."

"And your brother is going to get better."

"Yes."

"And I ..." The wind kicked up again, ripping the sentence away from her.

Jack pressed firmer into the small of her back. He needed her to finish that thought. The rest of his life depended on what she was about to say. "What?" he asked. His throat was like sandpaper, his words coming out entirely too rough.

Ella's eyes were limitless, pools that he could sink into and never find his way out of. Dark and mysterious, enchanting and beguiling. They were the true Sirens.

"There's something I need to tell you," she began. Pausing, she brushed the curls out of her face, tucking them behind her ears. "I have been hiding something."

"I don't care."

"Don't say that. You *will* care."

Jack shook his head. "I won't. Everyone hides things, Ella. It's not a sin or a secret. I've been hiding something since the moment I met you."

"What?"

Jack leaned forward, resting his forehead on hers. He filled his senses with her sweet scent, the lavender mixing with the salt air urging him to continue. "I don't think it's necessary for me to say it," he replied. "I haven't been doing the best job hiding it."

Ella drew away. Jack smiled ruefully, straightening his stance. He needed to see her clearly. He needed to see exactly how those brave, intrepid words affected her.

"Ella?" he asked.

Her frown deepened. She appeared to be working up courage. Had Jack said the wrong thing? Should he have let her speak? What could she have possibly done that would make her this cautious with him?

The gangplank rattled and feet slapped on the deck, reckless and unsteady. The voice that accompanied it was equally so. "Ella! Ella! You shouldn't be here! You, *you* there." Fingers snapped irritably. "You have no right to touch my fiancée!"

Jack twisted around, positioning Ella behind his back. A heavy man claimed center stage on the main deck, jutting a hip out in a flourish as if posing for a book about treasure-hungry buccaneers. He was younger than Jack, or greener at least, with a bush of dark brown hair on his head and a youthful, smooth chin that only needed a shave once a week. That chin was thrust into the air now, the moonlight glinting off its pale skin.

"Who are you?" Jack asked. "And who the *fuck* said you come aboard my ship?"

The man's hand fell off his hip as he shifted into panic mode. Evidently, he hadn't thought past his one gallant line. He craned his head past Jack. "Ella?" he said. "Ella, tell him who I am."

Jack heard Ella sigh. "This is Lord Lucas. A family friend—"

"Your *fiancé*!" he huffed self-importantly.

Jack lifted one eyebrow, drawing out the moment while rubbing the bottom of his chin with the back of his hand. "Hmm."

The gangplank groaned again as two more pairs of boots clambered onto his ship, unannounced and uninvited. This time, at least, Jack wasn't completely lost.

Fresh from their ball, Ella's sister and her large husband hurried to stand next to the young lord, their expressions equally contrite. "We are so, so sorry, Lord John—" the husband started, but his wife quickly cut him off.

Cordelia glared at her husband. "He's sorry," she countered. "Ella?"

Ella emerged from behind Jack. "Do you have to tell your husband *everything*?" she asked, tone venomous.

"I didn't think he would tell Lord Lucas."

Daniel huffed. "I didn't think it was a secret! You told me that Ella was going to see the ship. Lord Lucas asked where she was, and I told him."

Cordelia spun toward her husband, her frosty countenance making the poor man cower. "From now on, *everything* I tell you is a secret. Yes?"

The marquis nodded glumly.

Cordelia whipped back to Lord Lucas. "All right, my lord, let's get you home. You shouldn't have come."

"You're damned right," Jack interjected.

Lord Lucas shrugged off Cordelia's hand, his face mottled in various shades of red. One lonely vein pulsed in the middle of his large forehead. "I will not leave without Ella. She's mine, and I respect and love her too much to let her disgrace herself with this, this"—his sneer belittled Jack from head to toe—"*merchant.*"

An unexpected chuckle sprang forth from Jack. He'd expected *pirate.*

He folded his arms slowly, giving the impression of a man bored with a child's tantrum. *Merchant* didn't bother him; there was an entirely different word that made him want to pound the pompous ass through the deck floor. "She's … *yours?*"

It was spoken so casually and low that Lord Lucas could not mistake the chill. His Adam's apple bobbed up and over his starched, pristine collar. "Y-yes," he stammered. "We're engaged. Everyone knows it."

Ella groaned, covering her face with her hands. "We are *not* engaged, nor have we ever been," she growled through her fingers.

The lord scoffed, shifting his weight to his other foot. "Well, maybe not officially," he replied. "But it was going to happen. You know it and I know it." He flicked his head to Cordelia. "Your entire family knew it and wanted it, but then you had to go and ruin everything with your charade with Winchester."

Jack's ears perked up. Every hair on his body stood on end.

Again, Cordelia tugged on Lord Lucas's coat. "You've said enough. I think you should go to bed and sleep off all the drinks you had at the ball." She threw her husband a beseeching look, and the giant sprang to action.

He positioned himself on the other side of the lord, towering over him. "Ah, yes, let's go," Daniel grumbled. "This isn't the time."

Lord Lucas snorted. "It's the perfect time. I know what your mother is up to. The woman thinks she's Machiavelli, but I'm one step ahead of her. She thinks sticking Ella in that house with that man is going to elicit a proposal, but she's overplayed her hand."

He crossed his arms, lifting a haughty brow at Ella. "He'll never want you. You have to know that. He's a rake and a scoundrel. Do you honestly think he's going to be so grateful that he's going to make *you* his duchess? Hardly."

"Stop, please!" Cordelia cried.

"Why?" Lord Lucas asked with genuine surprise. He was a man of the *ton*, through and through. He actually believed his histrionics on this ship were gentlemanly. "Look what your mother's machinations have done! The duke's house is a den of hedonism, and it's clearly rubbed off on her! The old Ella wouldn't be caught dead here in the middle of the night, making eyes at the duke's brother."

Halfway through the lord's heroic speech, Jack had given up. He hadn't the stomach for Lord Lucas or his gallant attempt at rescuing. Instead, Jack locked on to Ella. She'd done her best, keeping up a steady, passionless expression, allowing the lord to throw his words and anger at her like freshly sharpened arrows. Her back straight, her shoulders pulled back, she permitted herself to be the bull's-eye for his frustration.

But then she flinched.

And Jack knew then that everything Lord Lucas was saying was true. About Ella and her mother. About Ella and Oliver.

Hypnotized by the moment, Jack watched a small, lambent tear pool under Ella's left eye. It sat there suspended above her cheek, defying gravity. But then her jaw clenched, and her lips trembled. And that lonely tear fell, leaving a shiny trail of truth in its wake.

Jack would have killed an entire army in retaliation for that tear.

One man would have to do.

Jack lowered his head, squinting at his clean, freshly scrubbed deck. "Hmm," he said to himself.

And then he charged.

Cordelia and Daniel had the good sense to give Jack a wide berth. Because when he brought his arm back, his swing was nice and wide. And when it made contact with the lord's face, it made the delicious kind of *pop!* that sent shivers up spines and put smiles on faces.

Jack's face, at least.

The lord screamed bloody murder and collapsed to his knees. But Jack needed more. He kicked the man's chest, waiting for the *thunk* of the flailing body to smack the deck. A more satisfying sound had rarely been heard.

Jack turned to the marquis. His voice still remarkably calm and bored, he said, "Take care of him for me, will you? I don't want his blood to stain my deck. Also, make sure his mouth stays shut about all of this."

Daniel nodded at once, as readily as any good sailor, and peeled Lord Lucas's body from the ground. Cordelia got halfway to her sister before Jack stopped her.

"Not her," he stated. His voice wasn't half so easy to control that time. "We have some things to discuss first. I'll make sure she gets home safe." He placed his hand over his heart and flashed a smile that could only be considered *piratical.* "You have my word as a gentleman."

Chapter Twenty

ELLA NEEDED TO hide. She watched Cordelia follow behind her husband, her steps slow and regretful. Was her sister really leaving her? *With him?*

The silence was deafening. The docks were busy, full of lively, drunken conversations, a few impromptu brawls, groups of men breaking into the odd sea shanty—but all of that was drowned out by what Jack was *not* saying to her.

Ella kept her gaze down. Fat drops of Lord Lucas's blood formed a small puddle in front of her, a gruesome reminder of who she was and what she'd done. The lengths she'd gone through for a man she didn't know.

A man she didn't even want.

Ella knew that now. Because the man she did want was staring at her with regret in his eyes.

She readied herself for the inevitable, knowing Jack would never show her how much she'd hurt him. His indifference, his callousness, would provide all the emotional pain he wished to inflict. And that kind of pain had the power to stay with someone long after bruises faded.

Jack's footsteps were measured and contained. From the corner of her eye, she saw him meander farther away from her, his hands clasped behind his back. Weathered and strong, this man was a contradiction. Dressed in his gorgeous black coat, shiny leather shoes, and snow-white shirt, he was the epitome of a duke's son. But something wild and unbridled lived underneath the expensive cloth. Something primitive and restless pressed against the fabric, pulling at the seams. Jack stretched his neck back and forth, his gold earring sparkling like the lone star in their cloud-filled night sky.

"Jack, I—" The words tumbled out of Ella's mouth, cut short when Jack spotted her across the deck. His cold blue eyes fastened on hers.

It was only a few seconds.

His penetrating gaze.

Her bracing fear.

And then he moved. It was all too fast. Jack was too quick.

Coward that she was, Ella shut her eyes at the last second, too afraid to witness his anger up close. She tensed as he reached for her, his grip hard, his arms like a steel trap.

And then his mouth seized hers. Soft and supple, pliable and wanting, Jack's lips formed to hers, kissing Ella like a man starved. There was no brute force in his kiss. Sweet and kind, Jack took her mouth like a gift, giving it the reverence and time it deserved. Giving her pure love.

Ella felt his hand climb up her side, landing at the back of her head. He maneuvered her, placing her at just the right angle so that he could deepen the kiss, suck on her bottom lip, coax her to open her mouth for his tongue. He swept inside the heat of her, tasting her, learning her.

Absolving her.

"Tell me it's true. Tell me you don't belong to my brother," he whispered against Ella's open lips. Both arms surrounded her now, as if Jack was afraid to let her go. He kissed her again and again, alternating sweet pecks along the side of her mouth with deep, sensual pulls that made Ella feel like he was stealing her soul from her body. She gave it up willingly. Anything to be held like this, to be cherished like this.

Ella placed her hands on top of his, a sob gathering inside her throat. "I don't," she rasped. "I never did."

The declaration spurred something in him. Jack's actions became hungrier, greedier. He kissed Ella with an abandon that made her head spin. She clung to him, knowing that the only reason she was still standing was because he was allowing it.

Ella tried to say more; she needed to explain. But his mouth was too demanding, his kisses too insistent. Jack hugged her to him, and through the hazy din of her mind, Ella felt his arousal. She shaped her hips around his, feeling his groan all the way down to her core.

Passion flamed all around them. This was no mere spark to tinder; this was a blaze that had the capacity to take everything down with it.

But guilt was a difficult thing to fling off. It stuck to Ella, prohibiting her from letting go completely. She wanted Jack. But after everything she'd done and hid from him, what could he possibly want with *her*?

Ella pulled back. Their chests heaved from the exertion. Were her eyes as glassy and passion-filled as his? Jack appeared lost, halfway between this life and the next. It scared her, but it also thrilled her.

He came for her again, and Ella placed her fingers on his lips. "Jack," she said, "I didn't mean for this to happen."

Gently, he grasped her wrist and pressed his mouth against the inside of her palm, the same palm that he'd massaged a short time ago. "I know. You meant to have my brother."

"No." She shook her head. "That's not ... I don't think ..." But it was true, wasn't it? This hadn't just been her mother's plan. She'd been complicit in its origins.

Jack chuckled darkly. A shadow passed over his face, and that fear that Ella thought had vanished reappeared to settle in the pit of her stomach. "It doesn't matter anymore," he went on. "The story has changed."

Ella fought for her voice. "Changed?"

Jack continued playing with her hand, separating her fingers so he could kiss them one at a time. When he reached the end, he took her entire finger in his mouth, biting it before setting it free. "You're mine now," he declared. "I'm meant to have you. That's it. And I mean to do it now."

Jack moved like a panther. Ella yelped as he lifted her in his arms.

"Where are you taking me?" she cried.

Jack's lengths were even, his steps never faltering as he stared straight ahead. "I'm taking you to my room."

"Why here?"

He cocked his head at her as if she'd just asked the most illogical question. "Because this is my home," he said matter-of-factly. "And now it's yours, too."

⟫⟫⟫✳⟪⟪⟪

JACK CARRIED HER below deck, the peeking moon and the glow of the lights lined along the docks giving way to darkness and obscurity. Ella was overcome by the sensation of floating, not just because she was tucked in Jack's capable arms, but because everything about this scenario felt like something she'd dreamed of before.

Ella strained to see through the shadows, hungry for details of the ship's vast underbelly, but Jack's familiarity made his movements too quick. It felt like they traveled through an endless network of skinny corridors and low ceilings.

Eventually, they came to the far end of the narrow passage. Jack turned to his side, nudging open the door and squeezing both of them through, careful not to knock Ella's hanging legs against the frame. Soon, a mattress gave underneath her as he carefully placed her down.

Ella leaned up on her elbows, watching Jack as he ventured to the small table to the right of the bed, lighting the oil lamp. At once it illuminated the intensity and determination of his handsome face.

Jack shrugged off his jacket, unbuttoning his waistcoat and linen shirt with impatient fingers. His gaze never left Ella. The more he stripped, the bigger he seemed to her. The room was small and tidy to begin with, spartan in its furnishings, but Jack and his composed hunger made it feel even tinier.

Grabbing the shirt from behind his neck, Jack tore it up and over his body, letting it float to the ground. Ella wondered if he could see the desire in her eyes. Did her hunger make the room seem small to him as well? Because the feelings coalescing in her body—from the soles of her feet to the crown of her head—vibrated with such stark longing that Ella couldn't stop herself from moving. She stretched her legs before curling them into her chest as she lay on her side, studying him.

It was no wonder that Jack never seemed comfortable in his coats and jackets. They stifled someone like him. His muscles were long and lean, sinewy and corded. They spoke of promise and experience. A man who could see things through. A capable man.

In the soft, faint light, his body glowed from days spent out on the water. A patch of rich golden hair covered his chest, only fading away when it was lost under the band of his trousers. He was windswept and dry, an amber gem with no polish. Jack was the whetstone, his abrasion used to sharpen others.

Ella's mouth went dry. It struck her that she'd never actually wanted to touch a man before. Yes, she'd daydreamed of men touching her, but looking back, that was a childlike, innocent notion, so very restrained and formulaic. Touching Jack like that would be blasphemous. He called for boldness.

Jack climbed on the bed. On his knees, he took Ella's hand. Chest to chest, he wrapped his arms around her, locking their halves together until their breathing found the same rhythm. His eyes were heavy as they scanned her face. "Do you know what we're about to do?" he asked.

Ella could feel herself turn red. Not sure what to do with her hands, she flattened them against his chest, surprised by how soft the tawny hair was against her palms. "In theory," she whispered, ducking her head. It was a little late for shyness, but Ella couldn't help herself. The way Jack was looking at her, as if he would utterly consume her if she'd allow it … It made her seem beautiful, desirable. Ella had never thought of herself like that before now, and it would take some getting used to. "I've never done this before. Will that be a problem?" She shook her head ruefully. "I mean, is that upsetting to you?"

Ella thought she'd hear laughter, something to assuage her enormous inadequacies. Nothing came.

Jack cupped her jaw and raised her eyes back to his. His expression was patient, his touch so very gentle and giving. "I *have* done this before," he replied. "Is that upsetting to you?"

"No!" Ella blurted, squeezing her eyes closed. Nothing was coming out right. Her voice, her body, her thoughts were all completely out of her control. She tried again, a nervous little giggle escaping her when she said, "I think I prefer it. *Someone* should know what they're doing."

The corner of Jack's mouth quirked up. His hands increased their pressure against her back and roamed up her body on a lazy path. She trembled as they ventured over the skin of her neck and got lost in her hair, picking and prodding the tight bun until it finally released, and her locks cascaded down her back. Jack's eyes flared as he buried his nose in the thick strands, his lungs expanded.

"I prefer you exactly as you are," he said, voice guttural. "And I like knowing that I'm the only man who's ever had you." He nudged her neckline off her shoulder, placing a chaste kiss in its wake. And then another. "And the only one who ever will."

Ella licked her lips, shivering as if she'd been dumped into a barrel of freezing water, but that didn't make sense, because she felt like she could combust at any moment. It was like she was in the middle of one of her fevers, out of her body, out of her mind.

And it was that idea that freed her from the torment of the unknown, the embarrassment of not living up to Jack's expectations. When Ella had been sick as a child, she hadn't been herself. Her family and doctor would tell her about things she'd said and done, knowing it was no fault of her own. It hadn't been the real Ella who was tossing and turning on her bed, mumbling incoherent, nonsensical things.

She could apply that logic now. Ella could allow this fever to rage. Let it overtake her, let it rule her mind and body this night. In the morning, she would remember that it was someone else, a different Ella. A character in a story. The woman she could only be with Jack.

Ella liked that idea. She liked it so much that she leaned into Jack, tracing her lips over his, once, twice, before canting her head and kissing him. She smiled as Jack opened his mouth on a slight gasp, then accepted his tongue like the prodigal son, home where it belonged, inside her.

"Get me out of this dress," she whispered, laughing when Jack immediately did as she instructed. He spun her around, working on the buttons, hindering his progress by laying sweet, heady kisses against her neck. Jack couldn't stop touching her. He'd unhook two buttons before his hands would slide to her front, palming her breasts through her gown, creating a delicious impatience that hummed throughout her body.

"God, I've wanted to do this for so long," he said against her ear, swiping the tender lobe with tantalizing licks, sucking on it as he pressed her bottom seductively along his turgid manhood.

Ella's mind swirled. A cacophony of sensations swarmed her as she tried to keep up. His hands were everywhere, inciting her. Inviting her. Slow as honey, measured and paced, not doing anything too quickly. Time was lost to Jack as he showered her with this new idea of wicked reverence.

"Jack," Ella said, finding his hands and prodding them back toward her buttons. His laughter was husky and devious in her ear.

"What?" he murmured.

The vibration of that one word sparked and reverberated down her body. Ella reached behind her, clasping the back of Jack's head. Twisting her neck, she caught him in a wet, open-mouthed kiss that signaled her growing eagerness.

"Fuck, you feel so good," Jack murmured. He broke free, wrenching her gown from her torso. Corset exposed, he reached inside the top of the stiff structure, palming Ella's breast, massaging it with the same erotic attention he'd paid to her hands in the carriage. She had considered that moment the most thrilling. She was wrong.

Ella fought for the words, but the more he caressed her skin, the more he pulled and plucked the tender nipple, the more fruitless the battle became. She was completely enveloped in him, covered and cherished.

She repeated his name. "Jack." It had become a benediction for her. "I want …" Ella couldn't finish the sentence. Because she didn't *know* what she wanted. Didn't know what to ask for or if she would ever find the courage to. Her body had ceased to be her own.

Jack licked the corner of her mouth, kissing a path down the length of her neck once more. With his free hand, he pulled up her skirts and explored underneath, palming the flesh above her knees before wandering north. "I know what you want," he said against her skin. "You want me to fuck you. To take you hard and fast and make you scream like the pirate you think I am. But I can't do that to you. Not yet."

Ella jerked straight against him when Jack's hand found the feathery patch of hair at the crux of her thighs. He cupped the entirety of her, rocking his hand up and down in a tantalizing fashion that made Ella's hips move in frightening, uncivilized ways. As if he were beckoning her with a hypnotic spell, her legs widened and she felt herself opening to him, inviting him to explore.

With two fingers, Jack found the seam of her sex, and he

rubbed the slick folds, all the while whispering every wicked thing he planned to do to her. "You'll only get the best version of me tonight, my love. The gentleman that you deserve. When I surge inside you, I will be delicate and careful, giving you every inch of me." His smile widened against her neck. "But don't worry. You'll still scream."

He spread her folds and dipped his fingers into her body. Ella's body tensed against the invasion. Jack bided his time, sucking on her ears more, explaining in vivid detail just how big she made him and how good it would feel when he made love to her, all while his fingers continued in their quest to make her comfortable, to help her body understand that he was the man it had been waiting for.

"Shh," Jack whispered. "Relax. I have you. You have nothing to worry about when you're with me. This is my job, Ella. Making you come. And you know how serious I take my work."

Dizzy and panting, Ella grabbed onto his promise, knowing Jack would never lie to her. She exhaled and defeated her resistance, giving more of her weight to him. Jack answered by releasing her breast and cupping her face once more, dragging it to his lips, where he filled her with his tongue, kissing her with a sweet passion that felt like a drug that Ella would never be able to live without. Still, his fingers worked her, slowly at first, and then deeper and faster. He used his thumb to circle the small, hidden pearl of nerves, and Ella cried out in his mouth, the electricity of the act staggering her so much that she couldn't participate anymore. Jack continued to hold her face, but even with her eyes closed, she knew that he watched her. Watched her open her mouth, watched her keen, cry, and shudder as something beautiful and blinding coiled and tightened deep within until there was nothing else for it to do but shatter. The overwhelming sensations sailed to every corner of her body, riding on the waves of her release.

It felt like she'd died.

It also felt like she'd never been more alive.

Limp and still in shock, Ella could only wait on her knees as Jack made short work of her clothing. With a few more flicks, he turned her to face him and slid the gown all the way down, lifting her out of it. He tossed it off the bed. Her chemise followed.

Jack's movements were still languid and unhurried, but Ella didn't think that would last. His hands shook as he settled her against the mattress. His color was high, his temples dotted with sweat as he rid himself of his trousers. Feasting on him wasn't an option. Jack spread himself over Ella, covering her completely. The soft hair of his legs tickled her calves, and his chest made her nipples pucker and strain. His size was daunting, but Ella tucked her fear away.

Jack held himself back, balanced on his elbows, but Ella wrapped her arms around his waist, pulling him closer. She wanted to feel that weight. Any opening between them was too much.

Ella's breathing had balanced out. She smiled at Jack, hoping to erase the divot that had developed between his eyes. Was he in pain? His member pulsed and throbbed between her legs as if it were more impatient than Ella. She undulated her hips and heard him hiss through his teeth. "I won't break," she teased. "You don't have to worry. I've always been a quick study. I'll catch on fast."

Jack's frown turned pensive. He smoothed the hair off her forehead, not speaking again until every last strand was taken care of. "You only have one first time," he replied quietly. "I want it to be right."

Using the backs of her hands, Ella caressed the flushed skin beneath his eyes. She had to do something. If he continued saying such wonderful things to her, she might cry. "It is right," she said, holding his gaze, "because it's you. It was always supposed to be."

Jack's expression darkened. He captured her lips for a blistering kiss, pulling her knees up on either side of him. His thrust was swift. Holding Ella's mouth against his, Jack embedded himself inside her, filling her utterly and completely.

Ella cried out. She froze from the abrupt pain, her body burning and contracting in defense. She lay underneath him, hating the way it felt like she'd been cleaved in two. Ella panicked. It wasn't supposed to be this way. She was supposed to *love* making love to him. This was supposed to be an earth-shattering revelation! Had she got it all wrong?

"Stay with me," Jack rasped, lifting himself onto his arms. He kissed the tears Ella didn't know she was shedding off her face. "Just stay with me. To the end."

Ella could only nod. But the pain wouldn't let up. It continued to throb even as Jack stayed motionless inside her. Frustrated by her poor aptitude for the act, she just wanted him to get it over with so she could fall asleep in his arms and burn this memory from her thoughts.

But Jack had other ideas. He kissed her, tugging on her lips until she giggled and kissed him back. He followed her neck down to her breasts, capturing a nipple in his mouth, swirling it with his tongue. And through all that, he kept peppering her with words. Telling Ella about the first time he'd seen her, about how hard his cock became whenever she'd scowled at him in her mother's drawing room. He told her that she'd ruined him for sherry, because every time he smelled it, he thought of drinking between her legs, eating her until she bucked and screamed.

And when Jack finally withdrew from her, Ella resisted the urge to stiffen. The pain began to ebb until she locked her arms around his middle, not wanting to endure the emptiness anymore. His body crashed into hers, creating a dance so seamless and infinite, Ella was reminded of water. They ceased to be two people. Their love, their coupling, was elemental, purely of nature. And the more she relaxed, the more she could lose herself in the transformation.

Jack rode her easy. Slow and measured, long and languid, he surged inside her each time like she was a holy site and he was making an offering. They became lost. Every few seconds one of them would blink and then they'd remember to kiss, but mostly they watched the other for changes, for insights, for details of pleasure to be stored away for future use.

Ella held Jack's head, keeping him close, fusing their souls just as completely as he'd fused their bodies.

Their love was peaceful for as long as it could be. And then it wasn't.

It was Ella's doing. She hadn't expected that spark to happen again. She'd thought this part was about Jack's fulfillment. But as his hips gained speed and he thrust between her legs, Ella's lower body pricked with knowing. Something grew. And grew and grew until her hips were pumping into his with more force and need. It couldn't be helped.

"Oh, God, Jack," she moaned. And he kissed her in response, making harsh, deep sounds in the base of his throat, also searching, beckoning for that ephemeral, cataclysmic end.

Ella arched off the bed as she screamed. Jack didn't kiss the noise away this time. She saw a pained smile before he roared his own scream, withdrawing from her body in time to spill himself in the sheets to her side. His back convulsed and swayed, all the strain and pressure seemingly evaporating as Jack found his release.

He collapsed on top of Ella, no energy to keep his weight from crushing her. She couldn't have asked for anything more. She hugged him, kissing his head when he let out an involuntary shiver as if he, too, had recovered from a fever.

Ella fell asleep thinking one thing: they'd absolved each other.

Chapter Twenty-One

J ACK JERKED AWAKE sometime near dawn. He'd been in such a deep sleep, and his body wasn't used to it. The small window in his quarters still showed no signs of light. Nevertheless, the faint scurrying of dockmasters and sailors, stumbling to their ships after a night of hasty sex, poor gambles, and sloppy decisions, alerted him that rising would be a wise decision.

He had been so excited to show Ella the *Siren* that he hadn't thought it through properly. She would naturally be mortified to slink past these scoundrels wearing her ball gown, giving every indication of what they'd spent the night doing.

Jack stretched his limbs, unable to keep himself from smiling at the memory. She would get over it. He wouldn't be apologizing anytime soon. He hadn't planned on making love to Ella, but it had been inevitable. She was his … the moment she'd glared at him.

Just like she was doing right now.

"I'm sore," Ella said, snuggling into his side, hiding the blush on her cheeks. Not *just* her cheeks. Jack would wait to tell her about that little discovery. Ella was so pale and fair that she would never be able to hide a thing from Jack anywhere in the vast lands of her magnificent body.

Fuck. Jack enfolded her in his arms, wondering if she could sense his cock's insistence. She'd just told him she was sore, and he was already throbbing against her like a young lad, so very keen and enthusiastic.

Her head popped up, her frown growing deeper. "I said I was sore!"

With a giggle, she pushed him away. Jack lifted his hands in a defensive motion, his grin as innocent as he could muster. "It's not my fault. I have no control of it in the morning. I promise."

"Then what do you do in the morning when I'm … I mean, when a woman isn't …"

Was she really asking him what he thought she was asking? "Um…" He coughed. "I deal with myself."

"How?"

Fuck me. Curious women are the devil. Jack grimaced. "I'll show you when you're not so sore."

Ella eyed him warily, and Jack was struck with her beauty once more. Her blonde hair was tousled around her head, giving her a lopsided halo. Her lips were plump and rosy, her body soft and pillowy. Her eyes warned of danger, but her light pink nipples pointed at him in invitation. Jack grazed the backs of his fingers against one, causing it to ripen even further.

Ella slapped his hand away, and he gave her a rascally grin. "All right," he said. "I could have controlled *that*."

Before she could scold him again, Jack rolled on top of her, kissing the morning drowsiness away. Secretly, he also hoped it would melt some of that soreness. The noises outside the ship clearly indicated it was time to go … but Jack could stretch it if need be.

Because he couldn't remember a time he'd felt this happy. And light. Like he could fly if he really put his mind to it. And it had everything to do with Ella. The way she'd given herself to him, trusted him to give her what she needed. Even now, she was building something wonderful inside him, something that could withstand hundreds of sieges and wars. That smile of hers—the one that said she was mildly irritated but also aroused—made him want to spill his seed inside her as well as spill his inner thoughts. She didn't make him want to be better; she made him want to appreciate who he already was.

"Tell me again. I need to hear you say it," he said, grinding his pelvis lightly against her cleft. Chagrined by his neediness, Jack lowered his head to her breasts, bestowing upon them lingering kisses, licking the swell of the mounds, one after the other in wonder.

Ella wrapped her arms around his neck. Jack's cock jerked from the possessiveness of it, the casual ownership. It amused him to think he was a horse, freshly broken. And content.

"Tell you what?" She grinned.

Jack had never considered himself so fragile before. After everything he'd seen his brother go through the past month … What he'd felt and done with Ella was nature at its most decadent, but nature was a delicate thing, needing perfect balance.

Jack's tender feelings were anything but balanced at present. The new rush of emotions left him raw, unprepared, and feeling so incredibly young.

He lifted his head from her chest. "Just one more time," he said quietly. "I need to hear that you want me—and only me."

Ella's eyes darkened with solemnity as she contemplated him. "One more time?"

Jack nodded. Laying his head over her heart, he listened as she told him the story of how she'd first met his brother at her family's ball. How she'd thought him handsome; how she'd started going to the park hoping to catch his attention. How one little comment she'd made under her breath changed everything.

It pained Jack to hear the contrition in her voice. If anything, he was used to people—women—grazing past him while latching on to Oliver. But he'd be lying to himself if Ella's story didn't affect him on a visceral level. Second place, he did not feel. But he still didn't completely feel like first.

Ella tightened her arms around him, using her nails to scratch at the base of his head. Jack moaned. If he could purr, he would have.

"Will we live here?" she asked, as if the idea had just come to her. Jack tried to read her voice. He couldn't tell if the thought excited or repulsed her.

"Do you want to?"

A thousand years seemed to pass as Jack waited for her response. When he couldn't wait any longer, he relented. "I can build you a house or buy one near your parents if you prefer." That worry of not being what a lady like Ella needed reared its head once more. "I'm not poor or homeless, you know. I've just been too busy to deal with it. I can afford any life you desire."

Ella regarded him curiously, as if she hadn't understood a word he said. "I know that." She tried to pull him back down, but Jack held firm. "It doesn't matter to me. I think living on a boat—"

"Ship."

Ella smiled. "Yes, ship. I think living on a ship with you would be the most amazing adventure. I couldn't ask for anything better."

Profound relief flooded Jack—along with annoyance that he'd turned into such a bear over the topic. He went down on his elbows, taking a piece of her yellow hair and brushing its ends against his fingers. "You deserve more, better," he muttered, lost in thought. "You were raised to want a certain life, and I won't let you toss it aside for me. You'll have that life, Ella. That and more."

Ella's expression was damn near sympathetic, like Jack had just told her that he'd had to put down his favorite horse. He didn't want her pity. He wanted her damned hand in marriage—now.

She straightened and placed a soft kiss on his cheek, and then the other, before reclining back on the mattress. "If you want to give me everything, then I'll take it. For your sake. But all I want is you, Jack. Forever."

"Only me, hmm?" He smirked, knowing full well that this

smug bravado he was showing was only for her benefit. Inside, he was nauseated with the kind of doubt that made one ill.

Ella pulled Jack down and took his mouth in a gratifying, bracing, melt-all-your-silly-fears-away type of kiss. Her lips shone with passion when she slipped away.

"Only you," she said in that lusty, low voice. Terribly suggestive.

Jack dropped his head with a groan. "I'm being ridiculous."

She laughed. "Yes, you are."

"But I'm not a duke."

"No, you're not."

"And you wanted a duke." His words were muffled in the valley of her breasts, but she heard him all the same.

Gently, Ella picked up his head until he looked at her. She was determined and fierce. She was also his. It didn't matter what she said next—nothing would change that fact for Jack. He would turn into the pirate everyone assumed he was and steal her away if he had to.

"The little girl in me wanted the duke," she said slowly, "because that was what she'd been taught to want. But I'm not that little girl anymore. I want you. Mr. Jack Sutton. But let's not forget about Lord John." She smiled shyly. "If he acts like he did last night, the gentleman can make an appearance at any time."

Jack laughed. It was laced with pain because his cock was pounding like the devil, but it was genuine. He ended the unnerving conversation with a lingering kiss.

He glanced out the window, sighing as a thin ray of light began to cut through the darkness. "We should go," he said. He tried to roll off, but Ella wouldn't let him.

"Jack," she said in that sexy little way that made his balls tighten. He closed his eyes, gritting his teeth through the discomfort. "Can I tell you a secret?"

"Hmm?"

Ella angled her lips toward his ear. "I'm not as sore as I thought I was."

LATER THAT NIGHT, Jack didn't know what had come over him. He decided to eat with the family.

Which meant he would have to use Herculean strength the entire dinner service pretending to care what his imbecilic uncles said while simultaneously acting like he didn't want to drag Ella to the nearest dark corner and ravish her senseless. It was damn near impossible.

Jack could wear a mask over his face and stuff his ears with cloth and he'd still smell the spiciness of her lovely skin, still feel the heaviness of her hair in his hands, still hear her life-affirming laughter.

He finally understood and commiserated with Adam and Eve's weakness. Forbidden fruit doomed a person because knowing something pure and splendid existed while never being able to experience it was torture of the worst kind.

But even with that dismal thought, the worst part of dinner was coming to the conclusion that Jack didn't completely hate it.

Yes, there were moments of the mind-numbingly absurd. For instance, as everyone was finishing their dessert, Ella had the ridiculous notion that Uncle Christopher should come to work for him!

Jack was struck mute, dumbfounded. Ella couldn't possibly think that just because he had encountered heaven in the ambrosia between her thighs, he would not chafe at the idea of Uncle Christopher working for Sutton Shipping.

Uncle Christopher! Who demanded a special dessert course after breakfast, lunch, and dinner, and once asked the carriage driver to take him all the way to London on a Tuesday afternoon because he "had a hankering for scallops."

But, shocking to Jack, his uncle displayed good sense. The man seemed just as perplexed by the unwanted suggestion—and the time it would steal from his schedule.

Uncle Christopher's bulbous nose scrunched up as he regretfully returned his spoonful of blancmange back to its bowl. "Nine o'clock!" he said, his voice shrill with astonishment. "In the morning?"

Jack observed Ella with avid fixation, waiting for that pleasant smile to crack. "Yes, of course," she replied, nervously shifting her eyes to him before returning them to the confused lord.

His uncle appeared to think on that. But then another question logically arose. "And I'm supposed to stay ... *all* day?"

Jack downed his glass of wine with an eye roll. "Yes, all day. *All day!* Because that's what work means."

That earned him a frown from the lady.

Jack didn't say anything more on the subject. He kept his remarks airy and perfunctory, determined to make it through the whole damn familial episode without losing his temper. Luckily there was Sonia, who was never at a loss for conversation. And Jack loved asking the girl about her time spent surrounded by artistic Italians and dramatic Frenchmen and then watching his mother shudder.

It was ... fun. Amusing. Lively. The food, the company, the conversations (most of them) were cozy. Jack hadn't felt this comfortable at this table since before his father died. It was the kind of atmosphere one could get used to. Like a comfy chair that sucked you into its pillows, making you rethink the need to ever get up.

It made one want to stay.

And then his mother had to ruin it.

Lady Evelyn's spoon landed in her empty bowl with a clink. She leaned back in her chair, patting her lips with her white napkin. Sonia, her little shadow, promptly did the same on her right. Lord Andrew, seated on her left, took the cue to finish as well.

Jack breathed a sigh of relief. *Thank fuck.* Now he simply had to sit and wait for Ella to happen upon a dark corner.

But the joke was on him, yet again.

"Oh, Ella?" the duchess said, perking up in her chair. "Oliver asked that you go to him after dinner. He's feeling so much better, and he wanted to know if you would read to him tonight. Would you mind, dear?"

"No … no, I wouldn't mind," Ella replied, gaining a wide, ebullient smile from the duchess.

Jack clenched the stem of his crystal glass and forced himself to keep his voice steady. "What changed his mind?" he asked. "Oliver has never wanted her before."

He grimaced at his mother's scowl. "That was a rather rude way to put it," she admonished him. "Apologize to Miss Ella."

Lowering his head, Jack murmured, "My apologies, Miss Ella."

"It's fine," Ella returned quickly.

"But what was the reasoning, Grandma?" Sonia asked. Jack could have kissed the girl and her limitless curiosity.

Lady Evelyn's eyes sparkled under the gold chandelier. "He just told me that he wanted her. I didn't ask why, though his memory must be returning, because he said that he knew she liked to read."

Jack placed his elbows on the table. "He said that? Oliver said that he *remembered* that she liked to read?"

The duchess flicked her hand out in irritation. "Yes," she said before hesitating. "Or maybe he said that he remembered *hearing* that she liked to read. That's hardly the point, Jack. We should take this as a sign that your brother is feeling ready to start living again. You should be thankful for that. You can get back to your boats."

She was right. He should feel thankful. But he didn't.

Sonia clapped her hands, and Uncle Andrew followed suit. At the last second, the man forgot himself and caressed the top of the duchess's hand before quickly sliding it back to his lap. Jack's mother flushed, and she angled herself away, toward Sonia, taking a shaky sip of her wine.

No one noticed. Only Jack.

He saw the whole pathetic thing.

Chapter Twenty-Two

SOON AFTER THE women retired from dinner, Jack took his leave and made his way to the library, bringing a glass of brandy with him. Along with the bottle.

He knew it was only a matter of time before Ella swept into that room, ready to make an expert decision on what to read to the duke. Did she know that Oliver preferred biographies over adventure tales? To be frank, Jack should have told her that if she really wanted to keep the duke's attention, she should read from the racing or boxing papers.

But even that annoyed him.

Because Jack didn't want Ella keeping anyone's attention other than his.

He heard her footsteps. Soft and determined, a short stride, though not hurried. Jack would know it anywhere.

Ella entered the room, making a sharp left. Jack's irritation pricked. She knew exactly what she wanted and where to find it.

He was only so happy to tell her that she was wrong.

"If you're thinking to lull my brother to sleep with your dulcet tones and a little Shakespeare, it won't work. He has never had any great affinity for the Bard."

Ella shrieked, her feet coming off the ground as she whipped around. Hand on her heart, she braced herself against the bookcase.

Jack grinned at her from his seat on the couch, taking a long drink of his brandy in an effort to stay composed. This was the first time they'd been alone since returning from London. He could probably recount the minutes if asked. Keeping a distance when no one was present to police him was remarkably difficult.

"You scared me!" Ella reprimanded him, brushing wisps of blonde hair off her face. "Don't do that!"

Jack's chest tightened. If she only knew how his cock stirred when she gave him those admonishing looks.

He hooked a lazy leg over his knee, admiring the heave of her bosom against her tightly fitted bodice. Tonight's dress was annoyingly prim, covering the pale, dreamy swath of skin that he'd licked and sucked so fully the night before. Had he left marks? Was that why the dress was buttoned up all the way to her chin?

"I didn't do anything," he replied. "I was here first. You came in and I made myself known."

Ella peeled herself off the books. "You knew I would be here."

His lips quirked. "Perhaps."

She faced the bookcase once more, tracing the spines with her fingers until she found what she wanted and slipped it from its row with a flourish. When she turned back to him, she wore a satisfied smile, hugging the book to her chest.

Jack arched a brow. "Are you going to tell me?"

"Why do you want to know?"

"I just do." He patted the cushion next to him. "Why don't you come over here and show me?"

Ella giggled. It was a short and breathy sound, a nervous reaction when danger was near.

Was Jack dangerous? Tonight, he certainly felt that way.

She shuffled toward the door. "You know I have to go. Your brother—"

"My brother can wait."

Jack watched her nibble on her lower lip and knew the war waging inside her. Ella wanted him. Jack could feel the magnetism between them, feel the animal attraction of their bodies across the staid room. The poor girl only wanted to do the right thing. Jack needed to reassure her that the right thing would always be him.

He placed his drink on the table and stood up with a sigh. He walked over to her, enjoying the way her eyes grew rounder with each of his solid footsteps.

Again, Ella backed up against the bookcase. Jack told himself to slow down; he told himself that there was no reason for such jealousy or possessiveness. But such rationalisms fell on deaf ears and a blind conscience. Because this woman was his, and everyone in their world was determined to make her someone else's.

Jack went for the book. After a mild resistance, Ella released it, and he peered at the cover. "*The Odyssey*," he remarked, unable to hide the surprise in his voice. He glanced up to find her watching him.

Ella shrugged. "I can't say it's one of my favorites …" She crossed her arms. "But it makes me think of you."

She sounded embarrassed, as if Jack had just caught her in some dark, secret act. The vise released in his chest, and he found his first full breath as it struck him that she wanted to think of him while reading to his brother.

Jack was an ass. His jealousy was mad and ridiculous. But most of all, it was childish. However, he was man enough to know it wasn't going away anytime soon. These irrational fears would stick with him the longer they stayed in this house, hiding their involvement.

Ella tried to take the book back, but Jack tossed it behind him on the rug.

Her mouth gaped. "What are you doing?"

Jack ventured to the door, closing it softly. Clicking the lock in place, he answered her, "I'm helping you."

Coming back to Ella, he reached for her face. Ella covered his hands with hers, her expression panicked. Nevertheless, she didn't push him away. "We can't," she whispered. "Not here. Everyone is in the drawing room as we speak."

Jack leaned closer, brushing his lips sweetly against her ear. "Then you'll have to be quiet," he whispered, flicking his tongue out, biting the lobe.

Ella's chest heaved; the squeak she worked so hard to temper hummed through her body. "I don't know if I can be." Her voice shook.

Jack wasn't sure if she could either, for that matter. She certainly hadn't been quiet on the ship, and it had incited him to no end. But it never hurt to *try*.

He lingered at her ear, using his nose to trace the whirling ridges. "You can because you have no choice," he continued. "You want to think of me when you read to my brother, yes?" She shuddered. "My method is much more thorough than reading a two-thousand-year-old book."

Jack lowered himself to his knees, pushing up her skirts with his hands, enjoying the instant way her body reacted to him. Ella's legs shook; the natural perfume of her sex lured him like a drug. Goosebumps erupted when he clasped her ankle and slid up her silk stockings, not stopping until they reached the promised land of milky skin. Using her skirt as a tent, Jack inhaled the heady richness, his mouth dry, his appetite whetted.

"Jack …" Ella wavered. Her hands dug into his shoulders. "I don't know—Oh, God!"

"Shh," Jack said against the soft hair guarding her core. Using the flat of his tongue, he licked the entirety of her, never knowing anything could taste so good. When her legs wobbled again, he came out from under the dress. "Don't you dare fall. You'll hurt yourself! Hold on to the damn bookcase."

For once the woman did what she was told—Ella latched on to the wooden shelves at her back. With her arms up, her chest arched out, she was the picture of a sacrifice. His very own

Andromeda. Her eyes were closed, her lips wet and pouty. The bun she wore was coming loose from being smashed up against the bookcase.

Jack cursed himself. He shouldn't have left the sanctuary of her dress. If a picture was worth more than words, this scene was a book that Jack would carry with him and read for the rest of his life.

He ducked back under her skirts, kissing the inside of Ella's thighs, tracing a path to her seam. Holding her arse, he lost himself in the act, licking and playing with her folds, using his tongue and mouth to tantalize the little bundle of nerves hidden under her hood, making her slicker.

Ella moaned from his exertions, and Jack didn't have the heart to shush her again. The erotic sounds spurred him on, making his lazy, lingering sweeps harder, faster. The more her legs shook, the more her breath pumped, the faster his rhythm, until Jack realized that he was merely trying to keep up. No longer passive, Ella undulated in his hands, rocking against his mouth, providing the beat to her need. Jack was the ship in her tempest, just trying to hold on and stay afloat.

When he felt her tighten, knowing the telltale signs were threatening to pitch both of them over the edge, Jack hopped to his feet, hiking Ella up in his arms while attempting to unbutton his trousers. In his awkward and messy movements, books fell from the shelves, littering the floor around them.

Unleashing his cock, Jack laid his forehead on Ella's, their chests expanding against one another, their faces slick with sweat. Jack's groan vibrated on her lips. "Bring me inside you, Ella," he said, his words wrecked and guttural. "I thought I could make you come on my knees, but I'm too selfish for that. I want to feel your release on my cock. I'll be better next time, I swear."

Ella's eyes flared, and her mouth opened on a gasp that quickly settled into a confident smile. Jack's neck went limp when he felt her timid hands searching for him. Tightening her legs around his waist, she righted his tip at her opening, nudging his pelvis in wanton invitation. "Don't ever be better than this, Jack," she rasped, tracing his bottom lip with her tongue. "I don't think I can take it."

Jack surged inside her. With one harsh thrust, he sheathed himself in her opening, muffling his shout in her hair. Ella molded to his body, tucking her head under his chin, where she panted and made scratchy noises from the back of her throat, biting the thin skin of his neck whenever a sound threatened to be too much.

There could be no restraint in this coupling. Ella's taste was on his tongue; her juices coated his shaft. Jack loved her with every fiber of his being …

But this was not the time for loving.

With one arm wrapped around Ella's lower back, Jack used the other to brace them against the bookcase. The weight and push of his hips kept them up and rocking as he plunged into her again and again, working them each to a nerve-shattering frenzy. Jack had never been so out of control, but all thoughts were forsaken. His body was merely a tool, used to bring her satisfaction. She climbed his body with her release, as if the very feel of the explosion made her think to fly. He was lucky she came first. Hearing her voice catch on that fateful moan, Jack felt his stomach clench, and he remembered to grab a cloth from his pocket, withdrawing from her just in time.

They stayed like that for long minutes, each recovering from the sensations, catching their breath and sanity. Ella was the one to bring him back to the present, taking his head and lifting him until they were both staring at one another again.

Jack grinned ruefully, a shyness barreling up through his wasted body. Up until then, their lovemaking had been controlled and measured, led by his discipline and experience. But there was nothing disciplined about fucking his woman against the wall. However, there was divine in the uncivilized, and Jack was positive he'd just experienced it.

Ella rubbed his hair off his face. It was unnecessary with his hair clipped so short, which made the act's intimacy even more apparent.

Righting his trousers, Jack leaned back for a quick, no-nonsense kiss that inevitably led to another, much longer one. Releasing her lips took a supreme act of will—alarming, since he could still see the tiny red marks on her neck from his wayward teeth.

"Do you feel better now?" Ella asked. Her smile was wide, her eyes knowing, and his embarrassment came back headfirst.

"Yes," Jack grumbled.

"Are we going to do this every time I have to visit your brother?"

Jack tilted his head, making a meal out of considering the question. He squinted while tucking a stray piece of hair behind her ear. "Maybe?" He laughed at his fragile ego. "Would you mind?"

Ella's smile dimmed, and she worried her lip. "Why don't we just talk to your family? I'm ready to tell them the truth. I know you're trying to protect me—"

"Shh, sweetheart, no," Jack said, wincing at the creases marring her brow. "I'm protecting you *and* the family. Oliver isn't as healed as my mother likes to believe." He exhaled, rubbing his forehead. "I'm sorry to ask this of you, but can you hold on for just a few more weeks? Please? Then the house will be so overjoyed by his recovery, they'll be more understanding of us and everything else."

Ella nodded, but he could tell she was putting on a brave face for him. Jack felt lower than a snake for causing her this suffering, especially after what they'd just shared. His throat tightened. "I promise I won't be pulling you into the library the entire time. If you're worried about that ..."

A smile tugged at the corner of her lips. "Oh, I don't think I would mind. Especially"—her pale lashes fluttered timidly—"if you do that again."

Jack's heart skipped. "That?"

A pretty flush bloomed up Ella's neck, masking his love bites, going all the way to her hairline. She looked down pointedly. *"That."*

Fuck, Jack was hard again. He had to create a rule that they could not discuss lovemaking after lovemaking had finished for at least thirty minutes—for self-preservation's sake.

"You liked it?" He already knew the answer, but he wanted to hear her say it.

Ella's neck snapped up. "Oh, yes," she replied. Her face wasn't pink anymore, more a *lobster fresh out of the pot* red. "I liked it. Very much."

Jack held the back of her neck and kissed her with all the intention and promise his body had to give. When he pulled away, Ella's embarrassment had faded enough for him to chuckle. "Adam and Eve," he murmured. And then he kissed her again, not stopping until the redness was gone for good.

Chapter Twenty-Three

ELLA'S LEGS SHOOK as she walked to the duke's room. She smoothed the wrinkles from her skirts and wiped little wisps of hair off her face. Her hand came away with a little sweat. She released a wobbly breath, trying to gain a modicum of serenity.

She wondered at Jack's behavior. Should she have been insulted by his blatant possessiveness? Did he actually fear she might spend a few minutes reading to Lord Oliver and fall back in love with him?

Back *in love*?

Ella knew now that the feelings she'd held for Lord Oliver were shallow at best. He'd been an *idea* to her. She'd used his handsomeness and the mystery and rumors he wore like a dark cloak to create a character that she'd always dreamed about.

It took Jack to show her that.

Now, he had to trust her.

Though she couldn't complain about his vigorous, thorough methods for retaining her attention.

Ella knocked on the door, opening it when a small voice told her to enter. Smells from that first, terrifying night in the townhouse smacked her in the face. The stench had followed the duke to Sutton Park. Biting and acidic, the odors burned her nose as she trod further into the dark room.

Oliver sat on the side of the bed, his arms braced at his sides, as if he'd been trying to lift himself to standing. He wore a red satin robe over his dressing gown, but the sash had been tied hastily and was threatening to come apart at any moment. As before, the light was kept to a minimum. Only one small oil lamp was lit near his bed, and it highlighted the anguish in his face.

"Do you need help, Your Grace?" Ella asked, maintaining her distance.

The duke's laughter alarmed her more than the smells. "No, no," he rasped. His arms were like sticks underneath his clothes, and his cheeks had sunken even further into his face. The duchess had said that he was eating, but Ella concluded his meals had been far from ample. His black hair had grown since she last saw him, though was still not long enough to cover the terrible scar on the side of his head.

Lord Oliver's gaze climbed to her, his expression so very bitter. "I tried to open the door myself and, well …" He lifted his arms helplessly, letting them fall back to his side with a desultory *thud*. "You see how well that went."

"It's fine," Ella replied, regretting the pity she heard in her voice. She tried again. "The doctors said that you're healing better than they ever could have believed."

The duke adjusted himself, sliding back onto the mattress. Even that minor action was a trial. When he managed to lean himself against the tufted headboard, he released an exhausted breath. "I'm a duke, don't you know," he explained. "And dukes always heal faster and better than the common man. Or, at least, that's what the doctors want to believe."

The grief that swarmed Ella surprised her; it hit her so much harder this time around. Seeing him close to death had been terrible, but hearing him speak in such a dismal, pathetic way was almost intolerable.

For long seconds, she stood in the middle of the large room, not knowing what to say. This man was used to everyone catering to him, giving him everything he wanted, filling his ear with promises and overestimations. And it hadn't been enough.

Sonia popped into her mind. The way the child had no compunction in telling the world what it needed to hear—or, at least, telling the world what she thought it should hear. And wasn't this household better for it?

Ella built up her courage. "It wouldn't hurt you, Your Grace, if you remembered that you're just a man. Healing takes time. Perhaps give it the leniency and respect it deserves, and it will do the same to you."

Her stomach clenched as Oliver's bushy black eyebrows pulled low. She tensed, waiting for him to throw her out of the room, but the edict didn't come. Instead, he brought his hand to his temple as if warding off an incoming headache.

"Sit down," he commanded.

Ella took the seat next to the bed. She did it at once, but also in a leisurely fashion that hopefully signaled ordering her about would not be tolerated. She held the book up, showing him the cover.

Oliver glanced at it from the corner of his eye and immediately sneered. "Oh, for fuck's sake. Anything but that!"

"It's *The Odyssey*," Ella said. "A classic story of man overcoming brutal obstacles. I thought you might enjoy it."

He crossed his arms with the impertinence of a child. "I have enough obstacles to face, thank you very much. I don't need to hear about that silly man's as well."

Dumbly, Ella let the book fall into her lap. Poor Homer. She'd expected more for him in this great house. "I can go look for another."

"Don't bother," Oliver grumbled. "Next time, just bring the racing papers. I'm behind on everything."

"All right," Ella replied quietly. She stared down at her lap, running her fingers over the book's smooth leather cover. After a couple more awkward, silent minutes, she got up from the chair and headed for the door.

"Wait," Oliver called out.

Ella turned to find him clutching his head again. His face was thunder as he caught her concern. "It hurts when I talk," he explained stiffly. "It also hurts when I walk and breathe. The only rest I get is from my sleep."

"Then let me go so you can get to it."

Ella attempted to leave again, but another "Wait!" kept her from getting far.

Sweat broke out along the duke's brow, and his fingers trembled against his head. Ella noticed the pitcher of water by the bed and filled the crystal goblet next to it. Sitting on the edge of his mattress, she held it out, waiting until he was ready to accept it. When the duke took it from her, she felt a fleeting sense of accomplishment.

"Thank you," Oliver said, returning the glass. Ella kept it in her lap, tapping her nails against the deep cuts in its side. But she didn't leave this time. She stayed right next to him. The man's features were haunted, his eyes ringed with dark hollows and infinite regret. Ella sensed a need in him, something that only she could provide: empathy.

Oliver laid his head back against the bed, blinking repeatedly at the ceiling. His Adam's apple bobbed alarmingly along his thin neck, like it might pop out. "I asked you here because I wanted to apologize," he said slowly. "I know you've tried to come before and I wouldn't let you—"

"It's fine."

Those emerald eyes shifted to her. "No. Everyone tells me that I have you to thank, but"—he hissed through his teeth, and Ella wondered if he was holding back tears—"I don't ... know you."

Ella's stomach dropped. Shame, unlike anything she'd ever encountered, flooded her. Even though she'd agreed to wait to tell the duke the truth, her conscience clawed at her from the inside, begging to be set free. She had to tell him the truth. *Now.* Jack would have to understand. She would make him.

"Your Grace—" She paused, waiting for her voice to catch up

with her newfound courage. "There's a reason why you think that—"

"Stop, stop," Oliver said, waving a hand between them. "You have to let me get this out while I can."

"But—"

Another impatient wave, which morphed into a pointed finger. "Not until I'm done," he warned.

Ella leaned back, squeezing the glass so tight that she worried it might break.

Oliver sighed wearily, that little exchange having eaten up so much of his energy. "I'm having difficulty remembering. Some things … little shards of time that happened over the past year. The doctors say they're coming back, but not fast enough for me." He gestured for another drink. Ella gave him the glass, quietly taking it back when he finished. "If you ask me the name of the servant who used to start the fires in my nursery when I was a child, I could tell you. Martha. But I can't remember the morning of the drive. Hell, I can't even remember the names of the horses that I drove—"

"Caesar and Mark Antony." She'd heard him scream them often enough on those Mondays.

For the first time, Oliver regarded Ella as if she were something more than a nuisance. "It would have come to me sooner or later."

Ella nodded. "Of course."

"But you … you're *not* coming to me. And the more you don't come to me, the more I realize that I might always be this way." Oliver shook his head. "No, please don't talk. Don't tell me that it's all going to work out. I have enough doctors doing that. I just wanted you to know. And that I won't shut you out any longer. I need you to help me to get better. Can you do that?"

Ella felt something graze her hand. Numb beyond measure, she realized that the duke had taken it, squeezing with what little power he had.

"*Will* you do that?"

Ella had never felt so hollow. So *less than*. And it was all her fault. She could blame her mother for starting this façade, and Lady Amelia for encouraging it, but this was all her doing.

Ella was on a horse, and that horse had bolted. Now *she* was in danger of drowning in the lake. And as she said yes to the duke and told him that she would do everything in her capacity to help him regain his health, she wondered if there would ever be a day when she believed that *she* was worth saving.

⫸⫷

THE FOLLOWING MORNING, Ella cornered Jack in the foyer before he could fly out the door. "We need to talk," she whispered, unsure of who might be nearby.

Jack's smile fell. "Can it wait?" he asked, wincing. "Sinclair sent me a note last night saying I needed to come to the office first thing. Can we talk after dinner?"

Ella rubbed her eyes. Sleep had been nonexistent, and she couldn't stop scratching her arms. Her skin felt too tight; nothing felt right. Ella told herself that she was overreacting, that everything would turn out for the best, but an unnerving sense of doom kept pricking her.

Jack swiveled his neck around them before leaning down to kiss Ella on the forehead. "I'll be back as soon as I can," he said before stealing a kiss from her lips. It was over before Ella could kiss him back. "Just wait for me."

⫸⫷

ELLA DID WAIT. For two days she paced every room in the house, but Jack didn't come. Eventually, he sent a letter saying he would explain when he returned, but he never mentioned when that might be.

Luckily, the duke didn't call on Ella during this time. She

dealt with the interminable hours of waiting by following Sonia around the house while the duchess tried out nannies, putting them through different unlikely, dramatic scenarios to see how they could cope with the colorful child. In forty-eight hours, grandmother and granddaughter had culled three, with a fourth not far behind. Even Ella had to admit the process had been entertaining, if not a little frightening.

By the third day, Ella was at her breaking point. A note from her mother provided just the excuse she needed to get out of the house and away from her overactive mind, which had begun to view the future in various shades of calamity.

On the way to the Weston townhouse, Ella finally managed to contain herself, ruminating on robust tea and Cook's famous lavender and honey biscuits. Ella would relax with her mother and let the woman harp on about all the comings and goings of the *ton*, all the drama that she thrived on and (sometimes) encouraged. Only a lazy afternoon like that could distract Ella from her doldrums and direct her attention to people other than herself.

The weight she'd carried like a pack mule felt lighter as Ella skipped out of the duke's carriage and ran up to the townhouse. Her smile was genuine when their ancient butler ushered her inside with his friendly, stoic demeanor. And the hug she gave her mother was strong and not at all forced as they came together in the drawing room before taking seats on matching rose settees, facing one another.

Lady Weston, in all her generosity, allowed Ella a solid five minutes to partake in the heavenly biscuits before the questions began. However, there was nothing relaxing about them.

The viscountess's features dimmed, her delight for the reunion fading into a businesslike intensity. "I spoke to Cordelia."

Ella's chewing slowed. "And?"

"She told me what happened after the ball."

Ella gulped the biscuit with exaggerated effort, her mouth impossibly dry. She was going to kill her sister. Of all the people in the world, why would Cordelia tell their mother about that night?

Lady Weston's mouth pinched as Ella remained quiet. "So, it's true. You let *the brother* seduce you."

Ella placed her teacup on the center table. "The *brother* is Lord John—the son of a duke, as you well know. And there was no *seducing*."

Or maybe there had been. Ella didn't know for sure. Seduction indicated something tawdry and wicked. She couldn't equate the word with what had happened with Jack.

"Son of a duke, but not a duke, is he?" Lady Weston pointed out sharply. "He's a shipping merchant. A captain. A businessman, for heaven's sake!"

"You say it like it's a disease, Mother."

Lady Weston's eyes widened, her pupils dilating until all Ella could see was black. "To you, it very well could be!" She reclined on the settee, tilting her head at her daughter. "Do you think I don't know what the *ton* says about me? What they whisper behind my back about my ambitions? Do you think I've ever cared?" She shook her head, not waiting for Ella's response. "No. Because I knew better. No one was ever going to look after me or my family better than me. And I'm almost complete. I only have my youngest, most stubborn daughter left."

Ella lifted her chin, feigning confidence. "And she is happily taken."

Her mother *tsked*, arching a brow. "In more ways than one, I can tell." Ella's mouth gaped open, but her mother went on. "Listen to me, daughter. I love you. I love you so much. When you were sick, I held your little hand, and I prayed to God to save you because I knew I wouldn't be able to make it if you left us. My beautiful little star. My tiny blonde light. You were a joy to this family, a missing piece the moment you were born. But then the fever took you. And it took *so much*. I know you don't want to believe it, but you aren't as strong as you think. Have you had any attacks since you've been away?"

Ella immediately thought to lie, but she couldn't. Her mother's shrewd countenance paralyzed her before she could try.

"That's what I thought," the viscountess said. She raised her teacup to her lips, her hands betraying a tremble. The lady placed it on the table and scooted to the edge of her seat. Her face was softer now, the natural effects of age highlighted in her downcast expression. "I know he seems like an adventure, sweet girl—"

"I love him." Ella had never said the words before. She'd assumed the declaration would make her stomach feel like it was filled with champagne, bubbles rising and popping happily inside her.

But it didn't. Not now. Not here.

And Lady Weston knew that. Ella could tell by the way her mother stared at her with fresh, aching pity. "He's an *idea*," she said. "A fantasy. But you were made to read about those kinds of lives, not *live* them. He doesn't even own a home for you. What happens if you have one of your flare-ups out at sea? Have you thought about that? Who will help you?" She pressed her hands together in front of her as if in prayer. "You have the chance to be a duchess. That is the life for you. Quiet, calm, controlled."

Ella's nose burned; tears began to pool. "Have you met Lord Oliver?" she asked helplessly. "Do you know about the life he used to lead? Because it sounded romantic in my ignorance, but now I know better. There's nothing quiet or calm about it."

"That can be his life *outside* of the home, but it won't be the way he acts toward you. A wife is afforded better." Ella could see how carefully her mother picked her words, and it made her heart shiver.

But it didn't change it. Ella loved a Sutton boy, and it wasn't Oliver.

"Will you try to stop me?" she asked, her voice breaking at the very end.

Tears were rare for Lady Weston. One didn't get as far as she had by giving everyone a front-row seat to her feelings. Nevertheless, her eyes glistened with disappointment. "No," she sighed.

"The last time I forbade you from doing something, you joined a cricket club. But I will ask you to stop and think. You're not a little girl anymore, Ella. Girls make decisions based on emotions. Women make them with their head. There's a reason why they say nothing is better than a good book. The real world wasn't made for happy endings."

Chapter Twenty-Four

J ACK COULD BARELY stand. He hadn't slept in days, ever since Sinclair sent him that dreadful letter. The *Dolphin*, one of Jack's new steam clippers making its return from Boston, had collided with a two-masted schooner as they navigated through the Thames. Oddly enough, the schooner managed to stay intact, but the *Dolphin* wasn't so lucky.

By the time Jack had made it to London, the docks were in a frenzy, every able-bodied man working together to pull sailors out of the water and salvage cargo.

And they were still at it.

It was only after Jack had made sure that each of his men had made it through safely that he finally peeked at the bottom line. Wrecks weren't as rare as he would have liked. All shipping companies took hits from time to time, but that didn't make it sting any less.

But it did mean he had to work harder.

Marching across the *Siren*, Jack barked orders as the afternoon sun beat down on his weary shoulders. His throat stung from the effort, and he took a second to recall the last time he'd let himself stop for a drink of anything. He couldn't remember. There was never enough time. The *Siren* had to finish loading and push off. Sutton Shipping couldn't sit still. Like a shark, it needed to keep moving if it were going to stay alive.

Jack tore off his hat, using it to wipe the sweat over his eyes. It was making his vision blurry. Or maybe it was the lack of sleep. All he knew was that delirium was slowly creeping in, because he looked out toward the warehouses lining the wharf and could have sworn Ella was standing there, parasol in hand, speaking intently with his business manager.

Then Sinclair turned to him, raising his arm high. When Jack continued to stare, Sinclair brought his fingers to his lips and let out a whistle that had most of the crew and dockworkers spinning his way.

Jack shook his head, replacing his hat. He hurried off the ship, never taking his eyes off Ella's apparition *or* losing his scowl.

Sinclair smiled for the first time in days as Jack approached. "Seems you've got a visitor."

Ella gave Sinclair a demure smile before turning to Jack. She was dressed in a light-blue day dress with an endless number of flounces on her skirt. She reminded him of a flower, the kind found in an open field, too beautiful to cut.

Sinclair drifted away. Jack might have said something to him; he didn't know. The effects of the past days hammered against his skull. His throat was still parched, but Jack didn't need water anymore—he just needed Ella.

The longer he stood there, the shyer she became. Ella twisted the handle of her parasol around her fingers, and it spun above her like a storm over the ocean ready to strike. "I was in town ... and I wanted to see you," she said, her voice thick. "Mr. Sinclair informed me of everything that happened. You didn't come home."

There was that word again. *Home* to Ella meant his brother's house. Jack now knew that *home*, to him, meant Ella.

"I'm sorry," he said.

She flushed. "You don't have to be sorry—"

Jack fell on her. In the middle of the screaming and hollering and ordering and catcalling and cursing that was whirling around them, Jack filled his arms with Ella. After a half-second of surprise, she melted into his embrace, resting her head in the little nook under his chin. They sighed together, exhaling deep relief.

"I was worried," Ella whispered.

"I'm sorry," Jack repeated. It was all he could think to say. He should have written a second letter. He should have explained. He should have considered her feelings.

Jack tried to stifle his irritation with himself. He would learn from this. His position came with so many unknowns, but he would have to change. He would have to do better.

But there was more to tell Ella, and Jack hated it more than he'd ever thought possible.

He drew away, keeping his arms at her hips. A whistle came from a bastard sauntering past, and Jack glowered at him until he was out of sight.

Ella let out a nervous giggle. "I shouldn't have come."

"No, I'm glad you did," he replied. "I have to tell you something. You're not going to like it. Hell, *I* don't like it, but I have to go. Only for a little while."

He rushed through the words, hoping they might lessen the bite. It didn't work. For her part, Ella remained composed and quiet as Jack told her about delivering cargo to Aberdeen, a relatively easy trip that in good weather took only a few days.

"Darby was supposed to do it," he explained, "but he broke his leg yesterday."

Finally, Ella blinked. "Was he in the collision?"

"No. The dunce fell down the stairs at a whore"—he caught himself—"tavern. Which only leaves me, at present."

Ella's lips pursed. "When will you be back?" Her voice was unbearably small.

"One week." Jack grimaced. "Two if the weather is bad."

"*Will* the weather be bad?"

"I'll tell it not to be," Jack teased, but Ella didn't find the humor. She continued to stare at him, two little divots furrowing deeper between her eyes.

She broke out of his hold. "Will you come home before leaving?"

Jack shook his head. "I *was* going to … to say goodbye to you, but now that you're here …"

Ella nodded, lowering her chin.

Why is this so difficult? Jack wondered. It was Aberdeen, for fuck's sake, not China! He'd be back before she could miss him. But that didn't make his heart feel any less hollow.

Jack curled his hand and used the backs of his fingers to caress the top of her cheek. Ella's eyes closed and her shoulders heaved. Jack studied her, sensing she was holding something back from him. There was an uneasiness in her, and it had been there before he had told her about the trip.

"Darling, did you need to tell *me* something?" he asked.

Ella's eyes snapped open. "No," she said, a little too quickly. She stepped away, replacing her frown with that damn demure smile once more. "I should go. You're busy."

"Not too busy for you!" Jack countered. Suddenly, he tore the parasol away and snatched her hand. More suggestive whistles sounded as he dragged Ella toward the *Siren*, but he didn't give a damn. He couldn't leave without getting to the bottom of this.

Jack weaved her past the dockworkers and loaders, past his nosy crew, who didn't even attempt to hide their curious expressions as he brought Ella aboard the ship and belowdecks. He didn't give one of them a passing glance, because Jack knew if he spotted one smirk or lewd gesture, he'd beat the man senseless, and he couldn't afford to do that with so many sailors on the mend.

Outside the captain's quarters, he felt her yank on his hold and say, "Stop! I shouldn't be here."

Jack did not listen. Instead, he opened the door and threw her inside the room. "*Here* is exactly where you should be, Ella."

She spun around to face him, her body vibrating. Her bonnet had come loose and was hanging half off her head. Her cheeks were flushed and her eyes brown and bright. But they were also intolerably sad.

Jack couldn't abide the distance. He came to her at once, untying the bonnet and tossing it to the ground. He wiped the stray curls off her face and then cradled her head in his hands. "I love you."

Ella's face came alive. Her features were severe as she studied him. "Why are you telling me this?"

Jack winced. He heard distrust in her voice, and he couldn't understand it. "Because I want to. I *need* to. I should have said it the night we spent here … and then every day after. And I won't make that mistake again."

But still, she remained silent. Jack had the notion that he'd just sliced open his chest with a blunt knife and must now suffer the consequences. He felt profoundly delicate, and there was nothing he could do about it. Ella was the only one with the power to stitch him back up.

She parted her lips, words coming a few beats later as if she were testing them out in her head first. "I told my mother about you today."

"Hmm." It was beginning to make sense.

Ella swallowed. "She doesn't like you."

Jack returned a winsome smile and shrugged. "Your mother is a smart woman."

"I told her I love you."

Jack's breath caught. He watched two little patches of pink paint the tops of her cheeks. "You're smarter than your mother."

"Am I?" Ella asked. Her tone was strained. A little hopeless. "Because I've given myself to a man who is not my husband. And he tells me that I should keep pretending to love his brother—"

"You know why!"

She nodded and pressed her lips together to stop them from quivering. "I need something from you, Jack. I don't know what. I don't even know what you can give me now, but I need … *something.*"

Jack yanked her toward him, enveloping her in his arms. He

held tight as the sobs came, feeling like the lowest man on earth. Because Ella was right. He'd asked for so much, and he hadn't given nearly enough. He kept his hand behind her head, smoothing her hair, ruining the careful bun until all the tresses poured down her back.

"I'll give you anything," he murmured. "I need you to know that. You mean everything to me. What do you want, Ella? All you have to do is tell me. You want a townhouse? A castle? I'll buy you the biggest you've ever seen. Everything I am, every-thing I will ever be, is yours." Jack kissed her forehead, her hair, her temples, desperately imprinting his words onto her skin, hoping they might soak all the way down to her marrow.

Ella's shoulders trembled as she pulled away. She wiped her tears with her fingers. "I'm sorry. I'm being ridiculous. I don't even know what I mean. I don't know what I want—"

"Marry me."

Ella blinked, more tears coursing down her cheeks.

After Jack had joined Callahan's crew, he'd been pressured to climb the rigging all the way to the top of the old clipper. He'd only been sixteen, and had never shaken so much in his life. But he'd done it, remaining on his precarious perch for as long as allowed, certain that he could see the end of the world from that glorious view. The wind had whipped through his hair and his clothes, turning him into another sail as the crew cheered on from below. The entire experience was exhilarating and terrify-ing. It was the first time he'd realized what it meant to truly feel alive. To be a part of something greater than himself.

Until now.

Ella's voice was soft when she answered him. But it wasn't lost.

"I would love nothing more than to marry you."

Jack tilted his head, his heart beating through his chest. "How about now?"

"Now?"

He smiled.

Ella's mouth twisted until she couldn't hold back her own. "How?" she asked.

Jack arched a brow, puffing his chest out as he raised his hands at his sides. "Did you forget that I'm a captain? And you just happen to be on my ship."

Ella laughed. "But that isn't legal, is it?"

"It is to me," Jack said quietly. "Say the words, Ella. And we'll be married from this day forth. If you want to wait for a priest and a piece of paper, we can do that too, but know now that when you leave this room tonight, in my heart, you'll be my wife. Forever and always."

Ella exhaled. Her face was impossibly open. Willing and trusting. Jack felt her hands climb his back, settling on his neck. She urged him closer, not giving up until his lips found hers. It was a tender and sweet kiss that whispered so many things, but nothing louder than *yes*.

"I love you," she said against his mouth, capturing Jack in a heart-melting embrace that left him shattered. Good intentions fled with inhibitions, and he locked her tight, claiming her lips, again and again, as passion flamed between them.

Ella walked backward, towing Jack with her. When her legs hit the bed, she fell back, laughing when he collapsed on top of her, unwilling to part for even a second.

Jack couldn't laugh. His chest hurt too much. Still fragile, he clung to her lips.

Ella's hands shook as she worked to rid him of his clothes. She was impatient and hungry, but Jack forced her to slow down. He wanted to string out this moment for as long as he could, because nothing could ever be better.

He stripped her with care, kissing every creamy piece of skin he discovered, cherishing it in the way that only he could. When Ella was bare beneath him, he imagined himself as water being poured over her body, baptizing her anew as his wife, touring her flesh like a pilgrim arriving at the Holy Land.

Ella cuddled him in her warmth, and Jack ran his fingertips

down the outsides of her legs from her hipbones down to her ankles, relishing the satin texture and the goosebumps he left in his wake.

Ella's hands curled into his back, her nails digging into his flesh while he turned to her breasts. Jack feasted on her taut nipple, tugging it between his teeth, devouring it until she let out those husky moans that drove him crazy.

They weren't in the eye of the storm—as their bodies and need became more frenzied, they became the whole storm. Ella waved and billowed beneath him, encouraging his exploration. Jack surveyed the slope of her neck, the long bones of her clavicle, the ridges and valleys of her rib cage. Her skin was slick and pink. Her tongue was restless as she captured his lips for another wet kiss that made the insides of his ears ring.

Breathless and heaving, they lost themselves in this moment, pushed by the swell of their desire to become one in all things.

Jack felt Ella reach for him, pull her thighs wider. She tightened her hold over his shaft, and his head immediately fell onto her shoulder as she guided him to her entrance.

He picked up his head to see her watching him. Eyes alight, her face damp, her features grave. Jack's cock wept as it stood poised at the threshold, but he held back. He used his entire body to rub up and down her length, sliding his cock against her folds, which grew wetter with each pass.

He chuckled, kissing Ella's desperate frown. "I'll give you what you want, my love," he murmured, tracing her heated lips with his tongue. "But not before you say the words."

Flustered, Ella shook her head. Her palms skated to his arse, and she tried to encourage him inside, but Jack was adamant. "Say … what …?" she asked.

Jack invaded her mouth, sinking his tongue inside before pulling away. But not far. His words vibrated against her lips. "Say that you, Miss Ella Chesterfield, take me to be your husband, to have and hold"—pulling her hands above her head, he twined their fingers together—"through sickness and health, from this day forward." Jack rocked his pelvis against her again, eliciting a harsh gasp. "Say it."

Ella locked her eyes on him. She licked her lips. "I take you, Lord John Alexander Sutton, to be my husband—"

Jack thrust inside her, biting her shoulder as she cried out. He angled his head toward her neck, waiting … not moving.

"To have and to hold," she continued, breathless, "through sickness and health, from this day forward."

Something inside Jack snapped. He straightened his arms at her sides, bracing himself as he pulled out of her tight passage only to surge into her again. His strokes were long and hard, lingering and sharp. He rode Ella, hiking her knees along his hips, driving into her, trying to reach her very center.

Ella cupped the side of his neck as she met his strokes, using the strength of her hips to copy his rhythm. "Tell me," she said, leaning up to place the command on his lips like a kiss. "Tell me."

Jack's body was lost to him, his mind even more so, but his heart was alive and listening. His heart knew exactly what Ella demanded of him.

He careened into her as he repeated the vows. The bed squeaked, their lower bellies slapped as he pumped and filled her with his commitment. Worshipping her with his body. "I, Lord John Alexander Sutton, take you to be my wife. To have and to hold, through sickness and health, from this day forth."

Jack couldn't wait any longer. Ella's telltale noises in the back of her throat warned that she was at her limit. Her walls pulsed and vibrated, quickening against his sensitive flesh as her back arched and she screamed. Jack wrapped his hand behind her head, picking up Ella until their noses touched. He used her breath to feed his own. "I will love you as no man has ever loved a woman. This, I pledge."

Then Jack let the water take him, and he relented to the abyss.

Chapter Twenty-Five

ALL THE WAY to Sutton Park, Ella worked on the speech she would give to Lady Evelyn about returning to her home. She and Jack had discussed that it might be easier for her to wait for him there, away from the pressures of his family. But the closer she came, the more she recognized how silly she was being. Lord Oliver had asked for Ella's help in his recovery. She couldn't leave without seeing it through.

Her days settled into a comfortable pattern. Ella spent most of her mornings with Sonia and Lady Evelyn as they navigated their never-ending hunt for a proper nanny, and in the afternoon, she met with Lord Oliver.

What they did was entirely dependent on how he was feeling. Sometimes, the duke pleaded with Ella to entertain him while reading the racing pages (which she begrudgingly did), while other times, he had the energy to leave his room. The first week was spent trudging up and down the hallway, regaining his strength and balance, and by the second, the duke was confident enough to navigate the stairs. Those days left him depleted and irritable, but Lord Oliver couldn't hide his pleasure at finally making progress.

Ella had to admit, the duke was the perfect companion for those who wanted to keep their minds busy. She rarely had time to worry about Jack even as the days dragged on. Lord Oliver was as entertaining as he was wicked. One of his favorite ways to pass the time while roaming the halls was to tell Ella about all the times he and Jack got into mischief when they were younger. Unfortunately, most of them involved tormenting their poor uncles.

Ella did not love the duke, but she did grow to genuinely like him. He was friendly and carefree, quick with a quip or a naughty joke. He was the kind of man who never said what he meant and never meant what he said. Ella's head always felt like it was spinning whenever he was near. But not in a romantic way, more like the way one felt when a misbehaving toddler came to visit.

At first, she had been apprehensive when Lord Oliver insisted that Sonia accompany her on her visits. In her eyes, the child seemed an exact replica of her biological father, just with a warmer complexion. But nothing paternal ever came from him as he teased and laughed with the girl. Soon, Ella understood that Lord Oliver was a man who enjoyed being around other people. He thrived on amusing them with his clever wit. He thrived even more on shocking them.

It was not lost on the duke that he'd been given a second chance. And Lord Oliver was keen to take it. Headaches still plagued him, and his nights were more restless than not, but a silver lining wasn't as far out of sight as he'd once believed. Ella had worried that the duke would ask her questions about their previous relationship, in hope of sparking his memory; however, those questions never came. He was too mired in his present, driven by his future. The past didn't seem important. When Ella proposed that Lord Oliver reach out to his old friends, inviting them to Sutton Park, he quickly closed down, his hand immediately retreating to his scar. The duke still wasn't ready to rejoin Society, not willing to do so, he said, until he was back to the man he was before the accident.

Even though Ella considered the duke a true friend, she hadn't the heart to tell him that that man might never return.

Lord Oliver had been through too much. He'd faced true struggle.

But she remained patient, optimistic. The man was finally taking steps toward reclaiming his home and birthright. She couldn't ask for more, especially when she remembered that it had taken Odysseus—the greatest hero of his age—far longer.

ELLA DIDN'T NOTICE the knock on the door.

In the drawing room waiting to go into dinner, she was mid-belly laugh. Uncle Christopher was delighting the group with a perplexing story about his first (and only) day working for Sutton Shipping. It seemed the poor man wasn't aware that there was such a thing as a work *week*, and he had been mighty put out when Mr. Sinclair sent him a letter the day after his first, inquiring of his whereabouts.

Lord Oliver, fully clothed in a jacket, cravat, and trousers for the first time in months, threw a tortuous look at his uncle, putting the room into hysterics, made worse by the friendly argument that ensued when Christopher attempted to defend his ignorant position. The duke eviscerated all points—with an insouciant smile on his face, of course.

However, Ella *did* notice when a grim-faced Carlisle entered the room, telling the duchess she was needed.

And the entire party fell completely silent when Lady Evelyn's scream rang out moments later.

Ella rushed into the foyer, stopping short when she spotted Mr. Sinclair, looking ashen and lost as the duchess sobbed against him, smacking her fists against his skinny chest.

"I'm so sorry. I'm so sorry." He kept repeating himself in a low, monotone voice that sounded nothing like him.

Ella's throat tightened, but she couldn't understand. As the scene played out in front of her, she couldn't shake the feeling that it was all a ruse, a theater act between amateurs—one with too much emotion, and one with too little.

Quietly, the duke walked past Ella, steady and stoic, as if his accident had never occurred. His shoulder brushed hers as he went to his mother. Crying out, the duchess turned to her eldest son. She clawed at his jacket for purchase, but her hands trembled too much. She collapsed to the floor in her pile of skirts, which had only started to be more colorful. A cane hit the ground, and Ella watched as Lady Amelia came up behind her. She knelt by her daughter, cocooning her in her thin arms.

Mr. Sinclair held out a letter to the duke before wiping his eyes behind his glasses. "It was a storm," he said in that odd tone, void of inflection. "Off the coast of Aberdeen. The men tell me that he was the last to flee, wanting to help everyone else first."

Lord Oliver kept his head down at the letter. "Did his body make it to shore?"

Mr. Sinclair sighed, his chest trembling. "No, Your Grace. He wasn't found. The sea is merciless."

The duke lifted his gaze from the letter. "So I've heard." Lord Oliver folded the paper with painstaking care and placed it in his inside pocket. "Edward, Christopher, Andrew? Help Mother and Grandmother to their rooms, please."

The men hurried to do as their nephew asked, their trembling hands the only signs that they were as affected as everyone else.

Mr. Sutton found Ella. His large eyes seemed imploring, almost like he was begging for forgiveness. But Ella just shook her head. What did all this *mean*?

The atmosphere appeared final. Something terrible had happened, and now … that was it. Lord Oliver had taken the news and hidden it away in his pocket. It was over.

A pain Ella had never experienced before wrenched her insides. The certitude of it tore at her. The idea that there was nothing to be done. Because *it* was done.

Jack was done.

Her breathing came on fast. Ella clutched her chest, her heart beating too quickly and shallow to be of use. She reached for the banister, hanging on the newel post as her legs lost their strength. She heard the duke's deep voice as he thanked Mr. Sinclair for coming. She felt the uncles shuffle by with the sobbing women. She heard some of the doctors—she didn't know how many—clear their throats as they watched this intimate scene from the periphery.

And then she heard Sonia.

The little girl's head was bowed, her hands closed into fists at her sides, as if she wanted to crush the overwhelming sadness before it had a chance to crush her.

That tiny, quaking puff of a cry broke Ella from her misery, and she scooped the girl up into her arms, holding her head against her shoulder.

Sonia cried on that shoulder as Ella climbed the stairs. She'd never know how the strength came to her, but her feet never stumbled. Her body didn't crumble once on the way to the little girl's room.

A maid looked on while Ella placed Sonia on her bed, swiftly joining her. She pulled the covers tightly over them before encapsulating the girl once more in her solid embrace. Ella didn't know how long they stayed that way.

Minutes or hours later, Sonia's tears slowed enough for her to lift her head out of the safe cavern of Ella's neck. Her small body shuddered from all the tears still waiting to fall.

"Do you think it was Charybdis or Scylla who took Jack?" she asked, her desolate voice ragged with emotion.

Ella stared into Sonia's innocent face, thinking of all the loved ones who had been stolen from the young girl—her mother, and now Jack, a man who wasn't her real father but wanted to be. She'd been cheated.

Ella caressed Sonia's hair off her face, urging it back on the tear-stained pillow. She gritted her teeth to steel her voice as she replied, "To keep him from you, it could only have been both of them."

She'd wanted to say "us."

Because Ella had been cheated as well. But she was the only one who knew it.

She held the girl long into the night, soothing her chills, humming through her tears, keeping the shadows from sinking their claws in too deep.

And finally, when Sonia's body couldn't take it anymore, it relaxed in its grief enough to fall into the sweet respite of sleep.

Then, and only then, did Ella fracture into so many pieces that it would be impossible to count. And she cried for Jack. Her husband. Her true love.

And the reality she'd tasted that must now go back to being just a dream.

Chapter Twenty-Six

GRIEF IS A devious thing, unnaturally smart. It waits. It plots. Patience is its tool. Dominance is its reward. For the uninitiated, it might seem careless or indifferent, but like a lion it can sit for days, biding its time for the perfect moment to strike. The moment of least resistance. The moment when a person is at her weakest but too busy pretending otherwise to know it.

That was when grief found Ella.

For days after the news, she ran herself ragged inside Sutton House, reacting to everyone else's sorrow. Her mission was to keep Sonia diverted, spend countless hours walking outdoors, and making sure a maid was there to take her place when she was called away.

Ella's sanity balanced on a tightrope. Her mind was at the razor's edge. But she couldn't stop.

She sprinted from Lady Amelia to Lady Evelyn, providing companionship for the women who had taken to their rooms. Ella told herself it was easy, since they didn't wish to speak; they used her because being alone was too much to bear.

Ella bore it.

And when the women used laudanum to drift off, Ella sat in the drawing room with the uncles, who'd commandeered the space to stay drunk and tell stories about their puzzling nephew.

With glassy eyes and slurred voices, they laughed about the impolite and prideful ways he'd treated them—while toasting to his adventurous spirit.

Ella knew they meant well. But she listened to their stories wondering how three men could know someone his entire life and never really understand him.

Lord Oliver was the only one who didn't need her. He hunkered down in his room once more, his doctors the only people admitted, and not very often. She contemplated knocking a few times but eventually decided to leave him to his gloom.

By that point, Ella was slowing anyway. Grief's tentacles were slinking around her on all sides, threatening inch by inch.

Until one day it happened.

Ella woke up and decided not to get out of bed. The result wasn't worth the effort. Her limbs felt like they'd been filled with lead, but her heart and head were impossibly empty. Food and drink didn't interest her. Neither did walking, nor listening to more badly recalled stories. She shivered uncontrollably while saturating her clothes with sweat. The blankets provided her only comfort, because they weighed her down. Like water rushing overhead, they dragged her deeper into the ocean.

It reminded her of the thought she'd once had about drowning, wondering if she was worth saving.

In the end, Ella just closed her eyes, helpless to stop it. Maybe she didn't even want to.

ELLA'S FEVER RAGED for days. In her erratic dreams, her parents came to her, clasping her hands to their chests, praying loudly in case the Lord was distracted. They talked to her, endless conversations about their family's happiest moments: her father teaching all of his daughters to fish in the country, Alexandra's first ball, Suzanne's first jump with her favorite horse.

Their descriptions became more vivid and frantic as they pleaded with Ella to remember.

Ella tried. She told them—shouted at them—that she was trying. But nothing worked. Nothing flickered inside her. Pain and regret and hopelessness trumped all.

And then she was floating. Riding. Sailing. Her head in her mother's lap, her feet curled in her father's. For a short time, the smell of decay and sorrow were gone. Lemon and lavender permeated once more. The sun's tendrils soaked through the curtains, creating magical dust motes dancing around the room.

Ella's room. Her childhood room. The room she'd slept in before.

Jack.

She remembered. But she didn't want to remember.

So she slept more, imagining herself with pale-white skin and ruby lips, encased in a glass coffin. It was comfortable being tucked away. Safe. And there she would wait. Until everything was different.

⟫⟫⟫⟪⟪⟪

A WEEK LATER, Ella's eyes creaked open. Her mouth felt like it had been stuffed with cotton; her throat burned. She was like a wet rag, soaked and wrung tight, and left out into the sun to dry.

She rubbed her fingers back and forth against each other, hating how sensitive the smooth skin was to the touch. She recognized it immediately. It had always been there to welcome her after she came out the other side of one of her fevers. It made Ella feel like she had shed her skin while she slept, and now she was a new person, forced to learn everything all over again.

A knock came to the door, and Cordelia sailed in, a tight smile on her face that fell the moment she saw that Ella was awake.

She stopped at the foot of the bed, her hands on her hips,

reminding Ella so much of their mother. "It's about time," she said, feigning irritation. Even in her wooziness, Ella could see the relief shudder over her frame. "You've had us worried. How do you feel?"

Ella's movements were sloth-like as she scooted herself higher on the headboard. Her muscles ached with disuse. "Tired," she groaned. "How did I get here?"

Cordelia tilted her head, her eyes narrowing. "The duke sent a letter after you became sick. Apparently all five of his doctors said that traveling would do harm, but Father wouldn't listen. They brought you home at once."

"I'll have to thank the duke," Ella said.

Cordelia nodded to the side table. "He's written every day. He's anxious for news."

Ella stared at the letters piled neatly in a stack next to a glass of water. "I'm sorry I scared everyone."

"Oh, Ella," her sister sighed, rounding the side of the bed. "It wasn't your fault. It wasn't anyone's fault."

That brutal, hollow feeling planted itself inside Ella's stomach once more. Her lips quivered. She bit them to get the words out. "Did he tell you ... about ...?"

Cordelia's lashes lowered. "Yes. We heard about Lord John. I'm so sorry, Ella. I know you'd come to care for him."

Ella grimaced. She scooted away from her sister, the events of the last few weeks rushing to the forefront of her mind. *Come to care ... come to care ...*

Again, Ella realized that her grief could never be shared. She'd have to see her way through it on her own. And though that thought made her even more exhausted, it didn't terrify her as it once might have. Because if anything, Ella was good at being alone. At least then she'd been safe with her books and daydreams. It was only when she'd allowed herself to believe in building a family that everything had gone awry.

She should have listened to her mother.

Cordelia's expression grew more and more worried. She

glanced at the door, and Ella was certain her sister would call for their mother any second. "Don't," she warned, giving Cordelia a pointed stare. "I don't want to talk to anyone right now."

Cordelia's frown deepened. She contemplated Ella for long seconds, before finally retreating from the bed. Her voice was lofty and light as she took her leave, saying, "We're here if you need us, Ella."

But Ella didn't need anyone.

And that belief flourished as the days dragged on. As did her bitterness. Ella's health improved, but her heart didn't. She hid in her room, pacing the carpet to while away the hours until falling into more depressive sleeps. She did manage to respond to Lord Oliver, thanking him for his attention. She asked about Sonia and the others. But she did not mention Jack. She couldn't bring herself to form the letters of his name, afraid that just seeing them might give her hope for something that would never be.

The duke surprised her by writing back the following day. And the next. His letters started to come as faithfully as the sun. It wasn't like before. He wasn't using Ella's pleasing nature to distract himself from Jack, as his mother and grandmother had. Ella sensed that Oliver saw these letters as a medicine of some kind. A tether—however small—holding them to the world. She wasn't sure if the medicine was for him or her. But, in the end, she could only assume that they both benefited.

Days and weeks passed with Ella keeping mostly to her room. Her mother, although worried, remained patient. She appointed herself to bring the duke's letters to Ella every afternoon, pocketing the small smile Ella gave her as a reward and a sign of better times ahead.

Ella allowed her mother to dream, but she knew better. Lord Oliver would recover, as would his family. He would carry on and marry and produce his heir, and a new generation would start all over again. Nothing as important as a title depended on Ella's future, and that reminder served her well. It meant she could mope and cry and hate the world and its callousness for as long as she liked.

However, some people weren't known for their patience. Some people couldn't be kept out, despite Ella's protestations. And a day came when she met her match in stubbornness.

There was no tentative knock on the door this time.

Ella was seated in her rocking chair in the corner of her room, a copy of *The Odyssey* in her lap. She'd been torturing herself, tracing its cover with her fingers, daring herself to open it.

Without warning, the door eased open, and the book fell out of Ella's lap as she shot out of her seat.

"Oh, good, you're alive," Lady Everly remarked dryly, regarding Ella from the threshold. She hitched her chin in the air before she stepped into the room. "By what Cordelia told me, I had my doubts."

Ella sputtered, unable to form words as her cricket club friend meandered around the room. Lady Everly's mouth remained flat and tight, her posture straight and unyielding while she inspected the stagnant life Ella had created within these four dour walls.

When the lady came to the bedside table, Ella saw her glance at the letters from Lord Oliver, staring at that spot a half-second longer than she had the others.

Ella willed herself to speak. "D-did Cordelia ask you to come? She shouldn't have done that."

Lady Everly waved her hand dismissively. "Your sister has done only what a sister should do. Do not blame the woman for loving you too much. Besides, it wasn't only her. I reached out to your older sisters as well. They said your illness had passed, but … something was still wrong."

Ella felt that old irritation surge. Again, her family thought they knew what was best for her, regardless of what she said. "They shouldn't have alarmed you. As you can see, I'm doing much better."

She lifted her hands to punctuate her bold words, but Lady Everly's unimpressed stare forced her to wrap her arms across her chest instead. Ella changed tack. "You've also been ill, I've heard."

A shadow fell over the lady's face before she could blink it away. "I was, yes," she replied stiffly. "I received some terrible news and stayed at my brother's home while I recuperated. It … affected me more than I'd expected."

If Ella could understand anything, it was that. "But I see you're better now."

Lady Everly smiled. "Yes, thank you."

Ella entwined her fingers nervously, thinking of things to say. She was out of practice with small talk. It dawned on her that she'd never entertained a friend in her room before.

"My mother shouldn't have brought you here," Ella said. "I could have met you in the drawing room."

The lady tilted her head swiftly, the blue feather in her bonnet wobbling. "Would you have? From what I've heard, you haven't left your room in days … weeks."

Shame burned Ella's cheeks, but it only fueled her anger more. "Is that why you've come, to deride me? Let me guess, Myfanwy ordered you to chastise me for missing the last few practices?" She turned her back on her friend, facing the window, finding solace in the muted scene. It had rained all morning, and black umbrellas peppered the sidewalk. "Tell her that I don't care. She can replace me. Please, *ask* her to."

Lady Everly chuckled, surprising Ella. "Oh, I won't be doing *that*. You can handle that on your own. Besides, Myfanwy's a little busy at present."

Ella glanced over her shoulder with a questioning look.

"She delivered her baby. A week ago. Jennifer told me. Said she named the baby Grace"—Lady Everly's lips quirked—"which I found oddly fitting for a daughter of hers."

Ella clasped her face, overjoyed and overwhelmed by the news.

"It's amazing, isn't it?" Lady Everly asked softly. "How life persists even when all else feels lost?"

Ella's hands fell from her face, her shoulders slumping. "I don't know," she replied wearily.

Lady Everly followed her to the window, flicking the lace curtain aside to peer out into the street. "I met Lord Oliver and his brother when I was very young. Did you know that?" she said, ignoring the hitch in Ella's breath. "I couldn't stand them at first, especially Oliver. Even for a duke's heir, he thought too highly of himself. But Jack"—a faint smile curved her lips—"he was more palatable, if a little too serious. I remember this one time when he decided to build a fort out in the woods of my father's estate. We all helped at first, me and Ollie, but soon we grew tired and bored, as most children do. We retreated to the house for biscuits and forgot about the whole thing. Much later, I walked back out to the woods to see what he'd accomplished. And he was still there! *So* intent. *So* focused. He simply wouldn't stop until he finished what he'd promised. Even at thirteen, I remember thinking about the man he would become, the passion he was capable of."

"Did … did"—Ella's throat tightened—"did you love him?"

The lady's eyes widened. "Jack? Good Lord, no. To be honest, he scared me a little with his quiet, brooding stares."

Ella smiled, seeing the young Jack as the lady described him. All long limbs and forbidding features, keeping everyone from his fort until he'd made it perfect.

Her stomach fluttered at the picture, and though it still stung and made her want to crawl under her sheets once more, it wasn't intolerable. She could handle it.

Lady Everly extended her arm, as if to pat Ella on the shoulder, but she quickly thought better of it and returned it to her side. "Yes, well … I just thought … I don't know what I thought." Frowning, she spun to leave, making it halfway across the room before hesitating. Confused, Ella watched the lady take a deep breath before turning back to face her. The brackets around her mouth deepened, and she sighed as if debating whether she wanted to say more.

"What is it?" Ella asked.

"When my husband died, I was miserable and lonely. And

that quickly gave way to anger and pain. After a time, I was so tired of feeling everything and anything that I just gave up. I chose to avoid it and ignore all the messy emotions plucking at my insides." She touched the brim of her bonnet, making sure it was still at the proper angle. "And that worked for a while. I was able to go outside again, meet with people without losing control and falling apart."

Ella's heart stalled in her chest.

Lady Everly continued. "But that made everything worse. Because that numbness bled into the rest of my life. I couldn't smile or laugh; I couldn't find joy anywhere. Hiding pain is just a way to keep it with you, safe and locked deep within. But there's no containing it, and soon it festers and spreads until there's nothing left." She winced. "The only way to heal is to feel the pain. You have to accept it, move through it. It's terrible; I can't lie to you. You'll want to die time and time again, but then … one day you'll wake up and the first thing you think about won't be how miserable you are. I promise you, Ella. All you need to do is get up. Every day. Again. And again. The rest will take care of itself."

Ella didn't have the energy to wonder how Lady Everly knew about her and Jack. Nor did she have it in her to be furious at Cordelia for probably telling Lady Everly. And she definitely didn't have it in her to hide her emotions from her friend.

Her vision clouded with tears as she covered the choking sob from her mouth. "What if I can't? What if I'm not strong enough?"

No one ever described Lady Everly as a soft woman—but that didn't mean she couldn't be. "You are. You just don't know it yet."

Chapter Twenty-Seven

THREE WEEKS AFTER Jack's death, Ella walked out of her parents' townhouse into Regent's Park. She couldn't hide any longer. And Lady Everly had been right—Ella hated every minute of it. She felt like Sonia on her first day at Sutton House: the sun was too warm, her clothes were too tight, the people walking past her smiled too much. But she felt a smidgeon of accomplishment as she retired to bed that night—she didn't force the pain away, though she did force it to share its space.

Then she woke up and did it again. And again. Venturing farther into the park and further into her old life again.

Determined to make amends with Myfanwy, Ella stopped dragging her feet and paid a call to the new mother—and spent a surprisingly happy afternoon watching how quickly and fully her cricket club captain had fallen in love with her baby daughter. Though it couldn't have been difficult. According to Myfanwy, Grace was the most beautiful, most wonderful, most intelligent baby that had ever been created.

Ella was enraptured enough to agree.

Of course, Myfanwy being Myfanwy, the blessed baby wasn't the only thing she was proud of. The Matrons had insisted that the annual match keep its date, despite Grace's delivery, which would leave Myfanwy unable to attend, since she was expected to stay home for a few more weeks, recovering from childbirth. But that would not do. Over a very stressful few days, she'd renegotiated with the club, delaying the match by another month.

Ella glanced at Myfanwy's husband while his wife recounted the stress. Eyes glassy from exhaustion, and with a face that hadn't been shaved in days, Samuel appeared ready to topple over at any minute. Ella wondered how much of that exhaustion was from the new baby, and how much was from Myfanwy's drama with the Matrons.

"Can you believe them?" she asked Ella while gazing lovingly at the baby girl in the crux of her arm. "They thought they would use my sweet, precious Grace against me. Ha! I would never allow that! They will simply have to wait." Her confidence faltered. "I still won't be able to play, but at least I can be there … to provide moral support."

Ella nodded. Myfanwy's moral support usually included a lot of frustrated yelling, but Ella was glad for it. Cricket wouldn't feel the same without Myfanwy there obsessing over it.

Later that night, Ella managed to get back to her room before the tears fell. It wasn't that she wasn't ecstatic for her friend, but seeing her profound contentment with her husband hit a nerve inside, reminding Ella of everything she'd lost. It had been a difficult day, but again she accepted the small win. She could have stayed inside, could have ignored Myfanwy and her new child, pretend the birth had never happened, but she hadn't. And just as Lady Evelyn had told her, she became stronger for it.

The following week, Ella started her morning as she did most others, crossing into Regent's Park just as the sun was climbing into the pale-blue sky. It had rained the day before and the grass appeared to be tipped with tiny, sparkling diamonds, and Ella had to watch her steps as she steered around all the puddles along the walking path.

She craved these mornings, when it felt like she had the entire park to herself. She didn't have to worry about keeping a pleasant expression on her face or pretending to be happy when she wasn't. She could just *be*. It was freeing.

But it never lasted. Slowly but surely, the park became lit-tered with fellow wanderers, and after a solid hour of exercise, Ella directed her feet home. She had the exit in her sights when a figure gave her pause.

Lord Oliver paced near the gates, dressed in a fine black jack-et and overcoat with a blue-and-green waistcoat peeking out underneath. He spotted her standing frozen on the path and tipped his top hat with a bashful grin.

Ella didn't have to try for a smile. She gave it willingly to her friend as she strode toward him, taking in all of his changes. The duke had put on much-needed pounds. His cheeks had more color, and his hair was filling in nicely from what she could see under his hat, even hinting at his previous curls. His smile was as audacious as ever, though Ella could sense a caution inside his deep-green eyes that hadn't been there before.

"Your mother said you'd be here," the duke said, his voice a little too high, betraying his nervousness.

Ella couldn't account for it. She eyed him curiously, wonder-ing if he was worried that he might run into someone he knew. "I like the quiet," she answered.

He nodded. "Yes," he said, pointing to his head. "I never knew it was such a luxury."

"Are the headaches still bad?"

"No, no, nothing I can't handle," he replied. "I can even listen to Mother and Sonia bang away now without fearing I might get sick. They're overjoyed to have a new admirer."

Ella laughed as the duke did what the duke did best: he re-galed her with stories of the family, humorous little snippets that he'd already written about in some of his recent letters. She was grateful for the meeting, but wondered about his true intention. It wasn't abnormal for Lord Oliver to ramble on, though it was odd when he did it with no sense of where he was going.

As he was winding down an anecdote about Sonia's new, fierce nanny, Ella couldn't contain her curiosity any longer. "Did you need something from me, Your Grace? Is that why you came here?"

"Ugh." He frowned. "Don't call me that. Not you."

"All right, then," she said slowly. "What do you want me to call you?"

His broad shoulders shifted; he gazed down at his feet. "Oh, you know, what everyone else calls me ... Oliver, Ollie ..." He tilted his head to her, his smile adorably sheepish. "Husband. We are engaged, aren't we?"

Ella's knees shook so much that she had to lock them straight. She could barely believe it. The Duke of Winchester was in front of her, staring at her with such blatant hope. For a fleeting second, Ella let herself get caught up in it. There was nothing stopping her from giving in to this temptation. Because he was a good man. A kind man. Marrying him would keep Ella from being alone; she could help raise Sonia and laugh with the duchess and place blankets over Lady Amelia whenever she fell asleep in her chair by the fire.

And through it all, Ella would always be reminded of Jack. And she would die little by little each day.

"Oliver ... Ollie," she said. "I can't marry you—"

"Oh, and why not?" He chuckled. "Because we were never engaged to begin with?"

Ella jerked back. "How did you ..."

"I think I've known for a while," he said, his tone unbothered, an attempt to reduce the sting. "Those damn doctors were right. I pay them enough for it. Everything *did* start to become clearer—everything except you. No matter how hard I tried."

Ella stepped toward him, the shame tearing at her. "I am so, so sorry, Oliver. You have to believe I never meant for any of this to happen."

He held up his hand, cutting off her pleas. "I don't need an apology, not after everything you've done for my family." He squinted. "But I wouldn't mind an explanation. Start from the beginning."

Ella gave him everything and more. She told him about hiding from him at her parents' ball, and then all those early Mondays. She told him about the accident and her verbal blunder, and how Jack had brought her to the townhouse, suspicious the entire way.

And the more she explained, the less weighted down she felt. Her conscience had been overwhelmed for so long that she'd forgotten what it felt like to be free of the nagging guilt.

When Ella finished, Oliver ruminated for longer minutes. His brows began to slant, and she worried that all of her talking might have encouraged one of his headaches.

The duke slid off his hat, twirling the brim round and round in his hands, instantly reminding Ella of Jack. The pain was instant and acute, and it consumed her ... until it left.

"Are you all right?" she asked.

Oliver's jaw tightened as he nodded. "Thank you for telling me that. It all makes sense now."

Ella continued to watch him. Her legs continued to shake, and she feared she might teeter over.

Oliver's expression was rueful as he raked his hands carefully through his short hair. He pointed his hat at her. "But that doesn't mean we can't still be married."

Ella caught herself in mid-teeter.

The duke went on, gaining speed. "I've thought a lot about it, Ella, and I think we match up well—*better* than well. I'm a new man with you, and I don't want to go back to my old ways. If there's anyone that can handle me, it's you. You could be a duchess. I would take care of you, give you everything you've ever wanted."

Ella shook her head, squeezing her eyes shut for a moment. "But I don't want anything, Oliver," she said carefully. "And I don't want to *handle* you."

He ducked his head, scowling. "That's not what I meant. You have to understand. I feel like my life is this puzzle and you are the missing piece. You can keep me on the straight and arrow.

You can make me the man I need to be."

Ella almost got sucked in again. To his promises, his eagerness, to his lovely green eyes. But his comment ate at her conscience. She'd heard someone use it before with her … being a piece to someone else's puzzle. Ella didn't want to be a piece in someone else's story. Not anymore. Lady Everly's acuity struck her once more. Two months—maybe even two weeks ago—Ella might not have had the strength to pass up this opportunity. But she did now. It had been growing inside her, callousing over the jagged cuts of loss. Marrying Lord Oliver would undoubtedly be an adventure.

But it wasn't the adventure she wanted. Ella didn't know what that looked like anymore. But she would use her newfound strength to recognize it when it came. And it *would* come.

"You're going to say no, aren't you?" he asked.

Ella grimaced, nodding.

Oliver nodded back, taking her reply with astonishing grace.

"You don't love me, Oliver. And deep down, you know that," she said. Ella walked to him, placing her hand over his heart. "And I don't want to make you into a different man. You're exactly the man you're supposed to be, and …"

"And you love Jack."

Ella pulled her hand away, but Oliver caught it, placing it back on his jacket.

His sad, knowing expression caused her lips to tremble. "I can't stop loving him." Her voice hitched. "Because I still feel him like he's still here. I'm sorry, but I can't—"

The duke tugged Ella into his arms, wrapping her in a bear hug. She sobbed against him, her shoulders quaking from the release of someone else she had kept inside too long. And she was grateful.

"I'd never ask you to," Oliver whispered in her ear as he continued to hold her.

For as long as Ella needed.

Chapter Twenty-Eight

JACK STALKED THROUGH the wharf, avoiding the shocked glances thrown his way. He could deal with curiosity, even confused gawks, but he couldn't abide the frightened confusion lining some of the faces. Like Jack was a ghost. Like he wasn't real.

He yanked his jacket lapels higher up his neck. What he'd been through had been real enough.

Jack was no stranger to devilish storms, but the one he'd battled outside Aberdeen would have made Poseidon run scared. In the last month, he'd had plenty of time to wonder if he could have done anything differently to change the course of that terrifying night, but he'd come up empty. When it came to brawling with the sea, sometimes you won, but most times you didn't.

And as Jack had flung himself off the *Siren* before the waves and rain could drag him down with it, he'd assumed that that had been it. He'd lost. Fair and square.

Even after he'd miraculously found a flat piece of detritus and held on for dear life, he'd known the end was near. With chattering teeth, he'd cursed the storm for hours before resorting to prayer, asking the Lord to provide Ella with the life that she deserved. Asking that maybe she keep a small place for him in her heart.

But the Lord was busy that night. Or just in a peculiar mood. Because Jack didn't die.

The following day he was fished out and carried aboard a whaling ship on its way to the Orkney Islands. The crew had been just as shocked as Jack was that he was still breathing after hours in the tumultuous Black Sea. And they were even more so when he was still alive the next day.

They'd left him in Stromness, beaten and battered, homesick and depleted. But incredibly determined. Jack waited two weeks for a ship to stop at the remote island. Luck was with him when a Hudson's Bay Company ship made port for supplies before finishing its final leg to London. Filled with a wide variety—from Canadians to Americans to Orknians and British—the crew was only too happy to show off their bountiful furs and pelts from their latest expedition and explain, in minute, grisly detail, how they'd trapped every last one. The ship delivered Jack to England six weeks after he'd left it—four weeks after he'd been declared dead. All in all, the journey back home had been comfortable and, more importantly, uneventful, though if pressed, Jack could have done without most of the Americans.

He marched into Sutton Shipping Company and found Jeremiah Sinclair seated at his desk, scribbling away as always. He was struck with an immediate pang of relief, grateful for life's tendency to not give a damn and always move on.

At the noise, Sinclair continued to look down at his ledger, but the pencil dropped from his fingers. Slowly, he brought his head up, blinking his huge eyes behind his round glasses. And then he smiled. "I knew you couldn't stay dead, Jack Sutton."

Jack grinned as Sinclair leapt from his chair, hauling him in for a hug that had him balancing on his tiptoes.

Sinclair pounded him on the back countless times before finally letting him go. "You're too skinny," he remarked.

Jack laughed. "What do you expect? I had to swim all the way back."

Sinclair *humphed*. "You swam, did you? So that's what took so long." He shook his head. "You pirates and the tales you tell …"

"And I'll tell you every single one later, my friend." Jack gave his friend a pointed look. "But I have some things I have to do first."

Sinclair nodded, catching his meaning. The men had known each other for too long to stand on ceremony. "Of course, of course," he said, pushing Jack back to the exit. "Get out of here. Go shout to the world that the mighty Jack Sutton has returned from his watery grave."

Jack grimaced, hesitating with his hand on the doorjamb. "Watery grave? I thought you'd have more faith in me than that."

Sinclair's expression fell. He paused, taking off his glass to rub his eyes before continuing. "What did you expect us to think, Jack? Some of your crew from the *Siren* made it to shore. They told everyone how quickly the storm had come over the ship. How catastrophic it had been." He sighed. "They said surviving was impossible. Not overnight in those waves."

Jack forced a wan smile, uncomfortable with the tilt to Sinclair's shoulders, as if the man had been bearing too much this last month. "Well, I did. And things are going to get back to normal. I promise."

He slapped Sinclair on the back, almost popping his glasses off his nose. The business manager poked them back in place with his finger before distressing Jack again with a pensive, hesitant look.

"What?" Jack snapped, chagrined by his loss of control.

Sinclair's mouth hardened to a line. "It's just … I had to tell your family. I was there. I saw what it did to them. To your mother … to Ella."

Jack's chest squeezed. There hadn't been one second throughout this ordeal when Ella hadn't been on his mind. Hearing someone else say her name out loud made him miserly, as if her name only was his to utter.

He flexed his jaw impatiently as he waited for his friend to finish his thought.

Sinclair went on. "The women collapsed and were taken to the rooms, utterly heartbroken. I swear to you, Jack, if someone told me they were still sleeping, I would believe them."

Jack nodded, resisting the pain that gnawed at him. The pain that *he'd* caused. Unconsciously he reached to twirl his earring, but found his earlobe empty. He remembered that he'd given it to the trappers as payment for taking him home.

Sinclair smiled, reading his mind. "You going to stop to get another one? Maybe a hoop this time. You actually seem naked without it."

Jack tried to laugh, but he couldn't make the sound. "I'm not a pirate, Sinclair. I'm a damned gentleman. I should remember that more often." He glanced over his shoulder, a smile finally finding his lips. "And I have a lady I need to wake up."

⇶⇷

EVEN WITH ALL the annoying looks Jack had received on the wharf, nothing came close to the disdain Ella's mother directed at him from her front door. The butler hadn't allowed him to come inside, and neither had his mistress. Something about his smell— which Jack had to admit, wasn't great.

Nevertheless, he suspected there was more to it.

"My daughter is not here," Lady Weston stated firmly, tipping her nose so high, Jack wondered if she could even see him.

"Where is she?"

"I'm not sure."

"When will she be back?"

"She didn't tell me."

Jack closed his eyes, praying for patience. Biting this woman's head off wouldn't help his cause. He needed her to like him—for Ella's sake.

Lady Weston's scowl could have sparked a fire. At this point, Jack would probably have to settle for the lady tolerating him.

"Can I leave a message?" he asked.

Lady Weston tapped lightly against her temple. "You can try, but my memory isn't as good as it used to be."

Jack shook his head with a bitter laugh. She was being impossible. And he wasn't exactly sure why. "Well, since we've met before, I assume you know that my name is John. It's short. Four little letters. Shouldn't be too difficult. However, if it is, it's no matter. I will return tonight. Thank you, my lady. Good day."

Jack turned with a grunt and was halfway down the porch steps before she called out, "Please don't!"

He twisted back to see the lady leaning on the side of the door, gripping the lace at her neck. Her face was blotchy, her eyes panicked.

Jack sighed, climbing the steps once more. "Don't what?"

Lady Weston pursed her lips. The disdain had gone, but it was replaced with something that Jack couldn't read. Fear? But what did she have to fear from him?

"Don't come back," she replied. "If you care about my daughter at all, you'll leave her be—"

Jack cut the space between them with one stride. "I love your daughter more than you'll ever know."

"Fine," the lady said, her voice oddly contained. It stunned Jack, because he knew her confidence came from the total belief that what she was doing and saying was completely right. "If that's true," she went on, "then you will listen to me now. Whatever happened to you out there, it almost killed my daughter. She was ill, and even when she recovered, she wouldn't leave her room for days and even weeks. She'd thought you were dead, and it made her want to follow you."

Lady Weston pushed away from the door, her chest nearly hitting his.

"But do you know who *was* here? Your brother. He writes to her; he walks with her. I know that he wants to marry her. He can offer her the life that she deserves, that she needs. You can't with all your roving and wandering and ... *ocean*. Ella is fragile.

She needs a house, her friends, her books. You don't have those things. So please, please, Lord John or Jack or whatever you call yourself, leave this house and never come back. Stay lost before you drag my daughter down with you."

Jack stared at the woman as she pleaded with him. Her lovely eyes were marred by anguish.

The urge to hate her was palpable. Because Lady Weston didn't know him. And she *certainly* didn't know her daughter. However, she did love Ella. And Jack could understand that. He took a moment, cataloging all the information she'd just fed him and allowing himself to forgive her. The lady didn't know this (and Jack certainly wasn't going to tell her now), but they had a long road ahead dealing with one another. Grievances couldn't be kept alive.

He cocked his head, scratching underneath his chin. "My brother accompanies her on walks?"

Lady Weston blinked. "Y-yes. He left his family at Sutton Park and has been spending more time in Town."

Jack nodded. He had so much yet to say. Explanations and apologies. Words pricked at the edge of his tongue.

But in the end, he only said one thing before going on his way.

"Hmm."

Chapter Twenty-Nine

JACK POUNDED ON his brother's door, shoving the butler out of the way the moment he gave him an inch. He snaked through the house, searching each and every room until he finally came upon the duke in his study.

Jack's fist was locked. He spotted his brother behind his huge, shiny desk, as if his accident hadn't happened, a drink in his hand, and he snapped. Jack wound his arm back to strike. Oliver didn't even have time to shout as Jack launched toward him.

Jack would relish the crack of flesh, the pop of bone beneath his fist. He hadn't punched someone in so long. It would be so delightfully cathartic. Until his attention got snagged.

That long and winding scar on Oliver's head screamed at him to halt. The pitiful thing was still pink and puckered, made even more visible by the fact that Oliver's curly black hair tiptoed around it as if reluctant to storm into its territory.

Jack's fist faltered, his intention abandoned.

His anger forgotten.

Oliver opened his eyes, his face still clenched in a wince. He released a stream of breath. "Christ, Jack. What a way to make an entrance."

Jack couldn't explain it, but he found that remark absurdly hilarious. Laughter escaped from his tight chest before he could stop it. He leaned back against the wood-paneled wall, giggling helplessly.

When his breath came back to him, Jack lifted his weary head. "Always good to see you, brother."

Oliver lifted his cut crystal glass to Jack. "And you," he replied. His eyes were shifty, wary, as if he still didn't believe Jack was in front of him. "Help yourself to a drink. Something tells me you deserve one."

Oliver attempted to stand, but he quickly fell back to his seat. Jack wanted to give him the benefit of the doubt and assume his accident was the cause, but he knew better. This wasn't his brother's first drink of the day.

Jack frowned at Oliver's glass. "I thought the doctors told you to give that a rest."

Oliver grinned, but it didn't reach his eyes. "Oh," he drawled, "you know what they say about old habits."

"They die hard."

"Unlike you, it seems."

"Believe me, the sea tried hard enough."

Oliver chuckled, leaning forward. "Tell me everything."

Jack shook his head. If he did that, he'd be stuck there for days. And he had come up with a laundry list of items he needed to complete before the day was out. "Later," he said. "First, you're going to tell me about Ella."

"What about Ella?"

Jack's fist started to itch again. He pushed his anger down. "You can't have her. She's mine. My *wife*."

A shadow passed over the duke's face, but he reclaimed his insolent expression. "That's funny; she never mentioned anything."

Suddenly, Oliver's scar didn't look so bad to Jack. It could certainly take a punch. "We have an ... understanding."

Oliver rolled his eyes. "Oh, I see. Christ, Jack, you couldn't bother to find a church before having her—"

Jack smacked the glass out of his hands. Crystal shattered

against the wall, dotting the carpet with tiny, shining pieces. Oliver regarded the mess with a frown, blowing out an exasperated breath.

"How fucking dare you say that to me after everything I did for you!" Jack seethed.

Oliver hopped from his chair, only to fall back again. "You stole my fiancée!"

"She wasn't your fucking fiancée, you stupid, spoiled arse!"

Oliver grimaced, jerking back as if the words had been a strike. He took a moment to right himself, folding his arms on the desk with careful, calculated precision. "And what about my daughter?" he asked quietly. "Are you going to deny that you stole her?"

Jack stumbled away like he'd climbed to the top of the rigging again and Oliver was the wind. "It … it wasn't like that."

"What was it like, Jack? Tell me," Oliver said, bitterly calm. "Did you think I wouldn't know? Did you think I wouldn't find out? No offense, brother, but you're not exactly the opera type."

Jack flailed. The decision had made so much sense to him at the time. Why was it so difficult to explain now?

"*Talk*, goddamn you!" Oliver boomed.

Jack's head wouldn't stop shaking. He dropped his gaze to the floor. "I didn't know what to do. The orphanage contacted you … Father had covered it all up—"

"Don't blame Father," Oliver cut in. "This was *your* decision! I can't blame a dead man."

"I know. I know, Ollie," Jack snapped. "But I didn't know if you were going to pull through, and I saw that little girl and wanted to give her a life, a real life."

"And you didn't think *I* could do that?"

Jack matched his brother's glare. "I didn't want her to be just another duke's bastard."

Oliver slammed his hands on the desk and came to his feet. "That wasn't your fucking decision to make. And you can't have her now. You would know that if you ever listened to me."

"What are you talking about?"

"That day," Oliver replied. "When I was on the stairs. I saw her. Even in a fucking state, I knew. It was immediate. Christ, Jack, she looks exactly like me. I told you she was mine."

Jack's mind was wrenched back to that day. He'd been so tired. He remembered picking Oliver up and returning him to his room. He remembered how hot and skinny his brother had been in his arms as he uttered those words.

"I thought you were talking about Ella. I thought …" With a curse, Jack ran a hand over his haggard face. "I thought I was doing the right thing. I'm sorry, Ollie."

Oliver squinted, giving his brother a long stare before eventually relenting. He tripped back into his seat. "I'm sorry too. About Ella. If it's any consolation, I didn't know she was truly in love with you until *after* I proposed."

Jack snorted. "I appreciate that, brother." He paused. "Wait, you fucking *proposed*?"

Oliver waved his hand in the air. "Don't worry; she refused. Said she would never stop loving you, or something just as saccharine."

"Good." Jack stretched his neck back and forth. And then he did it again. "So, are you going to tell Sonia, or am I?"

Oliver leaned back in his chair. "Don't look at me. You created this mess; you fix it. You *are* a lucky bastard, though. She'll be so excited to see you alive that she won't be able to stay mad."

Jack laughed. "There is that … there is that."

Oliver regarded him cautiously, growing serious. His sarcasm had played itself out. "You know, you could go back with me tonight. To Sutton Park. We could tell her together."

Jack nodded. He appreciated the subtle rebalancing of power. Oliver would always be the duke. And Jack would always not be. But they would forever be equals. "I will. *We* will," he added. "But I need your help first. That's why I came here." He tilted his head. "Well, I came here to punch you. And to show you that I'm still alive. And *then* ask you for help."

Oliver opened his arms wide and stacked them behind his head. "Jack Sutton, asking for help? That's impossible. What could I have that you don't?"

Jack scowled at his brother's theatrics and then winced. "A house."

Chapter Thirty

E LLA SWIRLED HER fork around her plate, shoving the roasted capon from side to side. With one ear, she listened to her father drone on from the head of the table, happily detailing his uneventful day, which, to Ella's mind, involved too much time at his club.

She was well aware that she wasn't being fair to her father, who had given her an abundance of affection and attention throughout her childhood. But lately, these moments came when she just felt so intolerably vexed. The forks and knives scraped too loudly on the china; the servants' shoes scuffled the floor too much as they brought the food up from the kitchen … Everything was just too quiet and measured, which made the atmosphere seem impossibly loud.

"That's all very riveting, dear," Lady Weston told her husband, pausing to chew her meat. Her gaze flickered to Ella. "Ella looks very pretty, doesn't she, Henry?" she asked, smiling at her daughter so intensely, Ella couldn't find her eyes. "I think you've finally put on the weight you needed. Your cheeks aren't quite so pale anymore."

Lord Weston blinked at his daughter as if studying her for the first time. "Ella always looks pretty," he answered matter-of-factly, before returning to his food.

"Oh, I know!" his wife replied with a little laugh. "I just think that whole nasty fever business is finally over and done with." She pointed the tip of her knife at the ceiling. "Onward and upward, as they say."

Ella returned a wan smile, giving her mother just the encouragement she needed to continue.

"I didn't see Lord Oliver here today. Did I miss him?"

Ella shook her head. "No."

The viscountess desperately tried to moderate the intensity in her voice. "That's too bad. I was growing rather used to his visits. And I can tell how much he adores walking with you."

Ella rolled her eyes, placing her fork on her plate. She tucked her hands in her lap and faced her mother. "He's only done it twice," she replied tartly. "It's hardly a routine."

"But it *could* become a routine," Lady Weston said. "And wouldn't that be lovely?"

Ella received no satisfaction out of hurting her mother, which was why she stayed silent in the face of her enthusiasm. Her mother's poor hopes would be crushed soon enough when Oliver started showing interest in a new, pleasing young lady. Ella would deal with her then.

Lord Weston thumped his wine glass back on the table. "That reminds me," he said, picking up his knife once more, "the duke's brother, you know, the one who everyone thought had died at sea ... well, apparently, he's *not* dead! It was all anyone could talk about at the club today. Someone saw him walking around Mayfair this morning, right as rain. Or something like that."

The floor dropped out from under Ella. She gripped the edge of the table, her knuckles going white from the effort. Jack was alive and in London?

She shook her head. Her father must have heard wrong. It wouldn't be the first time.

"What did you say, Father? You didn't mean Lord Oliver's brother, did you?"

"The very one," he replied, distracted by a pea that wouldn't stay on his fork. "He owns the shipping company, correct? Lord … John?"

Ella nodded.

Lord Weston stabbed the pea with the fork, pointing it at her with relish. "Then *that's* the one." He bobbed his head, tickled by the fact that he'd been the source of worthwhile gossip.

Those tiny champagne bubbles were back, popping inside Ella's stomach. She released her hold on the table, staring at her plate in wonder. Everything seemed so much brighter, more brilliant. The carrots had never been more orange, the peas never more succulent, the capon's skin never more crisp and buttery.

She could hardly stay in her seat. Her chest threatened to burst; she needed to dance. She needed to sing. She needed to find Jack—

Her mother's knife screeched across the plate as she sawed through her little chicken. "Yes, I know, dear," she said evenly, giving her husband the same smile she'd just given Ella, albeit more strained.

"You *know*?" Ella snapped. "What do you mean, you know?"

Lady Weston wouldn't raise her head. She focused on cutting everything on her plate. She wasn't even taking bites—just cutting and cutting, again and again, until the food was reduced to little bits of unrecognizable clumps. "I mean, I saw him."

"What do you mean, you *saw* him?" Ella's tone was so severe, Lord Weston straightened away from his plate.

Lady Weston huffed, finally dragging her attention away from her slaughter. She tilted her head at her daughter petulantly. "I mean he came by today. You weren't home."

Ella's stomach dropped. "Well … is he coming back? When?"

Lady Weston shrugged through her growing agitation. "He didn't say."

"Where did he go?"

"I don't know."

"How did he look?"

"I don't remember."

"Mother!" Ella slammed her hands down on the table and lifted herself to standing. "What. Did. You. Do?"

"Nothing!" her mother cried, glancing at her husband like she was begging for reinforcements.

Lord Weston got the hint. "Ella, sweetheart, sit down. What's gotten into you?"

Ella hissed out an exhale as she reclaimed her seat, but continued to shake her head. She ignored her father's question and snatched up her knife and fork. "Were you *ever* going to tell me?" she said, digging her knife into the capon. Limitless amounts of nervous energy coursed through her, encouraged by raging, maniacal anger. She had to do something. So she sliced a piece of the chicken and shoveled it into her mouth. Chewing felt good. It was a tangible release of her frustration and hurt.

"Of course I was going to tell you," Lady Weston said breathlessly. "Honestly, Ella, you act like I kept this from you on purpose."

Ella arched an eyebrow at her food, too busy working on another bite to look up at her mother. "Oh, I *know* you were keeping it from me."

"Ella!" Lord Weston barked. "Do not speak to your mother that way." He turned to his wife. "I know you think the fever is over, but I'm not so sure."

Ella chortled, forking more food into her mouth. "I'm not ill," she said in between chews. "I'm *upset* because Mother treated the love of my life like a dog at her door. The poor man has survived the impossible and come all the way back to me, and he's still not good enough for you."

Lord Weston threw up his hands. "The love of your life? Lady Weston, what is she talking about?"

"Nothing, dear."

Ella glared at her mother. "Don't you say that. Don't you hide what you've done. *I love him.* I will always love him. You said you wouldn't stand in my way. Why did you do this?"

Lady Weston watched helplessly as Ella added another piece

of meat to her mouth. "Ella, slow down," she exclaimed. "You need to calm yourself. I'm not standing in your way. I'm just asking that you rethink it … What about the duke?"

"I don't want the duke!"

Ella's attention flicked to the hallway. She thought she'd heard something—men's voices—but her mother wasn't finished arguing her side.

"I would just like you to give him more of a chance—"

Ella could no longer contain her fury. "I don't have a chance to give. I love Jack. I want Jack. And if you won't give us your blessing, then I'll—"

She stopped, dropping her utensils. They clanged against the china as she grabbed her throat. She tried to swallow, but something was stuck. Ella breathed, but she couldn't get any air through. Her body panicked. She jumped to her feet, knocking her chair over. She leaned over the table, coughing and hacking, doing anything to get the food dislodged, but nothing worked. Her parents crowded around her, patting her back, screaming for help, urging her to keep trying. Her father hacked at her shoulder, but all it accomplished was shoving her hips into the sharp edge of the table.

She clawed at her throat. Her vision swam. Her head became fuzzy. She stumbled into a wall … and the wall moved.

Ella looked up to see what was in front of her, and only had a second to realize it was a person before his hands spun her around. Three sharp *whacks!* hit her back right in between her shoulder blades, loosening the clog in her throat at once.

Ella heaved in a massive breath, spitting the capon onto the table as her industrious mother threw out a linen cloth to cover it. Ella couldn't stop coughing. Her throat felt stretched and fiery. Her lungs ached from the pressure. All eyes were on her as she settled herself, her chest heaving from the frightening episode.

And then everything went quiet.

And her parents weren't looking at her anymore.

Slowly, Ella turned around to find Jack standing behind her, his hand still palming her shoulder. She blinked, wondering if she'd died and this was heaven.

But then she saw Oliver, with his relieved, roguish grin, step out from behind his brother and knew it couldn't be.

"Are you all right?" Jack asked. Ella was still lost in her fog. She stepped away, and Jack dropped his hand from her shoulder.

"Well, we came right in time, didn't we?" Oliver announced, sharing an awkward chuckle with only himself.

Jack frowned. "Ella?" She couldn't stop staring at him, marking all the little differences she could find. His blond hair was longer. His stark face was skinnier. He desperately needed a shave. And his ear—

"Where's your earring?" Ella blurted, fighting away the tears that had already started to well.

A reluctant smile curved Jack's lips. "I had to sell it."

Ella was having a hard time following him, which made the tears impossible to stop. "What do you ... what ...?"

He pulled her into his arms. "It's all right, Ella. I'm here. I'm not going anywhere."

Ella melted into him, filling himself with the musky pine smell that she'd thought was gone. He rocked her gently, his hand on her back, the other behind her head. And all the while her skin hummed with the budding awareness that this was real. Jack was truly holding her.

She heard someone clear his throat. *Oliver.* She glanced over her shoulder to see him stride toward her father. "And how are you, Lord Weston? How was your summer?"

"Oh ... ah ... very good," her father stammered, no doubt uncomfortable with his daughter being held so familiarly by a young man in the middle of his dining room. "And yourself, Your Grace?"

Ella giggled from the absurdity.

If nothing else, Oliver knew how to be diverting. He kept up a steady flow of conversation while Ella regrouped.

When her tears waned, Jack released her slowly, his expression still stony and cautious. So very Jack. "I'm sorry," he said quietly. "I never meant to hurt you."

She reached out to his face, trailing her fingers from his temple all the way down to his jaw. "Is it really you?"

He nodded, his Adam's apple bobbing over his necktie.

"I'd hoped for so long …" Her voice broke.

Jack captured her hand. "I love you," he murmured. "And I plan on doing it for a long time, sweetheart, but I think now I better speak to your father. Can you let me do that?"

Ella laughed, nodding as she turned to the group, fiercely gripping Jack's hand.

"Father? Mother?"

Jack stepped forward, granting her parents a sharp, perfect bow. "Lord Weston, may I have a moment of your time?"

Ella's father looked hopelessly adrift in his own home. "Oh, yes, that would be fine"—he glanced at his wife—"I think?" Lady Weston gave him a stiff nod. The viscount turned back to Jack. "We can go to my study or—"

"Oh, I think we're past privacy, don't you" Oliver quipped with a grand smile. "Let's stay here. We're already so cozy."

Jack shook his head at his brother.

Lord Weston was no match for the duke. "That's … all … right …" he replied, though it sounded more like a question. Lady Weston rolled her eyes, nodding again.

Jack lowered his chin. "My lord, I am here to ask for your daughter's hand in marriage—properly." Ella squealed. He gave her a bashful smile before continuing. "I came to know your daughter while she lived at my brother's estate. Very quickly I realized that she was everything I could ever want in a wife. She is beautiful and kind and intelligent. She's the kind of person that listens, truly listens." He paused. "Now, I know you had better people in mind, and I don't blame you for that. But no one will ever love Ella more than I will."

Jack's cheeks ballooned as he blew out a breath. Ella grinned, wondering if he'd ever said that much at one time in his life.

As they waited for Lord Weston's response, Oliver claimed the floor and slapped a folder across Jack's chest, forcing him to catch it before the contents scattered. "Ah, yes," Jack added. "I know my lack of home ownership has been an issue in the past, but my brother can confirm that I purchased two townhomes this afternoon: one right next door and the other a little farther down on the crescent. Both have sizeable libraries. The people currently living there said they could be out as soon as needed."

"The Earl of Braintree? Out?" Lady Weston gasped.

Jack grumbled, "My brother thought it showed excellent taste."

"The plasterwork was phenomenal," Oliver assured the room. "Truly master craftsmanship. First rate."

"What?" Ella squawked. She dragged Jack into the corner as Oliver detailed the homes to her very avid mother. "I thought we were living on your ship?"

Jack's eyes turned down. "Sweetheart, the *Siren* is gone."

"I know *that*," she said. "But a different ship, *one* of your ships. What happened to that idea?"

"I'm trying to give you a life, Ella. A solid, respectful life, one that you deserve."

"I deserve you!" she countered. "And you're not going to stick me in a house while you go off to sea. I won't do it. My place is with you!"

"Who said anything about sticking you anywhere?" he exclaimed. "We'll live in it together. And when I have to be at sea, you'll come with me there, too."

But Ella wasn't hearing him. It all sounded so final. So tame. "I won't have you giving up your passion just for me. First it was the earring, and now it's being a captain—"

"Will you forget the damn earring?" Jack barked. "I'm not giving up anything. I'll still sail, but not as much. Sinclair's been after me for years to stay on land and"—his mouth twisted as if he'd swallowed a nail—"*mingle*. I've put in my time. And now all I want is to make you happy. I deserve that."

Elle's neck wilted from the sweetness. She knocked her fist lightly against his chest, pouting. "But you're a pirate at heart."

Jack chuckled. "Maybe so, but I'm also my father's son. And I can't make him proud by running myself to death."

Ella's argument faltered. "Will you at least consider another earring?" she asked.

"Whatever you want, sweetheart." He towed her back to the group.

"It should be bigger, shaped like a skull or pirate's chest!"

"Of course," he said, grinning. "Anything else?"

Ella looked at her parents, who were completely in the duke's thrall. Oliver commanded their attention, making her father laugh and her mother shriek with joy. But Ella wasn't fooled. She saw the glint in his eye. He loved it just as much. Oliver was in his element, flirting with Lady Weston over expensive wine, delighting her with his good taste and flair for just about everything. The lady's excitement matched his own. In fact, Ella realized, her mother was getting *too* excited.

By one property in particular.

Ella adored her family and was thrilled to combine it with Jack's. Loneliness would be a faint memory. But there could be *too much* of a good thing.

Ella twisted to Jack, capturing his head with her hands. "We are *not* choosing the townhouse right next to my parents. Hmm?"

Jack smiled and, despite their audience, swept in for a long, passionate, promising kiss. "I couldn't agree more, my lady. I couldn't agree more."

Epilogue

L ADY JO EVERLY hung in the shadows outside the servant's
entrance. She pulled her hood longer over her head.

It was late. The moon nestled behind the plummy clouds in
the coal-colored sky and animals she dared not imagine skittered
about in the many crevices behind the massive townhouse.

But she knew the butler would be awake. Hazard of his trade.
Though the man he served was altered, the butler's habits could
not be. Being ready at all hours—especially the late ones—was
what the position called for. And Carlisle had served the
Winchester family his entire life. He was one of the best for a
reason.

Which was why Lady Everly only had to knock once—and
only lightly—before she could hear the footsteps marching on the
other side of the door.

Nevertheless, as good as Carlisle was, even he couldn't hide
his surprise when he came upon her face that evening.

"Lady Everly," he said, quickly regaining his composure.
With supreme effort, he un-furrowed his brow. "It's … ah …
well, it's late."

"I'm well aware of that," she answered readily.

The firmness in her tone helped to settle the butler's apprehension. He pulled his shoulders back and lifted his chin. "He is

not expecting company, my lady."

At the mention of Oliver, Jo's confidence began to falter. It had taken her days—weeks—to muster the courage to come to this place, and now all she yearned to do was flee back to the safety of her home, locking her heart back behind the bars she'd caged it in all these years.

But she'd come this far …

Jo stepped around the butler, entering the kitchens. Even though everything was cleaned and put away for the night, the warm smells of spices and baked bread twisted her stomach in knots. It smelled like a home. A home that, at one point, she had been sure would be hers. *Theirs.*

Jo shoved the emotions to the far reaches of her mind and turned back to the butler. She smiled, but knew it was weak. "The duke hasn't expected me for quite some time," she said evenly.

Carlisle shook his head, his expression painfully hopeless. "My lady—" He hesitated. "He's not well enough for visitors …"

Jo ignored him, making for the stairs. "Oh, come now, Carlisle," she tossed over her shoulder. "When have I ever been a visitor?"

EVEN IN THE moonless night, Jo found the room easily, remembering which step squeaked, which floorboard groaned. Carlisle followed her the entire way, but he gave up trying to stop her. He remembered too.

This time Jo didn't knock. From what she'd learned, Oliver wouldn't answer anyway. All of London was talking about it. The headaches. The opium. The changes in the man who used to be the life and breath of every *ton* event. The way he'd hidden away like some monster in the attic. A fairytale prince who'd angered the wrong witch and now had to live out his existence as some horrid half-thing.

Jo crept into the room. Behind her, Carlisle sucked in an anxious breath, but instead of scaring her, it incited her to go on and close the door after her.

Goosebumps immediately erupted under her layers of clothes. The room was freezing, with the long, heavy curtains swaying fitfully against the half-open windows.

Jo's nostrils itched from the colliding smells. Caustic and sterile metallic scents mixed with sweat and the fruity hints of wine. Sure enough, Jo spotted an empty bottle on the table near the bed, along with a smaller amber bottle next to it. She didn't need to guess its contents. For years, her mother had used opium to find sleep. Most of London used the miracle cure in one way or another.

But Oliver hadn't. Not until now.

Jo had waited long enough. Finally, she let her eyes venture to the body lying motionless in the bed. Her hands clenched at her sides as she took him in. It had been months since they'd shared a space, and she had to stifle a sob as she witnessed all that had changed in him. He'd lost so much weight. The bedding covered him like a shroud, seemingly pressing Oliver into the mattress. His face was gaunt, the skin pulled tight and waxy along its many angles. His eyes sank deep into their sockets, giving him a skeletal effect that came close to breaking her.

But it was Oliver's hair that proved to be her undoing, yanking the sob from her throat. Jo had heard the doctors had shorn it away to ascertain the damage to his skull, but knowing and seeing were two different things. Oliver appeared so young and fragile lying there in front of her. He'd believed himself to be invincible. He'd been so sure of himself that Jo had believed it as well.

Slowly, she reached out toward the jagged scar on the left side of his head but stopped short of tracing the horrid mark. Inky hair sprouted at its edges, but like stubborn grass that wouldn't grow in certain spots, it refused to hide the craggy wound.

Jo stumbled back. The ground started to waver under her

feet. She was off balance and the small amount of food she'd forced herself to eat earlier in the day threatened to come back up.

She'd told herself she could do this, but she'd been wrong. It was too much. Too soon.

But then it hit her, and Jo righted herself instantly.

Oliver had always been too much, too soon. It was what had made them perfect for each other. It was also what had ruined any happiness they could have had together.

Jo inflated her lungs and sat on the bed, perching herself near Oliver's side. His breathing was smooth and calm in the deep throes of opium-induced sleep. He wouldn't wake up. He would never know she was here, which was the entire point.

"I'm sorry it took me so long," she said softly. "I didn't know if you'd even want me to come or what I would say to you." Jo smiled wistfully. "I still don't."

Before she could stop herself, Jo ran the back of her fingers over the edge of Oliver's cheekbone. Her lips quivered at the sharpness.

She pressed herself to go on. "For the longest time I hated you. Maybe I still do. But even still, I couldn't stay away. I tried. You have no idea how hard I tried. But when I learned that you could have died …"

Tears fell onto the bed. Jo swiped them off her face, annoyed at the emotion she couldn't contain. "I realized that I couldn't go through this life without your knowing the truth."

Jo leaned forward. She came face to face with Oliver, stopping just before her lips skimmed against his own. His wine-sweetened breath fanned her mouth and a multitude of memories—of happier, more innocent times—spanned across Jo's memory. His strong hands holding her hips … his inappropriate whispers in her ears … his stares from across ballrooms that told everyone that she was her and only hers. Forever.

The words began to waver as Jo continued. "I do hate you; I hate you so much because of what you took from me—what you took from us."

Jo's neck felt impossibly weak. She yearned to rest her forehead on Oliver's as she used to. However, that was a bridge she dared not cross. She came here to do one more thing, and then she would leave knowing she'd left nothing behind.

"But I didn't come to tell you that I hate you, Ollie. Besides, you already know that." Jo closed her eyes. "I came to tell you that I love you. I've always loved you and I always will. You were the only one for me. For the longest time, I thought we were made especially for each other. That God had designed this exquisite pair to show the world what perfect love could be. And we, in our infinite humanity, wrecked it."

Jo stared at his mouth. She was tempted. So tempted. One last kiss to hold close. To remind her of being young and sweet and helplessly in love.

But she pulled away. Because Jo wasn't young anymore. Or innocent. Or even sweet. She was a grown woman. Finally ready to move on.

She stacked her hands in her lap, feeling sheepish. Silly. Her voice came out deep and gruff. "So, now you know. I will love you forever. It's not worth much, but take it for what you will. Get better, Oliver. Live. For my sake. You owe me."

Then Jo got up from the bed and left the room. She didn't look back. She wouldn't let herself.

It was done.

OLIVER WAITED FOR the door to close. And just to be sure, he waited a few more minutes.

Only then did he open his eyes.

And smile.

And utter to himself, "Well, I'll be damned."

About the Author

I'm a lifelong reader of romance novels. Some of my earliest memories are of sneaking into my mom's room at night and stealing any books I could find.

After moving around quite a bit, I've finally put down roots in New England with my two sons and husband. I've always been a writer, starting out in newspapers, but it wasn't until my sons began going to school full-time that I began working toward my dream of becoming a romance author.

I enjoy crocheting toys for my kids, hiking with my Saint Bernard, and watching Real Housewives on the couch with my very old and very fat pugs.

* 9 7 8 1 9 6 7 1 6 9 6 6 5 *